DIAN'S GHOST

Acclaim for Justine Saracen's Novels

"*Mephisto Aria* could well stand as a classic among gay and lesbian readers."—*ForeWord Reviews*

"Justine Saracen's *Sistine Heresy* is a well-written and surprisingly poignant romp through Renaissance Rome in the age of Michelangelo. ...The novel entertains and titillates while it challenges, warning of the mortal dangers of trespass in any theocracy (past or present) that polices same-sex desire."—Professor Frederick Roden, University of Connecticut, Author, *Same-Sex Desire in Victorian Religious Culture*

"Saracen's wonderfully descriptive writing is a joy to the eye and the ear, as scenes play out on the page, and almost audibly as well. The characters are extremely well drawn, with suave villains, and lovely heroines. There are also wonderful romances, a heart-stopping plot, and wonderful love scenes. *Mephisto Aria* is a great read."—*Just About Write*

"*Sarah, Son of God* can lightly be described as the 'The Lesbian's *Da Vinci Code*' because of the somewhat common themes. At its roots, it's part mystery and part thriller. *Sarah, Son of God* is an engaging and exciting story about searching for the truth within each of us. Ms. Saracen considers the sacrifices of those who came before us, challenges us to open ourselves to a different reality than what we've been told we can have, and reminds us to be true to ourselves. Her prose and pacing rhythmically rise and fall like the tides in Venice; and her reimagined life and death of Jesus allows thoughtful readers to consider 'what if?'"—*Rainbow Reader*

Waiting for the Violins "...was a thrilling, charming, and heartrending trip back in time to the early years of World War II and the active resistance enclaves. ...Stunning and eye-opening!"—*Rainbow Book Reviews*

Visit us at www.boldstrokesbooks.com

DIAN'S GHOST

by

Justine Saracen

2016

DIAN'S GHOST

ISBN 13: 978-1-62639-594-7

This Trade Paperback Original Is Published By
Bold Strokes Books, Inc.
P.O. Box 249
Valley Falls, NY 12185

First Edition: March 2016

Credits
Editor: Shelley Thrasher
Production Design: Susan Ramundo
Cover Design By Sheri (graphicartist2020@hotmail.com)

Acknowledgments

I first wish to acknowledge author Farley Mowat for *The Woman in the Mists*, his excellent biography of the very complicated Dian Fossey. Good reading for anyone who wants a balanced account of her troubled yet inspirational life.

On the personal level, I'd like to thank Dr. Sandrine Lambot, my local veterinarian, for providing a list of supplies a jungle vet might need, and Velvet Lounger, for information on radio reception in the mountains. My warmest thanks go to my editor and friend Shelley Thrasher, for plugging along with me, draft after draft, adding wisdom at every go-around. And I will never forget our Alpha, Radclyffe, who holds the whole enterprise on her shoulders while managing to keep her own creative wellspring flowing.

Dedication

For Dian Fossey, courageous,
and crazy enough for gorillas to die for them.

Chapter One

Harlem, New York City
December 12, 1993

Fury, of a sort she'd never known before, seeped into her like water through sand. Her heart pounded so violently it was all she could hear, that and the sound of her deep in-and exhalations. Yet she was powerless. She'd found their revolver, but the empty basement offered no one and nothing to strike out at.

Then she heard their footfall on the iron stairs. At first she froze. Then, as they approached along the corridor, she stepped aside to where the opening door would cover her. In the long moments before they entered, fear evaporated and her whole consciousness distilled to will. Inhibition, reason, self—all gave way to a bright pinpoint of rage and to a single savage thought: revenge.

The door opened, and she swung around it to face the figures silhouetted against the light. Startled, one of them reached into his jacket, but too late. She fired twice into his chest and he toppled backward, his automatic still in his hand. Behind him, the second man lurched back down the corridor, but she stepped over the crumpled figure and snatched up the automatic to pursue him.

The fleeing figure twisted awkwardly while he ran and fired wildly, the bullet striking the wall behind her. When he turned away, she fired three times into his back, bringing him to a halt. He dropped to his knees and then fell to the side.

She stood, panting from excitement, holding the automatic in one hand and the old revolver in the other. Her mind cleared as she calmed, and with a brief glance back at the nightmare room that had driven her mad, she formed a plan.

The first man who lay at her feet was corpulent, but she had to drag him only a short way. She placed him slouching against the wall and facing toward the second man, who lay some twenty feet away. She wiped down the automatic with her shirt and set it back into his plump hand.

She wiped the revolver clean of her prints as well, then nudged the second man with her foot. When he gave no sign of life, she pried his automatic from his hand and folded the revolver into his curled fingers.

Now, to the casual eye, it looked like the running man had mortally wounded the fat man, but with his last breath, the fat man had shot back, killing the other one as he fled.

If the NYPD detectives were as competent as they were portrayed on television, her feeble attempt at staging would be for nothing. But maybe they wouldn't be. Only the third gun would discredit the scenario she'd created and would have to disappear. She slipped it into her belt under her sweatshirt and jacket.

The rest happened with dizzying speed. She had only reached the top of the basement steps when she crashed into a bulky black man passing on the sidewalk. A second later, as she grunted an apology, she heard police sirens.

A distant shout of "Stop!" told her officers on foot had spotted her running, but she turned into the first alley and sprinted the entire block up to 119th Street. The December-evening darkness gave her a chance, as well as the construction site on the corner at Manhattan Street. Dodging between a crane and a cement truck kept her from their line of sight for only a few moments, but it was enough to give her a head start.

She turned a corner, sped down another block, then made a right on 120th. Just ahead was Morningside Park and she hurled herself toward it. She took the stone steps two at a time, cursing inwardly when, out of the corner of her vision, she saw one of the policemen pursuing her on foot.

Slowly, the distance between them increased as they crossed the park, and she forced her aching legs up the stairs to the higher elevation of Morningside Drive. She reached street level again, but damn, another squad car was speeding toward her with siren and flashing lights. Halfway down 120th street, she realized she was nearing the buildings of Columbia University.

Fuck. Another siren from another squad car, this time careening down Amsterdam Avenue. She had to get off the street.

Desperately, she flung herself onto a walkway between two buildings and took an abrupt right turn. Two students were just emerging from a doorway, and she caught the door before it closed.

An empty corridor stretched out in front of her, then bent left. She stopped for only a second to remove her jacket and wool cap and then took off again. Crumpling the two articles into a ball, she stuffed them into a trash bin at the end of the hall. Her long hair, damp from running, fell to her shoulders and seemed to slow her down.

"He went in here," someone said from behind the corner she'd just turned. Just ahead was a staircase. Her chest aching, she was tempted to run down, but that's what her pursuers would expect. She forced her tormented legs to run up, grateful that her sneakers concealed the sound of her footfall. If only she could reach the top of the flight before they saw her.

On the next floor another empty corridor. Could she hide in a classroom? No, she'd be trapped. She swung left, but oh, Christ, it dead-ended in a double door. Out of options, she yanked it open.

An auditorium, full of students listening to a presentation. A few heads turned as she entered, pulling the door closed behind her. She forced herself to stop and stroll unhurriedly along the rear to the nearest aisle. At the bottom of the aisle, students stood in a line in front of a microphone asking questions, so she attracted little attention as she strode down a few rows and fumbled past a dozen knees to an empty seat.

Her hair was disheveled and she sweated, but once seated, she forced calm on herself and breathed with long, slow inhalations. Two seats away from her, a woman with a blond ponytail glanced over at her, apparently puzzled, then smiled politely. Dana smiled back, then feigned intense interest in the speaker at the podium.

"...that question all the time. But I don't have an answer, so please forgive me if I do not comment here on Dian's death and simply talk about the gorillas she loved."

Ah, Dana thought. Gorillas. Unexplained deaths. The speaker must be talking about Dian Fossey's murder. She remembered the movie. Ironic, a question about a murder, when she could still feel the gun handle pressing into her ribs. She should have tossed it, but she'd had no chance.

Focus, Dana. Focus. She had to blend in. And when it was over, she'd melt into the crowd and file out with all the others onto the campus. Her breathing was almost normal now, and it looked like she'd managed to escape.

Someone asked another question, something about qualifications.

The speaker held out open hands as if to accept all offers. "Intelligence, endurance to hardship, love of animals. A degree in one of the life sciences would help. The projects run from three months to a year, though if you can do the work, we prefer you to stay longer. Rapid turnover is bad for the gorillas."

The sound of a door opening drew her attention toward the rear of the auditorium. Shit. Cops, two of them. She snapped her glance back toward the stage, trying to remain anonymous, inconspicuous. Why was Blond Ponytail watching her? She straightened up and tried to appear earnestly engrossed in the scene onstage.

But the show was over. A gray-haired gentleman had come to the podium and was droning platitudes of thanks. Polite applause followed, and the sound of closing notebooks, the thuds of spring-loaded auditorium seats, the murmur of people departing. This was her chance.

But the traffic out of the hall was ominously slow, and no one seemed to be moving. What the hell was holding things up? She scanned the room, her throat tightening as she saw the reason.

All the exit doors but one were blocked, and the two officers had taken up position on both sides of it. They were checking student IDs and searching backpacks, even patting down the male students.

Apparently they assumed their suspect was male, and she was grateful that she'd worn a woolen cap that morning. Still, she couldn't risk filing past them with a pistol in her belt under her shirt, and with Blond Ponytail watching her with such interest, she couldn't wipe the gun clean and leave it on the floor. What now? She swept her glance around the auditorium looking for another way out. There was none.

Indifferent to the police presence, a gaggle of students had gathered around the speaker. If she joined them, maybe she could even get rid of the gun someplace. She edged toward the back of the group, hoping to find an open backpack she could slip the automatic into. Nothing offered itself.

Dana fidgeted, conscious that the others carried books, purses, knapsacks while she was empty-handed. She skirted around the periphery of the group that slowly shrank as students received answers to their questions and moved away. A nervous glance over her shoulder told her the line to the police checkpoint was getting shorter, too. Crap. Like a wild animal in a snare, she could move but was still trapped.

Finally she stood in front of the speaker with only Blond Ponytail at her shoulder.

Dana saw a slender, attractive woman in her late thirties, in a dark-blue pants suit. Her light-brown hair was cut short, and she touched it nervously as she spoke. Wide, well-formed lips were pressed in a tight smile, as if she was forcing the last bit of congeniality when she really wanted simply to leave. Reading glasses hung on a silver chain over her chest, giving her a pedantic look, but her large brown eyes showed, or perhaps feigned, interest in what Dana had to say. And what *was* she going to say?

"Um, I just wanted to…uh…meet you. I've heard so much about…um…the work with the gorillas."

"I'm happy to hear that." Another tight-lipped smile. "What did you think of the presentation?"

"Um…I liked it a lot." Shit, how long could she bluff? It had focused on something about gorillas, and all she could remember was the movie with Sigourney Weaver. "Well, I'm glad someone is publicly addressing the problem of endangered species."

"Was I inspirational enough? I mean, did I make life in a rain forest in the middle of a politically unstable country sound appealing?"

What country? Uganda? Congo? Rwanda? She couldn't remember. "Yes, I thought so."

"Rwanda must be a real challenge," Blond Ponytail said behind her and reached past her to shake hands with the lecturer. "I just want to say how much I've always admired Dian Fossey and respect what you're doing to carry on her work. If I didn't have a Master's Degree in Criminal Justice to finish and a great job offer…and an old dog I can't abandon, I'd jump right in."

A dark-blue shape came into view from the edge of Dana's vision, and her heart began to thud again. She pressed her arm against her side, flattening the bulge of the automatic pistol. As if the conversation itself could somehow surround and protect her, she blurted, "I had a dog, too. A gray-and-white husky. It's shattering when you lose them."

The speaker glanced at her with momentary warmth and sympathy. "Yes, it must be," she said, then shifted her attention back to Blond Ponytail. "Criminal Justice, how interesting," she said. "All that courtroom drama."

"Not really. I'm majoring in Forensics. You know, dead bodies. Law itself is a little disappointing. So many conflicts between what's legal and what's moral. Like what to do about wildlife poachers, for example."

The speaker seemed to brighten. "I know what you mean. Rwanda's gorillas suffer from that legal weakness. Well, perhaps you can come for a short stay in the summer. We have all kinds of jobs, and I'd welcome anyone with your enthusiasm."

One of the officers, Hispanic, almost handsome, had joined them, while his partner still examined the students at the exit.

"Is everything all right, Officer?" the speaker asked.

"We're looking for someone fleeing a crime scene and have reason to think he came in here. Did you notice any latecomers, anyone who might have burst into the room in the middle of your lecture?"

"I'm afraid I can't be much help, Officer. I could hear students trailing in at the start, but after that, I was just too focused on my talk. Really, the audience would have noticed latecomers more than I would have."

The officer looked directly at Dana. "Did you notice anything?"

"No, nothing at all." She hoped her voice wasn't too high, though she was panicking inside.

"What about you? Did you see anyone running in, maybe out of breath?" he asked Blond Ponytail. Dana felt the quick glance of the other woman like a pinprick.

"Uh, no. Not really. I was pretty much engrossed."

Dana could have kissed her.

"Thank you," he said, obviously disappointed, and strode back to his partner to take up position again at the door. Crap, they weren't going to give up.

Blond Ponytail was talking again. "I'll keep in touch. Karisoke sounds fascinating."

"That would be great. Just write to me—Kristen Wolfe. Karisoke Research Center, Ruhengeri, Rwanda. Someone brings the mail up to us every couple of days so it should reach me eventually."

Ah, finally, the dark-haired speaker had a name. Kristen Wolfe. Nice. And she looked a bit like the British actress Kristin Whatshername. Compact, intense. An idea bubbled up from Dana's churning unconscious. "This research project you're looking to staff…"

Kristen's attention swung back toward Dana. "It's not really a research project, rather more a combination study, anti-poaching, and general gorilla monitoring." She started packing up her materials, snapping a loose-leaf notebook shut, unplugging her slide projector, rolling up the extension cord.

Dana did a lightning calculation. Actually no calculation at all, since two dead men were lying in a basement a few blocks away, and sooner or later New York's Finest would trace them to her. If they didn't arrest her in the next five minutes.

"I'd like to join you, Dr. Wolfe."

The lecturer all but snapped to attention. "You're serious? You don't have a job or a school term to finish?"

In the corner of her vision, Dana could see the policemen patting down another student who had walked up from the front row. Right. They were looking for a gun, and she was carrying one.

"I finished my degree at Amherst a couple of months ago and have been looking for a job. I could leave any time."

"Degree? In what field?"

"Uh…biology," Dana lied. If she had to show credentials, she was cooked. "Here, let me help you with that." She lifted the projector with its tray of slides and extension cord and tucked the entire bundle under her arm, as if to prevent anyone taking it from her. It pushed against the hidden automatic, which in turn pressed into her side. "We can talk on the way out. Do you have a car?"

"Oh, no. I'll just take a taxi back to the hotel, but it would be lovely if you could help me flag one down." Kristen slid her notebook and papers into a wide bag on her shoulder and stepped off the platform into the aisle. After a brief handshake with Blond Ponytail, she focused her full attention on Dana, obviously choosing the bird in the hand over the one in the bush.

"And your name is…?"

"Oh, sorry. Dana Norland." She offered her hand, and their handshake seemed to seal the transaction—and her rescue.

They marched together up the aisle where the officers still flanked the exit. Carrying the slide projector and slides, Dana kept up a stream of talk. Like a congressman on a filibuster, she rambled on about anything she could think of. "Do you have medical facilities, or should I bring along the usual first-aid kit? I don't have any medical conditions, but you never know. What about other supplies? I can bring paper and a portable typewriter, if necessary, obviously not electric. And clothing. You said rain forest. That means rain gear, which I have, of course. I wonder how the gorillas put up with it." Dana kept up a verbal storm.

From out of its center, Kristen nodded at the officers and they nodded back.

Keeping in step with her, as if absorbed into the glamor and authority of the lecturer, and the appearance of being her assistant, Dana and her gun slipped unmolested past the police.

CHAPTER TWO

Dana let herself into the ground-floor Harlem apartment of Tony and Emily Bailey. "I've got a job," she announced as she closed the door behind her. She was going to have to tell a lot of lies in the next few days, but that remark, at least, was true. Old school friends of her mother, they'd let her live rent-free for two months in their spare room, and so she owed them at least that.

"Terrific! Where is it?" Tony shuffled toward the entryway in his slippers. "I thought your job interview was tomorrow."

"It was, but something much better came up." She averted her eyes. "Something overseas. I answered an ad in the newspaper, a shot in the dark, kind of."

She rubbed warmth back into her arms, glad to be indoors after jogging through the streets without hat or jacket. If Tony noticed her lack of winter clothing as she strode past him into the living room, he didn't say so.

"A job abroad. That's great! What country?" White-haired and grandmotherly, Emily greeted her from the sofa. "Doing what? With whom?" She shooed the cat from her lap, drew Dana down next to her, and peered over her reading glasses. "Tell us all about it!"

Dana had half worked out her story on the way home. She hated lying, but if the police came around asking questions, she had to leave no trail. "England. University of Manchester. They need someone to work in the lab."

"Lab work. But isn't your degree in Classics?" Tony looked puzzled.

"Yes, but I had a minor in Zoology, and besides, the job is just simple stuff. Cleaning cages, taking notes, etcetera."

"Strange that Manchester can't get one of their graduate students to do that," Emily said, twisting sideways to face her.

"That's what I thought, too. But some international agency is funding the project, so they want people from all over. I didn't ask too many questions. I'm just glad to have a job that doesn't involve typing letters for accountants."

Emily nodded understanding. "When do you start?"

"As soon as I can get a visa and work permit. Just enough time for me to clear out my room and put everything in order. Fortunately I already have a passport."

"An international job. Your mother would have been so proud." Emily tilted her head and studied her. "I see her every time I look at you, with those deep-brown eyes and her cute mouth that turned up a little at the corners. She always looked like she was smiling even when she was just reading a book."

"Really? It's nice to hear I'm carrying around a little bit of her in my DNA."

"It's true, though now you're *actually* smiling, and I'm so happy to see it." Emily touched her wrist. "I know, taking care of your mother all that time really took the spirit out of you. You were always somber. And then, just when you were trying to start out fresh with a new job, Nikki disappeared. I'm so sorry for you. But he might still turn up. That happens all the time." She touched the cat that rubbed against her ankles, as if there were some connection.

Dana glanced away for a moment, trying to calibrate the right expression. She cleared her throat, trying to sound neutral, like someone who still had hope. "Yes, he could. And I know you'd look after him until I can make arrangements for him. It's good to have friends like you."

Emily squeezed her hand. "Will you go with me next Saturday to St. John's? Perhaps that will cheer you up. It's a combination Winter Solstice and Feast of St. Francis, you know, the Blessing of the Animals. It'll be lovely."

Dana was puzzled. "Solstice I can understand. It's coming up in a week or so. But isn't the St. Francis thing in October?"

"It is, but Reverend Morton was sick in October so they moved it to December. It's such a wonderful spectacle, the mass and then all the animals. Miss Kitty has been looking forward to it all year. Haven't you, dear?" She scratched the cat's neck, eliciting a soft purr.

"Last year it was a complete zoo." She laughed brightly. "You never know what'll turn up. Oh, please, dear, say you'll go. I have passes for two, and Tony can't sit on those hard benches because of his back."

Dana closed her eyes for a moment. Her life had turned into a horror movie, and the last thing she wanted just then was to sit in a church and watch a parade of people with their pets. But she'd just lied to the kindest people she knew and felt guilty. "Yes, all right," she said wearily and forced a smile.

On a Saturday morning at 10:45, Amsterdam Avenue was dreary. The rain had just stopped, but the sidewalk was full of puddles, and Dana and Emily had to watch the ground to avoid them. Cars shussed as they passed on the partially flooded street, a depressing rainy-day sound. Nonetheless, holding a harnessed but somewhat puzzled Miss Kitty, Emily was ebullient.

"Aren't the Christmas decorations pretty? I know, they put them up far too early, but they do make everything so festive. It's a shame you won't be here for actual Christmas, but I suppose Solstice will have to do. Anyhow, your mother would be pleased that I've dragged you to Saint John's."

"Really? I never thought she was religious. Not even when she was dying."

"No, not in the 'love Jesus' sense. But she loved the cathedral. We went to concerts together a few times, after you left for Amherst. But when she found out she had cancer, she got caught up with the treatment and we never went again." They walked awhile in silence. "I miss her, don't you?"

"Of course I do. A feeling my father seems to lack completely. He never once appeared when she was dying. I know it was a bitter divorce, but you'd think he'd have a drop of kindness."

"Don't worry about him, dear. He's got his job and a new young wife, and you don't need him. I'm sorry you had to lose a year of college, but obviously you were able to make it up later."

"Yes, but being gone a year sort of broke the flow. When I went back, everyone seemed so young and self-absorbed." She glanced up. "Well, here we are."

The Cathedral of St. John the Divine rose up in front of them in its splendor. Vaguely Gothic in style, it had been under construction off and on for half a century and still had scaffolding around its south tower. Its double main portal was flanked on both sides by a row of statues. Saints, she supposed. Wasn't it always saints?

They joined the crowd climbing the stone steps and fell into step with an elderly woman leading a dachshund and a portly man holding a box of kittens.

It was a relief to arrive inside, away from the damp winter air, and while Emily showed their passes to the attendant, Dana glanced around at the landmark cathedral that she was seeing for the first time inside. She was impressed.

Chapels in a variety of styles ran along both sides, and candles burned in racks in almost all of them. Halfway down the nave, Emily claimed seats for them both on the aisle, and while others filed past them, she turned to gaze up at the rose window. It was, she had to admit, magnificent.

"Nice, huh?" Emily smiled. "I knew you'd like it."

"I'm guessing the stage isn't always there." Dana pointed with her chin toward a wooden platform some twenty feet square at the center of the transept. Folding chairs and music stands stood in long rows on both sides. At that moment, the chamber orchestra filed in and the musicians took their places. Immediately following them, some hundred people in choral gowns streamed in and lined up in two groups on either side of the platform.

The last person to arrive, in a dark suit, was obviously the conductor. At his signal, the chorus sat down and the orchestra tuned. The cathedral lights dimmed, leaving the congregation in murky twilight while, on a screen hanging over the orchestra, an image of the full moon appeared.

Dana had never heard of the *Missa Gaia*, but the opening sounds gripped her immediately. The howling of a wolf in a four-note cadence sounded eerily over their heads and was repeated in the saxophone. In the darkened church, it was a powerful evocation of nights in the wilderness in the absence of men. The sobbing of the dog-ancestor was unbearably plaintive and caused her chest to tighten with grief.

The following movements of the mass interwove soft jazz with New Age sounds and were nothing like any of the traditional masses she'd heard. But then Mozart or Verdi would never have considered inserting a wolf's cry into their Kyrie. The jazzy rhythms and occasional solo saxophone were a pleasing celebration of the solstice and the return of the light, and she was able to quiet the voices that murmured in the back of her mind. Until her escape from New York, that's what counted. Her visa had arrived just that morning, so it was now only a matter of days.

After the final chords of the Go Forth in Peace sounded, the lights came up and a man in a green chasuble climbed the steps of the pulpit. Dana felt her peace of mind dissipate into annoyance. A sermon was the last thing she needed.

But the reverend surprised her, as the mass had done, for his theme wasn't the transcendent but the world itself. One of the great discoveries of the last century, he said with some drama, was evolution. And it had enriched and glorified the story of creation more than any scripture could.

"This is the wondrous tool that God has taken to not only create a world, but to let it metamorphose in infinite variety. Life is a kaleidoscope of forms, and we as humans are but bright spots in that interplay, spots that have been gifted with introspection and understanding. But with understanding comes responsibility. We are not the masters of earth but its guardians. The other creatures are here, not *for* us, but *with* us, and it is a test of our worth that we recognize ourselves in them and care for them."

The message was an appealing one, and though the niggling skepticism at the back of Dana's mind made her wonder whether malaria mosquitos, parasitical worms, and bubonic bacteria counted as God's creatures, she appreciated the general earth-friendly approach. Besides, the sermon was mercifully brief, and he followed it by an explanation of the Feast of Saint Francis and the Blessing of the Animals. The latter did not include parasitical worms or lethal bacteria. In conclusion, he invited the congregation to process with their creatures past the altar.

Dana leaned toward Emily. "Go ahead, join the procession with Miss Kitty," she urged. "If she can endure being surrounded by dogs without panicking, she deserves a blessing. I'll wait here for you to make the circuit."

"All right, dear." Emily stood up, clutching the elderly and none-too-happy cat to her chest. "You can tell me what you saw when I'm back."

As Emily stepped out of the pew into the moving line, Dana sat down again and observed the procession. It was amusing to see the menagerie that filed down the central aisle of the nave, and she was able to forget the fear and horror and confusion of the last week.

An endless line of people carrying cats and dogs shuffled by, but also goats, a pig, parrots: a ringneck green, an African grey, and a white cockatoo with its crest raised in agitation. Following up the rear were the larger creatures: a young camel, a donkey, and a miniature pony. Two men held capuchin monkeys on their shoulders, but she saw no larger primates, and she was relieved. For all its benevolence, a crowded church was no place for creatures as intelligent and sensitive as a gorilla or a chimpanzee.

How strange. She hadn't yet set foot in Africa, had never even laid eyes on a live gorilla, but already she cared about them.

Emily finally made the circuit past the altar and returned to their pew. Miss Kitty's claws were deeply embedded in Emily's coat, a clear sign she'd had quite enough beatitude that afternoon. Rather than wait for the procession to come to a close, they made their way along a side aisle to the narthex and back to the street.

The rain had started again and blew toward them. Emily wrapped her coat around Miss Kitty while Dana linked arms with her and held the umbrella over them both. "How did you like it?" Emily asked. "Did it reconcile you a little bit with religion?"

Dana shrugged. "Whether they're God's or nature's creatures, animals have emotions and can suffer, at least if they have consciousness. And if we have any moral sense at all, we shouldn't want to cause that suffering or benefit from it."

She thought for a moment. "Hmm. I wonder if the good reverend eats meat?"

Emily chuckled softly. "If you're looking for hypocrisy you won't find it. I know for a fact he's a vegetarian, but not a dogmatic one. He recognizes that people have eaten meat for thousands of years, but they've also been abusing and enslaving each other that long, so that's no excuse. If you asked him, I think he'd say morality consists in people thinking about the implications of what they do and considering the bigger picture."

"Implications? Hmmm," Dana said, then fell silent and hunched forward into the wind.

Chapter Three

Ruhengeri, Rwanda
December 24, 1993

The twenty-two-hour trip, with long wait times in Brussels and Kigali, had left Dana ample time to brood. In the previous ten days, the "event," as she came to think of it, ran through her mind in an endless loop in monochrome, like a jerky silent film. The nightmares plagued her sleep, endless variations of the same aching dread, of falling, sliding, tumbling down through a tunnel toward some pit of nameless horror.

The days were slightly better, though she'd sleepwalked through them, keeping up a façade of normalcy and cheerfulness, concealing her numbness and confusion. The whole episode was so beyond-her-experience awful, she couldn't integrate it into her understanding of herself and so forced it into some deep cellar of her mind where she hoped it would wither. Instead, it banged on the walls, demanding to be recognized, and she was a fugitive from that part of herself long before she fled the country.

She glanced through the window of the tiny ten-passenger plane and studied the unpaved runway of the Ruhengeri airport, flanked by green. Here, finally, was Rwanda, raw and fecund, where she'd have new tasks, new people, a new identity.

When she descended the steps onto the dusty ground, the chill in the air surprised her. How could a country so close to the equator be so cold? The sky was overcast, and a damp breeze blew through her hair and she was glad she'd heeded Kristen's advice to wear a heavy jacket. Exhausted and grimy, she wondered if she'd be allowed a bath and a nap before the trek up the mountain.

She passed along the narrow walkway to the uniformed official who functioned as customs control, fetched her luggage, and plodded with the other passengers toward the wire fence that marked off the airfield.

Some dozen people waited, though all but one were Africans. The only white woman was presumably Kristen. "Welcome," she said, as Dana came through the gate. "How was your flight?"

"All right. Long." Dana set down her suitcase and took a deep breath. "It's a relief to finally arrive."

"Any problems? Is everything in order?" Kristen asked.

Dana studied her host, surprised at her appearance. She'd looked so academic, so schoolmarmish in the Columbia lecture hall. Now, in khaki trousers and shirt, and without her glasses, the schoolteacher had metamorphosed into a female Indiana Jones. The difference cheered her.

"Yep. Inoculations, visa, health check, local currency, clean underwear. Ready to go."

Kristen chuckled. "Glad to hear about the underwear. Socks, too? You'll probably need those more."

"Five pairs, all the same color, in case one gets lost in the washing machine."

"Washing machine? Ha. Good one." Kristen glanced down at the suitcase.

"Here, let Mukera carry that thing," she said, and a stocky African in a green-wool ranger's uniform stepped forward.

He seemed in his twenties, friendly and rather handsome. He smiled, revealing a row of beautiful large white teeth, though one of the two in front was broken in half. With a quick nod of greeting, he lifted the heavy bag with obvious ease and turned away.

Kristen followed him and Dana hurried to catch up. A moment later, they stopped in front of a mud-splattered gray Land Rover.

"Um. Will we be going directly to the campsite?" Dana asked hesitantly, her hopes for a long hot bath evaporating.

"No reason to stay in town. We've already done the shopping." Kristen opened the rear-facing door and Mukera slid the suitcase inside, then jumped in next to it. Just as Kristen closed the door behind him, an open truck carrying men in camouflage uniforms careened past them. A few of the men seemed to glower at them as they swung by, and the automatic rifles they clutched added menace to their gaze.

"What's that?" Dana asked under her breath, as if the soldiers could overhear. "I thought the civil war was over."

Kristen nudged her toward the front of the Land Rover. "It is, officially. But the rebel Tutsis held Ruhengeri for a short time, so the government sends troops in now and again to monitor the area. Don't worry. We're up in the mountains, and none of that has anything to do with us."

Dana tucked the information into the back of her mind as Kristen started the motor. While they rumbled along the uneven street, she glanced up at the overcast sky. "I didn't expect it to look like this."

"You mean so dreary?" Kristen snorted again. "Everyone expects all of Africa to be hot and sunny. But we're at a pretty high elevation, and most of the Virunga volcano range counts as temperate rainforest. More often than not we wake up to thick fog, and it rains a lot, especially in spring and fall. You'll get used to it."

They drove through Ruhengeri without stopping, raising a cloud of dust behind them as the military truck had done. Traffic was unregulated by stoplights, but the lack of motor traffic obviously prevented serious accidents. Still, the street was filled with men pushing wheelbarrows or bicycles, women balancing wide bundles on their heads, children, and the odd mongrel or goat. Avoiding them took some dexterity, and Kristen's calmness, as she swerved around them, was reassuring.

They were out of town in fifteen minutes, bumping along the roads between cultivated fields. Women with babies strapped to their backs looked up as they passed, then bent back to work again. Finally they stopped at the end of a road near a wide expanse of cleared land and a row of corrugated metal sheds.

"This is the car park for vehicles bringing people into the Parc des Volcans. From here on, however, it's all by foot."

"By foot," Dana repeated softly, gazing wearily up toward the steep wooded flank of the mountain. Of course. What else had she imagined?

Mukera unloaded Dana's suitcase, a large cardboard box, and two lumpy backpacks. They stood together with their goods surrounding them while Kristen drove the Land Rover into one of the sheds, padlocked the tin door, and rejoined them.

"I'm afraid you'll have to handle your own luggage. Mukera and I will be carrying supplies." She slid her arms through the straps of a backpack that appeared to hold canned goods and other groceries. Mukera, for his part, lifted the larger backpack onto his shoulders and hoisted the cardboard box onto his head.

"Can you manage?" Kristen asked Dana, though the question was obviously rhetorical. It was either manage or leave the luggage behind.

She knew, at least vaguely, that Karisoke was somewhere up in the Virunga range and that reaching it would require some hiking. But she hadn't counted on having to lug her own baggage. Glad that she'd crammed all her worldly goods into a single suitcase, she loaded it onto her back and rested it on her knapsack in much the way Mukera did his box.

Immediately after the car park, the footpath climbed steeply upward and the trees became denser. Worse, the ground was wet, and in places, the soil simply slipped away under her feet, leaving her in ankle-deep puddles. Strange and alarmingly large insects and worms appeared, and she flinched as they buzzed past her or slithered under her feet. The worms, particularly, were terrifying, as thick as snakes and a foot long.

They slogged through swaths of nettle and walls of bamboo, coming out on the other side upon rocky outcroppings or forty-five-degree mud slopes.

She labored on as long as she could, but after half an hour, she halted, panting. "Please. Can we rest, just a few minutes? I could have done this without the suitcase, but not with."

"Sure, we can rest awhile. Sorry for loading you up that way, but we have only one porter at the moment. Usually we have three, but we'll be feeding a lot of people tomorrow, and the two others are collecting the heaviest supplies from Gisenyi."

Gratefully, Dana let the suitcase glide off her back, and she dropped down onto the spongy earth at the side of the trail. "Ah, right. I lost track of the date. It's Christmas Eve, isn't it? Strange, one doesn't usually associate Christmas with Africa."

"I know, but most Rwandans are Catholic, and they take the holiday as seriously as Americans do. Anyhow, you'll meet the whole staff tomorrow when we have our celebration. It's not as big a deal as when Dian was here, but the men have come to expect something, and I try not to disappoint."

"You give them gifts, too?"

"Yes. That's what's in the box Mukera's carrying. New uniform shirts and boots, fabric for their wives, and candy for their children." She checked her watch. "Anyhow, if you're rested, we should get going."

Dana moaned. "You mean we're not there yet?"

Kristen snorted. "Not quite. It's a two-and-a-half-hour hike if you do it without stopping. But it doesn't get dark until six, so we can rest again if you need to." Kristen's smile seemed sincere, unlike the one she'd worn after her Columbia lecture.

They set off again at a pace Dana knew they'd slowed on her behalf. Mukera was silent though he showed no sign of fatigue. Was he pleased to have a rest or annoyed at the delay?

"Is there any chance we'll see gorillas on the path?" she asked between pants.

"Not likely. They rarely come this far down the mountain, and we don't want them to. Any casual contact with the local people is dangerous to them."

"Who *are* the local people? I did a little reading and know about the tribal differences, but only the names. Everyone in Ruhengeri looked the same—that is, African. But that's my ignorance, isn't it?"

"Ignorance isn't a sin if you get rid of it. The differences are important to the Rwandans, and you'll notice them after a while. Rwanda had a caste system with the Watutsi—or Tutsi, as they call themselves now—traditionally filling most of the government positions. That's changed, but it'll take too long to explain how. The ordinary Tutsi are cattle herders, and a lot of the national park has been cleared for them to graze their cattle."

Dana was puzzled. "But I mostly saw farms coming from Ruhengeri. No cattle, only people working in the fields."

"The farmers are largely Hutus, and as you can imagine, there's tension between them as to what land is used for what."

"Are people still living in the forest? Like in the *National Geographic* stories? God, I really am ignorant."

"Yes, a smaller people, called the Batwa, or the Twa. They're traditional hunters and gatherers and probably the original inhabitants, who predate the arrivals of the other two groups. They keep to their little villages, but they're the most trouble for us."

"Why's that?" Dana shifted the position of her suitcase, but it didn't help. Her neck and back and legs still ached from the unfamiliar weight, though talking kept her mind off the pain.

"When the land at the foot of the Virungas was declared a national park, and the animals were made off-limits to hunting, they became poachers."

"Poachers? I always understood poachers to be people who shot rhinos for their horns and elephants for their tusks. It never occurred to me they could be hunting to survive."

"Well, they do both. When they hunt in the park, they set traps for hyrax and bushback, which they eat, but those traps also maim and kill our gorillas. The most relentless hunters are Sebahutu and Munyaro, from different villages. They've been arrested repeatedly, but the system is pretty corrupt, so they always buy their way out again."

"And they're not just hunting to feed their families?"

"Some do, and you could excuse that. But Sebahutu and Munyaro are the visible part of a vicious industry that supplies the horn and ivory markets, and are wiping out whole populations of wildlife. They also harvest gorilla parts for collectors."

"Gorilla parts? What do you mean?" Dana already had an inkling.

"The hands, feet, and head of a gorilla, especially of a silverback. People pay a lot of money for them. They can also sell the fingers, tongues, and testicles to the witch doctors for their magic. Horrendous, isn't it, to think some people are so indifferent to animal suffering?"

"Or entertained by it," Dana added somberly, but Kristen's dreadful narration went on. "They kill them in a particularly horrible way, too. If the hunters come upon a trapped animal, to keep their gunshots from being heard, they'll kill it with their dogs and spears.

But it's almost as bad when the hunters don't come. The animal stays trapped for days, and if it manages to break the rope that holds the trap, the wire snare is still around its hand or foot. The limb becomes gangrenous, and the poor creature dies after weeks of agony."

"My God," Dana said, muted.

"So that will be one of your jobs, to go out on snare parties and bring them in." Kristen stood up. "Anyhow, let's get going. We still have a long way to hike." She stepped onto the trail again.

Mukera got to his feet as well and, with a powerful sweep, swung his box onto his back. With considerably less grace, Dana hauled her suitcase up to its precarious, painful place and resumed slogging over the rugged terrain. She brooded on what Kristen had said.

How many white men had come to Africa to kill wildlife and been applauded for it? Countless thousands of lions, leopards, elephants, rhinos, and buffalo, sacrificed to the ego of some European or American needing to prove his manhood. Had the animals they hunted managed to kill any of them first? One or two, maybe. Not nearly enough. A fury rose in her, and the appalling memory flickered to life again. To dispel it, she talked.

"What do you do for light? Kerosene lanterns?"

"A notch up from those, but the principle's the same. They're pressure lamps, or Coleman lanterns, and don't give off smoke. In general, you get used to living with less light, the way our grandparents did."

"Oh." Dana fell silent again. Whatever other bad news Kristen might have could wait until her feet, buttocks, and back were no longer aching.

Finally, when Dana thought she could bear no more, the steep slope leveled off to a gentle incline and they entered a sort of woods. Hopeful, she quickened her pace. She'd been staring at her feet, but now she looked up and saw increasing numbers of a slender tree with an umbrella-shaped crown. The bark, which seemed to always be peeling away, was reddish-brown, and the branches were hung with moss.

"What lovely trees. What kind are they?"

Kristen slowed her pace. "Hagenia. Yes, they are pretty. The Rwandans use them for practically everything—medicine, carving, carpentry. The fauna seem to like them, too." She glanced up toward a brightly colored bird that fluttered from one of the branches.

A layer of mist covered the ground, thick at the bottom and more diffuse in the air above it. Like dust, it gave substance to the beams of afternoon sunlight that sliced in diagonally between the trees. Birds chirped, distant monkeys screeched, and other invisible creatures clicked, sang, hissed, gurgled. In that one moment, Dana understood why people came to Africa and stayed.

Just then Kristen halted. "There's Karisoke just above us," she said. "Home."

Directly ahead of them lay a long expanse of open ground. The path they were on bifurcated toward north and south, and beyond the separation she could see a wide meadow. On both sides, huts were widely separated, like a village of people who wanted nothing to do with one another.

"I had imagined it much smaller, you know. Dian's cabin, a fire pit, a few tents, all in a little jungle clearing. But it's much more civilized. More like a summer camp."

"Well, it was more primitive when Dian first arrived, of course, but over time, people brought up materials and hammered together a few structures. Yet don't get your hopes up. We still have no plumbing, and we heat and cook with wood stoves."

"Where do you get your water? Do you collect rainwater?"

"Fortunately, no. A stream runs along the edge of the camp." She pointed south. "On the other side of that thicket. The housemen will usually bring it up to your cabin in buckets for cooking and washing, but you might sometimes have to haul it yourself."

"And toilets?"

"Outhouses. More exactly long-drop loos. Behind each cabin. You'll get in the habit of keeping old shoes and a flashlight by the door for night visits. Come on. I'll show you to your new home." Kristen started up again along the path that curved northward.

Some hundred yards along the way, they crossed another path where Mukera turned away from them toward what was presumably a supply shed.

They continued until Kristen stopped before a small cabin with a porch. "This has the richly poetic name of Middle Cabin and will be yours while you're here. The toilet is off behind it."

Dana nodded, reserving judgment until they were inside.

The porch creaked as they stepped up onto it, and Kristen unlocked the door, then handed over the key. "It might be a little dusty," she said, shoving open the door that was not quite square. "But the men put clean linen on the bed, and you shouldn't find any unwelcome creatures nesting in the dark corners."

Dana stepped in and glanced around with misgiving. "You mean bats, snakes, rats?" Dana tried to make light of the idea, but Kristen's expression told her that yes, all three were possible. *Great.*

The interior was spare, with a single bed, a wooden table and chair. Open shelves hung along one wall, and a primitive wardrobe stood along the other. An iron stove on a metal platform took up the center of the long wall. Boxy and functional rather than quaint, it had a wide pipe rising to the ceiling. That, she supposed, would be her primary source of heat, and since the air of the cabin smelled dank, she'd need to learn how to use it quickly.

Kristen glanced around the interior as if seeing it for the first time herself. "The moldy smell is from the rain, of course, but it'll dissipate once you get a fire going." She pointed to the shelves behind the iron stove. "The cabin has the basic equipment for cooking and eating, though in the next couple of weeks, you may want to add a few personal things from the shops in Ruhengeri or Gisenyi."

She tapped the iron stove and brushed off some dust. "As for food, twice a week, our head porter goes down the mountain with outgoing mail and our grocery lists and returns with the mail and supplies. He's doing that now, in fact. Of course, anytime we're in Ruhengeri or Gisenyi, we always bring back as much as we can carry."

"What's available? What do Rwandans eat?"

"Potatoes, carrots, other vegetables, some canned goods. We do get eggs from the chickens, and if you don't mind eating it with powdered milk, we have plenty of porridge."

"No chips and beer, then?" Dana quipped.

Kristen snickered. "Depends on what you mean by beer. The camp men brew their own variety, called *pombe*, but sorry, no chips.

In any case, all trash goes either into the compost heap in the back or into the stove to burn."

She opened one of the cupboards and lifted out something flat and heavy, wrapped in a plastic bag. "This is your main hardware. A portable typewriter. Manual, of course. We keep it in plastic when no one's using it. Don't want the interior to rust or attract spiders."

Setting the portable on the table and brushing off her hands, Kristen moved toward the door. "I've got to sort out the things we brought up to the camp, but I'll heat some soup in an hour or so. Why don't you stop by later? My cabin's the one right before the footbridge over the creek. Just follow the path down between the fences and you'll see it. In the meantime, I'll let you unpack and send one of the men with a load of wood for the stove."

Lifting her hand in a gesture of good-bye, she went out, leaving Dana a bit nonplussed in her new cold, dank home.

To dispel the disappointment, she unpacked her suitcase, realizing that, in spite of its weight, it carried far too little for long-term camping. Obviously, she needed to make another trip down the mountain to purchase the things she lacked. And she'd have to learn how to cook on a wood stove. How long could she subsist on instant soup?

A knock roused her from her funk, and she opened the door to a stocky African with a receding hairline and a slight potbelly. Her New York City prejudices regarding black strangers at the door caused her to pause for a fraction of a second. Then, embarrassed, she stepped back to let him in.

"Oh, you've brought wood. Thank you. Can you show me how to start the stove?"

He came inside with the kindling but didn't seem to understand what she'd said.

Rubbing her upper arms to signal "cold," she pointed toward the stove and opened the front cover.

He grunted understanding, or maybe disapproval of her communication skills, and knelt in front of it. He seemed to tinker for a moment with a vent under the stove and then built a teepee of wood and straw in the chamber.

Frowning, he glanced around, obviously looking for something, and she realized it must be matches. A jar of them stood on a nearby shelf, and with a slight pride of discovery, she took it to him. Obviously she'd guessed right, for he nodded, drew out a match, and ignited the tepee. As soon as the wood caught flame, he inserted a couple of larger chunks, closed the cover, and stood up.

"Oh, thank you," she said again, laying a cold hand on the iron to savor the first waves of warmth.

Silently, he nodded again and let himself out.

Alone once more, she pulled the cabin's one chair up in front of the stove. Damn. How was she going to speak to the staff? What had the other students done? Would she have to pantomime everything she wanted to say, like a game of charades? She imagined herself standing in front of them. *Noun, two syllables, name of a food.*

Had she let herself in for a new kind of isolation?

CHAPTER FOUR

At least she would eat that day, Dana thought as she strode along what she hoped was the correct path. Ah, yes. Just ahead was the footbridge and, to the right of it, a hut somewhat larger than her own. Wood was piled up against one wall, and next to it a wire pen held chickens. Clever idea. A regular supply of eggs and the occasional fresh roasted poultry—unless you were sentimental about chickens.

She knocked and Kristen opened the door, releasing a cloud of warmth rich with the aroma of fresh garlic. "Welcome to the manor house," she said.

Dana stepped in and gazed around the interior, noting that Kristen had a wood stove, somewhat like Dana's but with two holes at the top rather than one. A battered copper kettle sat over one of them, steam wafting from its spout, and a covered pot, presumably the source of the garlic aroma, stood on the other.

"Pretty cozy here. Heat feels good, too." She rubbed her hands and held them over the iron stove.

"A fire makes a big difference, doesn't it? Did Kanyara bring you the wood and show you how to light it?" Kristen lifted the pot lid and stirred the soup, a charming contradiction in her khaki field clothing and a little white apron.

"Kanyara. That's his name? Yes, he showed me, but I'll have to develop the knack. I tried to talk to him, but I guess he speaks only Swahili."

Kristen chuckled sympathetically as she laid out mismatched soup bowls on the table. "The language they speak here is Kinyarwanda, and you'll pick up a few expressions in time. But I think Kanyara was just pulling your chain a little. The camp staff all speak French to some degree or another." She gripped the pot with two ends of a towel and carried it from the stove to the table. Dana pulled up a chair and sat down opposite her.

"Ah, yes, I read about that in a traveler's guide, so I brushed up on my college vocabulary. Silly of me not to try it. Oh, that smells good."

Kristen lifted the lid. "Black bean soup. I made a batch of it yesterday, with beans and whatever vegetables we could collect from the garden." She ladled a generous portion into both their bowls.

"I was wondering what I'd be eating while I'm here. Is this part of the regular cuisine?" She tasted a spoonful. "It's delicious."

"When you're cold, tired, and hungry, everything tastes wonderful. Which is good, because cooking anything complex is a challenge. Beans and rice store well, so I eat them a lot, along with corn, potatoes. I also try to keep a garden, but the heavy rain and the occasional passing wildlife make it an uphill battle. Here, have some of the bread. I brought it up today, and it won't stay fresh long."

Dana ripped off a corner of the flat bread and dipped it into her thick soup. It was the perfect comfort food.

"Now try this. See what you think of it." Kristen took up a pitcher and poured something cloudy into Dana's glass. After a moment the particles settled to the bottom. "It's the pombe I told you about, a kind of beer made with bananas and millet. The Rwandans drink the whole thing, including the stuff at the bottom, but feel free to leave it."

Dana took a sip of the grainy beverage and found it unpleasantly sour. "I'm not much of a beer drinker, actually," she said, setting it aside. "Is it safe to drink the water?"

"Not until you become acclimated. But I'll make you some tea." Kristen got up to lift the steaming kettle from the stove.

"Please forgive me for my ignorance about Karisoke." Dana spoke to Kristen's back. "All I really know is what I saw in *Gorillas in the Mist*. And I seem to recall that Dian made up the name as a combination of the peaks on each side of us: Karisimbi and Visoke. How accurate was the movie?"

Kristen returned to the table with two mugs. "Not very. She was here for some eighteen years, and the movie had to cram all of them into two screen hours, so it couldn't tell much. Also, the director seemed to care mostly about how glamorous Sigourney Weaver made gorilla-watching and how much she was in love with her photographer. But yes, Dian named Karisoke, and it began simply as the base for her study. Over time, it expanded to include research by other people, some of which had little to do with her. It's still called Karisoke *Research* Center, but after the death of Digit, her favorite gorilla, Dian focused heavily on anti-poaching. And since poachers hunted everything, the place also became a de facto sanctuary for wildlife: bushbacks, duikers, hyraxes. We even had a flock of African greys pass through for a few days. I'd have loved to keep one as a pet, but that's the very thing that has decimated their population in Rwanda."

When the kettle began to hiss, Kristen lifted it from the stove and poured the boiling water into a porcelain teapot with a rose pattern on it. The teapot, too, seemed at odds with the rugged field scientist. She stirred it gently for a few moments, then came to the table and filled their two mugs.

Inhaling the fragrant Earl Grey steam, Dana studied Kristen's face. In the low light of the Coleman lamps, the resemblance to the British actress of the same name was striking, though this Kristen was a little less immaculate than the actress and at the moment had a few particles of something black hanging in her hair.

On a whim, Dana reached over and plucked them off. Holding her fingertips close to the light, she examined the flecks. "Bean pieces, looks like. Sorry to invade your space. I thought it might be something alive."

"I guess I stirred the soup a little too aggressively. It was courageous of you to reach for things you thought were bugs. A little risky in Africa."

Dana smiled. "I'm good with moths and spiders, too." She shoveled another spoonful of soup into her mouth. "Mmm. You're obviously a good cook. Will you prepare something for tomorrow? You talked about a Christmas celebration."

"Ah, yes. That's a tradition that Dian began, and although it's less elaborate these days, we do have a common meal and I give presents to the men. With the few grants we depend on, I can't pay them much, so I buy them some of their equipment with my own money, like Dian used to."

Dana winced slightly at the irony. "Though it didn't completely win their loyalty, did it? I mean, one of them killed her."

"That seems less and less likely, but it's not worth going into now. It's a long, complicated story. She was a complicated woman."

"I gathered that from my reading. Are the stories of her shooting and torturing people true?"

"She did kill a couple of cows the Tutsis had let loose in the park. She never shot any people, though I think after the death and mutilation of Digit, she was capable of it. For her, that was the same kind of crime as killing and mutilating a child. She saw no moral difference between animals and people. In fact, once, when the Batwa had taken her dog, she kidnapped one of their children and held him until they brought the pup back. For her, the two were the same."

Dana glanced away. "I can sympathize with that."

"So can I. But that view made her a lot of enemies, both among the more sensitive types on her staff and, of course, among the Rwandans."

"I wish I'd known her." Dana thought for a moment. "Would it be possible to see her cabin?"

"To find out if it's haunted?" Kristen chuckled softly. "Sure. I'll take you there now, if you like."

The cabin was larger than the others and sheltered attractively by graceful hagenia trees. They stepped onto the narrow front porch, and Kristen unlocked the door. "This place was kept sealed as evidence for nearly a year, until the case was resolved." She said the word resolved with obvious sarcasm. "Then we had to wait for her next of kin to collect all her belongings. So for the longest time, no one used this place. Later, when we had to put guests here for lack of space, they usually didn't like it. You can't blame them. No one wants to sleep in a bed where someone was murdered."

The cabin smelled of mold and had the gloom of all abandoned places. Kristen's lantern illuminated only the spot she held it over, and otherwise haunting darkness surrounded them.

Holding the lantern aloft, Kristen walked in a circle around the front room that, by camping standards, must have been quite luxurious. Though sparsely furnished, it did have a full fireplace with bookshelves on both sides. That they were empty added to the overall grimness. To the left, a step down led to what was probably a dining space, with a table and an iron stove. To the right was a kitchen, with a worktable and cupboards.

Kristen led her to the other side of the fireplace and made a similar circuit, casting light on a bed, a set of drawers, and yet another stove.

"That's the bed they found her on?" Dana winced at the thought.

"Yes. I guess you read about the way she was killed."

"By a machete blow to her head, right?"

"They call it a *panga* here. It belonged to her, in fact. She'd taken it from a poacher some time before."

"I understand one of her trackers was arrested for the murder. Someone she'd fired."

"Yes, though they really had no evidence pointing to him. He already had a good job with another mountain-gorilla project. The authorities simply had to come up with a conviction, so they declared that two people, who were almost certainly innocent, had conspired to commit the murder. The other one was a white assistant who had arrived shortly before. He was never arrested, though. It's generally assumed that the US State Department and the Rwandan government arranged for him to escape to avoid a trial visible to the entire world."

"So, it was poachers?"

"Also very unlikely. The Batwa are a small people, almost pygmies, and they're not known for face-to-face confrontations with big white people. Dian stood head and shoulders over them. They're adept at poisons and would have had endless opportunity to poison her food or kill her in the bush. Crashing through her cabin wall and trashing her room after hacking through her skull is just not their style."

"So who could it have been?"

Kristen held the lantern at her side now, and the semi-darkness around them added to the grimness of her narrative. "People have been whispering for years that Protais Zigirazo, the brother-in-law of the president, ordered the murder. The locals call him Mr. Z. He was prefect of the province covering both the park and Karisoke, and he's stinking rich from illegal businesses, animal trafficking, that sort of thing. It seems now evident that he hired assassins, because she'd threatened both to expose him and to stop gorilla tourism, from which he was getting a lot of income."

"Has anyone tried to arrest him?"

"We have a lawyer attempting to reopen the case, but you can imagine how the courts here work." She shrugged in a way that was meant to change the subject and brushed dust off one of the bookshelves.

"It's strange. A hundred people have been all over this cabin—police, family. They've pretty much stripped the place clean of her personal items. But I still sometimes run across things that belonged to her."

"Like what?" Dana imagined a hairbrush or a sock.

"I'll show you what I found last time I was here." Two steps brought her to the chest of drawers, and she slid the top one open. "This thing." She held up what at first looked like a shrunken head, but when Kristen brought the lantern closer, Dana could see it was a rubber Halloween mask. A rather grotesque one, with pendulous blue lips and bulges under the eyeholes. Moles and pimples populated the skin, and a ragged red scar ran down one cheek.

Kristen laughed. "She used to wear them or post them near the gorilla nesting sites to scare off poachers. They hung on branches all over the mountainside, and for a long time, they seemed to work."

"Good idea, though kind of creepy."

"Creepy? Why?"

"Well, fake-scaring people is part of Halloween. You go 'boo!' and everyone laughs. But wearing them to convince people you really are a monster, that's a little strange, don't you think?"

"Funny. That's what her friend Rosalind said."

"Well, whoever Rosalind was, she was right."

"Rosalind Carver. Dian's best friend, who ran a flower plantation at Mutera. Still does, I think, though we've lost touch. She was the one person who remained a friend through all those eighteen years, and she hated Dian's masks. She claimed they brought out the worst of her demons. I always thought it was the exact opposite."

"I'm not sure what you mean."

"On the outside Dian was this angry woman who presented a coldness, even a hostility that kept everyone at arm's length. But she had a flame inside her, a righteousness in the purest sense, that you could see in her eyes. In a way, it was the best part of her. When she wore the monster mask, it was another wall of separation, a reduction of that passion to something trivial. Either way, Rosalind tried to dissuade her."

"I think you both must have loved her."

Kristen dropped her eyes. "Well, yes. We both wanted to take care of her. Not that it did her any good." She dropped the rubber mask back into the drawer and slid it shut.

"Miss Kristen." A dark form stood on the porch just outside the open door. Kristen approached him with the lantern, and Dana saw an old man with a cap of white hair and a slight stoop.

"Buffalo is in the camp, near our food store," he announced. "The men throw sticks at him, but he doesn't go. Maybe if you shoot your gun—"

"Yes, of course. I'll be right out." She turned to Dana. "This is Senweke, our senior tracker, who's been at Karisoke since forever. He can tell you anything you need to know. Anyhow, sorry to end our little tour, but I have to go scare off a buffalo."

"Can I help?" Dana followed her out onto the porch and watched as she locked the door behind them.

"No. I'm sure a gunshot in the air will send him running. Here, you can take the lantern. Let's continue our conversation another day, all right?" Without waiting for a reply, she set off at a jog beside the African.

Nonplussed, Dana stood on the porch for a moment, watching what might have been comical. A slender, delicate woman jogging into the darkness with an old man—to scare off a buffalo that outweighed them both tenfold.

What should she do now? Then she remembered the gorilla cemetery she'd read about that was close by Dian's cabin. It couldn't be that difficult to locate. In fact, stepping carefully up the gentle slope behind the cabin, she quickly came upon the patch of grass and grave markers.

She was surprised at how many there were. She counted some fifteen wooden stakes rising from the grassy ground, and each one held a wooden plaque. Somber, she wandered among them, holding the lantern over each one, trying to imagine the dark creatures lying beneath them.

Uncle Bert, Macho, Kweli, Nunkie were names she remembered from reading Dian's book, but others—Marchessa, Frito, Leo, Kazi, Kurudi—she didn't recall. The last one brought her to a halt. It was Digit, whose death was the beginning of Dian's passion, some would call her madness, that changed research into a crusade.

Dana ran her finger along the wooden plaque. She understood the outrage and disbelief, the desire for revenge. Killing a creature who understood love and who offered it back was an atrocity.

And there, a few steps away, was the stone circle that held the grave of Dian Fossey. With a last caress of Digit's marker, she stepped into the circle, then knelt to hold the lantern closer to the double gravestones with their metal markers, one in English and one in Kinyarwanda.

NYIRAMACHABELLI—
REST IN PEACE, DEAR FRIEND,
ETERNALLY PROTECTED IN THIS SACRED GROUND,
FOR YOU ARE HOME WHERE YOU BELONG.

She sat on the soft ground and brushed bits of mold from the raised letters. "You'd have done it too, wouldn't you?" she asked the grave marker. "If someone had killed Digit for pleasure and made a film of it for amusement and profit, you'd shoot him too. I'm sure of it."

As clearly as if the spirit of Dian Fossey were standing right next to her, she sensed a rough smoker's voice reply, *In an instant.* A wave of relief came over her for the first time since she'd fled the hideous basement. Here was a woman who shared her sense of justice. If nothing else, at least two of them burned with it.

The fine mist that had hovered in the air thickened to rain and forced her to return to the cold comfort of her own cabin. The ashes still smoldered in the stove, and with a bit of straw, she managed to rekindle them. She huddled over the slowly growing heat. *Two of us against the world.* She repeated the comforting thought.

But one of them was dead.

CHAPTER FIVE

Dana had the nightmare again, the blood dream that had plagued her since the horror in the basement. Once again she stumbled in the dark, this time in a room, searching for a light switch. But the wall was smooth. She stepped farther in, hands held out, and the floor was sticky with blood. Something dead lay at her feet, and some ominous presence stood behind her. Metal clanged against metal—a machete. She turned to face it blindly, and when the mortal blow fell across her face, she awoke with a silent scream.

She lay awhile, bewildered, until awareness returned in stages. First that she was in Africa, in a cabin at Karisoke, that she was working for Kristen Wolfe, and last, that whatever job she was supposed to be doing, she was late for it.

She lurched out of bed, threw on her clothes, laced up her hiking boots, and dashed out the door. She half expected to find an angry Kristen on the path tapping her wristwatch, but the entire camp was still. Baffled for a moment, she started for Kristen's cabin and then remembered, it was Christmas Day.

She exhaled relief. She wasn't late for anything. Checking her own watch, she noted it was ten o'clock. Good. At that hour it wouldn't be impolite to knock on Kristen's door.

Kristen opened it, fully dressed and with her glasses atop her head.

Dana smoothed back her hair, which she realized she hadn't yet combed. "Good morning. I woke up, guilty that I wasn't out on the trail at the crack of dawn, but then remembered what day it is. Sorry if I'm a little rumpled. Do you have anything planned for me to do?"

Smiling her amusement, Kristen stepped back to admit her. As she entered, Dana smelled the aroma of coffee and turned toward the stove where the pot stood.

"Would you care for some?" Kristen asked. "It's from a couple of hours ago but should still be good."

"I'd love some. Do you have sugar?"

"On the table." Kristen filled a fresh mug for Dana and added hot coffee to the half-filled mug on her desk. "Ordinarily work starts at dawn, but you're entitled to a lie-in on your first day, especially when it's Christmas. None of the men are working today either. In fact, they'll be arriving soon with their families to start cooking."

"I'm relieved to know I haven't screwed up already. Can I do anything in the meantime? Baste the turkey, put the rum in the eggnog or Christmas carols on the stereo?" Dana stirred sugar into her coffee and took the first sip. It wasn't bad, though a little stronger than she was used to.

"Thanks for offering, but no to all of the above. The women will concoct something out of beans and sweet potatoes, and the men will finish brewing enough pombe for them all. As for Christmas carols, I think you'll find the Rwandans do just fine with their own music. But if you want to occupy yourself while we're waiting, I'll give you a rundown on gorilla care."

"That sounds perfect. I have a lot to learn."

Kristen took her cup from the desk and sat down at the table across from Dana. This morning she had the schoolmarm look again, with her glasses on a chain. When she peered closely at something, they moved from her chest to her nose, then to the top of her head.

"To start, I'm sending you out tomorrow with Senweke, our oldest tracker. He even worked with Dian, so he knows more about gorillas than anyone. He'll show you how to track them and interact with them without getting hurt or hurting them."

"How many gorillas are out there, anyhow? How are they doing?"

"When Dian started in the late sixties, the mountain gorillas were all but extinct. She was determined to save them, no matter how many enemies she made doing so. And she succeeded, almost single-handedly. Today we estimate about six hundred throughout the Virungas, though Karisoke studies only about a hundred of them."

"They live in family groups, that much I know. Dominated and protected by a silverback." Dana wanted to make it clear she'd done her homework.

"Yes, and the interesting thing about the silverback, at least if he's accumulated females, is that his role as family head is primary. He defends his infants ferociously, and that's why any live capture of a young gorilla, say, for a zoo, always involves killing the silverback as well as the mother." She took a long drink of coffee to let the lesson sink in.

"On the other hand, if he *is* killed and his females migrate with their babies to other groups, the new silverbacks will almost always eliminate the foreign infants to bring the mothers back into estrus."

"Hmm. Like lions do. How often do the females have young? I mean under ideal conditions."

"About once every three years. Which means she'll be tending to her infant for most of that time. The babies can eat vegetation from the age of two but have to learn from her which plants to eat and how to strip off the bark, etc."

"What group will I be monitoring? Will it have any infants?"

"Ultimately, you'll be reporting on all of them, but to start, Senweke will take you to group four, Ndengera's group. Their home territory is relatively close to camp, and they're well acclimated to humans. Then we'll send you off to meet the other groups. Eventually you'll be able to recognize them as individuals by their nose patterns, their scars, or their behavior."

The high-pitched shrieking of happy children interrupted their conversation. "Ah, well. I guess it's starting." Kristen went to the door. "Sure enough, the families are here and the men are bringing in the pombe."

Dana stood behind her, watching the Africans arrive. At the front, two men bore between them an enormous clay pot hanging in a net from bamboo shoulder poles. Behind them, half a dozen women came dressed in brightly patterned fabric wrapped around the lower body and gathered at the waist, with a second piece draped diagonally over the shoulder. Each woman seemed to have her own pattern, for no two were the same.

The women waved as they passed, unsuccessfully calling their cavorting children to heel. Like mothers everywhere.

"In no time at all, they'll have a huge fire going and their stew will be ready. Our contribution, by the way, is a raisin cake." Kristen pointed with her head toward a square metal pan covered with a cloth on a shelf. "I made it this morning."

"A real cake? How do you bake a cake on a wood stove?"

"Pretty much the same way you do in an oven. You just pour the batter into one pan and cover it with another one. You have to keep the lower pan a little elevated so you don't get the pizza-dough effect, but in general, it works fine."

Dana wandered over to the cake and poked it gently. The surface gave and then rose again in the normal way. "Amazing. Were you raised by Amish or something?"

"No, but my husband and I used to camp a lot, and you learn tricks like that."

Husband. The word was like a slap. But she should have expected that. How could such an attractive woman not have caught the attention of men? And belonged to one.

Suddenly she lost interest in the cooking lesson. "Uh, maybe we should head over there. Can I carry something?"

"Sure. What about the cake? I'll bring the gifts." Kristen disappeared into the bedroom and returned with the cardboard box Mukera had carried up the mountain.

"I hope they appreciate you for doing all this," Dana said, opening the door with her free hand.

"I hope what I do shows how much I appreciate *them.*"

A fire was already burning in a circle of stones near the men's house, and someone had set a ring of stools, chairs, and empty crates around it. The men welcomed their employer with enthusiasm and offered warm handshakes to Dana as well. Only the children watched silently, eyes intent on the gift box.

Senweke emerged from the men's hut and made a ceremony of offering them a cup of the new pombe. Kristen took a long swallow and handed the pot to Dana, who feigned drinking and wiped her mouth with the back of her hand. "Merci," she said.

"It's time for introductions," Kristen said in French, then muttered to her in English. "Don't worry if you can't remember their names. I'll remind you again later." When she turned to the nearest man, she spoke again in French.

"Dana, this is our head porter, Gwehanda, and his wife." She pronounced a name of five or six syllables. Dana didn't try to repeat it but smiled warmly and shook the woman's hand. In return, the woman bowed and spoke a long unintelligible phrase, presumably in Kinyarwanda.

"She's wishing you Merry Christmas and Happy New Year," Kristen said.

"*Merci et joyeux Noël*," Dana responded, in linguistic compromise. By then another one of the staff had stepped up. A stocky man, with a potbelly and a wide grin. A portly woman stood behind him.

"This is Kanyara, one of our housemen. He's the one who built your fire yesterday. And this is his wife." And again came the multiple syllables. Dana responded with the same good wishes in French.

Two men stepped up together, neither with a wife in tow. Both were slender, with narrow skulls and long, straight noses. One was light-skinned and angular, with slightly awkward movements, like a teenager whose body had grown too fast. His companion was the color of dark chocolate, though pale patches under his eyes gave him a sort of radiance. He was more graceful than his friend, but enormous ears compromised his rather aristocratic beauty.

"These are two of our trackers, Nemeye and Ntampaka," Kristen said. Dana needed to know these names and tried to memorize them, but then forgot them again immediately. Obviously, she'd have to come up with some nicknames.

The ritual continued until Dana had met the entire staff and all the visitors to the party, at which time the dinner of beans and sweet potatoes was served. Bowls of various dimensions appeared and the stew was ladled out, first to Kristen and Dana, the honorary guests, and then to all the others.

The buzz and chatter died down as everyone began to eat, and Dana cautiously took her first bite. The concoction, unlike the pombe, was surprisingly good and very filling, though it could have used some salt.

The men took turns adding wood to the fire, ensuring it burned high to counteract the cool late-afternoon air. Dana swept her gaze around the harmonious gathering of Hutu porters and housemen, Tutsi trackers, and two white foreigners. This is how Africa should be, she thought.

She glanced across the fire, where Kristen sat chatting with Senweke. His cap of white hair and the pipe he smoked gave him an air of aged wisdom, one he deserved, for no one could deny that he knew more about Karisoke than anyone.

How pleasant to watch the two of them in lively conversation, ignoring age, nationality, race. Maybe it was the celebratory fire that crackled between her and them, but Dana felt a wave of affection for them.

She was startled as one of the women took her empty bowl from her hands, signaling the end of the meal. Another woman came behind her handing out small blocks of the cake Kristen had made that morning.

"My friends." On the other side of the fire, Kristen had stood up and was calling attention to herself. She delivered a little speech, mostly in French, with a few phrases in Kinyarwanda, and then began to distribute gifts. She began with the children, handing out mints or gumdrops or Tootsie Rolls in little bags, the kind that people gave trick-or-treaters on Halloween. The women came next, each one getting a length of bright fabric, presumably enough to make one of the colorful skirts they favored.

Then the men were invited up and handed their new shirts and rubber boots. Last of all, she presented a small box to Senweke. Bowing from the waist, he opened it and lifted out something coiled. Letting it unroll, he displayed it to the crowd, a belt with a brass casting for a buckle. The figure was hard to make out from a distance, but Senweke announced "a gorilla" and bowed again to show his gratitude. The other Rwandans applauded, but when it became clear that the gift-giving had ended, they stood up and began clapping and chanting.

Dana could make no sense of the words, and the chant could have been anything from nonsense syllables to an epic poem. It was surprisingly melodic to her Western ears, and she was sure, if she knew the tune, she could have sung along with them.

As if on cue—though perhaps it *was* a cue—the women and girls gathered in a cluster beside the fire and began to dance to the rhythm of the chant. While the men continued clapping and singing in unison, they swayed gently, twisting arms and shoulders, bending and swooping, following a complex pattern of movements.

After some ten minutes of the graceful female ballet, the men leapt forward and the women backed away, taking up the musical accompaniment. The male dancing was more jerky and energetic, with hops and leaps and stomps, and they whirled in a dizzying fashion. This too lasted for some ten minutes before the women leapt back into the fray, providing a sort of counterpoint, the women resuming their soft swaying while the men wove among them leaping wildly. Even the children seemed to know all the motions, the boys and girls executing the steps assigned to their gender.

It was a thrilling spectacle, with the dancers' loose clothing rising and falling with every leap and turn, and Dana could only imagine how it would have looked on a wider stage.

After perhaps half an hour, the drums took priority, and only a few remained dancing to the rhythms of the drum dialogue. Two drummers became three, and three became four, the rhythms ever more complex. They drummed in syncopation, like a difference of opinion in a language that preceded speech and rendered it unnecessary. The beat continued for the next hour, becoming ever more frenetic as the dancers consumed their pombe.

Gradually, a mist settled over the camp, the bright afternoon sky giving way to a dark, overcast sky that threatened rain, until the only spot of light and warmth was the fire. All around them were the blurred outlines of trees—the mysterious, magical, dangerous forest—and the drumming seemed to be their excited heartbeat. The fire was their solace, their clarity. Someone tossed a few more logs on it, causing it to throw up sparks.

Dana's every sense was engaged—by the colors of the women's clothing, the rhythmic drumming against the background of chatter, then by the smell of the wood smoke and the perspiration of the dancers, and finally by the taste of the pombe, which on her second try wasn't so bad.

Her attention returned to Kristen, who still sat with Senweke on the other side of the fire. Perhaps fatigue and jetlag had made her a little dizzy, but Dana found everything romantic and beautiful— Kristen, Senweke, the dancers, the sense of community. On her first day as a fugitive in Rwanda, she had come upon a fragile and precious harmony, held together by the spirit of a single fascinating woman. Dana sensed the presence of Dian Fossey and knew she smiled.

At that moment the mist condensed to rain, the droplets hissing on the burning logs. Under the light rainfall the Rwandans gathered their drums and pots and children. Kristen stood up, and after a series of handshake and shoulder pats with her staff and their wives, she came around to Dana.

"What do you think of our Rwandan Christmas?" she asked as they walked side by side away from the men's house.

"I think I want a gorilla belt buckle."

Kristen laughed. "You can get one yourself next time you're in New York City. I bought it in a novelty shop in Greenwich Village."

"I'll remember that. But yes, I thought it was a wonderful celebration. Is Christmas always so cheerful at Karisoke?"

"Generally, but it always has a somber note as well, at least for me."

"Why's that?" They were at the crossroads where Kristen's path diverged from the one leading to the middle cabin.

"Tomorrow is the anniversary of Dian's death. I never forget that. Never." Kristen kissed her quickly on the cheek. "Merry Christmas, Dana," she said, and pivoted away down her own path.

Chapter Six

December 26, 1993

"Bonjour, Senweke," she said as she opened her door to the senior tracker. He wore his new shirt and rubber boots, which contrasted sharply with the mud-splattered cotton pants tucked into them. The canvas sack he carried on a strap diagonally across his chest had also seen better days.

"Bonjour, Miss Dana," he said, detached but polite, like a man who knew his own worth. What thoughts lay behind his cool manner she couldn't guess, but it made her both proud and humble to know her first foray into gorilla territory would be with a man who had tracked for Dian Fossey. She'd memorized the French expressions she'd need for ape-and-jungle situations but, for the rest, would have to resort to French 101 sentences. Embarrassing. She sensed Senweke had much to teach her and she regretted now that she hadn't studied more.

She drew on her own boots and rain jacket, laid her camera strap over her shoulder, and joined him in high spirits. With any luck, today she'd meet her first free gorillas.

Senweke walked slightly ahead of her to an area above the camp, saying little and responding to her remarks with "Oui" or simply with a grunt. But when they crested a ridge some forty-five minutes later and the foliage became dense, he slowed his pace and bent forward, studying the ground.

"Ah, voila," he said finally, though in his Rwandan French, it sounded more like *Ahwallah*, and halted.

He swept his palm along the surface of a nearby bush. "You see the broken stems? The gorillas have passed. The stems always break in the direction they are traveling. If you get close, you can smell them."

But when she bent down to sniff one of the leaves, he tapped her on the shoulder and said, "This time you do not need. Look over there?"

She peered through the brush where he pointed and saw animal feces. Flies buzzed around them and they gave off a barnyard odor, similar to that of horse droppings.

He touched them with his toe. "These tell us much. They smell normal, so the gorillas travel slowly, nothing chases them." He knelt on one knee in front of the feces and motioned her down next to him. This animal is healthy but not too big. A female, maybe. Ah, look over there."

Slightly ahead of them a smaller pile lay off to the side, lighter and looser.

"Her baby," he added. "They stopped here yesterday."

"How can you know all that?"

"Not so difficult. Gorillas leave a trail all the time, and when they are healthy and not afraid, their dung is solid. A big animal leaves big dung and a small animal less. The flies, but no fly eggs, tell us it is recent. Also, with the rain, after two days, it dissolves."

That made sense. "And when they are sick or afraid?"

"When they run away, they leave diarrhea, and it smells very bad. This way you know if you are following a group that is running." He stood up and resumed the climb.

"Interesting," Dana said, following him. "Funny. I never saw that in the Tarzan movies."

"Tarzan?"

"Nothing. A silly story. For American children. So…what should I do when I see a gorilla?"

"Become like a gorilla. Sit down and make noise like this." He grunted in soft, throaty rumbles. "Don't reach out your hand, and don't stare at them. And if they charge at you, don't run away. It is probably only display."

Dana thought for a moment. "Probably? What if it's *not* display?"

"Then run away," he said, resuming the march.

They hiked for another hour among trees and dense undergrowth, alternating with open ridges and exposed rock, and she tried to maintain his pace. Her legs and feet were beginning to hurt again, but she was determined not to whine.

Senweke abruptly stopped hacking with his panga and halted. Puzzled, Dana peered from behind him. All she saw at first was the usual foliage but then realized that it wasn't growing naturally. It seemed to have been gathered into rough circles that had depressions at their centers. She looked farther and discerned half a dozen such circles.

"Gorilla night nests," Senweke announced and stepped forward cautiously. "Keep going but slowly," he added in a subdued monotone.

"Do you see them?" she whispered. The air began to smell a bit like old sweat, and she shivered with excitement.

"Yes, up ahead. Come closer. Let them see you and then sit down. Don't try to hide."

She took another step, peered through the underbrush, and caught her breath. Four bulky black creatures, sitting in a tight group, turned their heads idly toward them but seemed unperturbed. Gorillas! Her first gorillas. Right there in front of her. She was both thrilled and nervous. What if she did something wrong and they fled? Or displayed?

But they merely kept on plucking stalks of something that grew around them and stripping off the outer skin.

One of them...she could hardly believe her luck...suckled an infant. A bundle of pitch-black fur that she calculated weighed as much as a two-year-old child, it turned at the sound of their arrival. Enormous brown eyes gazed toward her, and the movement of its little head caused the nipple to slide from its mouth. Wiry hair grew in a halo around its head, giving the little creature its look of astonishment.

Behind them, two juvenile gorillas wrestled, alternately barking and huffing. Three other adults squatted under a bent hagenia tree, focused on their lunch.

"Oh, how wonderful," she murmured. "But where's the silverback?"

"Over there, watching out for them." Senweke whispered, pointing with his chin.

The largest of the gorillas sat on a low tree branch just above the family group. He turned his head to glare at the intruders for a moment and then yawned, revealing a vast and terrifying maw with canine teeth larger than her thumb.

The threat was subtle and efficient, and he seemed to know it, for he stood up and turned his back, and his massive square buttocks twitched, as if to show contempt for the trespassers.

"Which group is this?" Dana asked in a low voice.

"Group four, the closest one to the camp. The silverback is called Ndengera, and the blackback over there with the females is Ngabo. He is the son or brother of Ndengera, so he is allowed to stay, even though he is a grown male. Soon he will be a silverback and will have to go."

"The others are females?"

"Yes, Inzozi, Kundu, and the mother Amahoro. The juveniles are the children of Inzozi."

"Rwandan names. No more Uncle Bert and Flossie, eh?"

"No. No more American names. They are Rwandan, these gorillas."

"How old is the baby?"

"A year and a half. We think it is a female, and her name is Mwelu. She will drink her mother's milk for another year, but she begins to eat by herself. You will learn their names and faces to keep notes on each one."

"Yes, of course. I'll start now." She slid her notebook and pen from inside her jacket and noted all the names, with details and little sketches to help her distinguish one from the other.

Ndengera had a strip of gray across his thick brow ridge, though it might have been common to all silverbacks. She couldn't be sure. Ah, there was something that distinguished him. The last finger on his right hand was a stub, and she wondered what injury had caused it.

"That one is Inzozi?" She pointed to the smallest of the females, and Senweke nodded.

"She has a torn ear. Good way to identify her." She noted the fact in her record book.

"And that one is Kundu. She is older and not afraid of people, but she steals your things if you do not watch out." Kundu placidly chewed some kind of plant stem.

But it was the mother gorilla who held her attention, as she slid her infant to her lap and gazed skyward, like some simian Madonna. "Amahoro is rather pretty, isn't she? I mean, as far as gorillas go," Dana observed, and made a simple sketch of her long sloping snout and thick upper lip. The juveniles were harder to distinguish, though one was larger and noisier than the other.

Lastly, she sketched the infant Mwelu with her huge, dark eyes and the smooth, black mountain-gorilla equivalent of a pug nose.

While she sketched, glancing alternately at the faces and back at her drawings, the two adolescents neared and began to romp around her. After checking that everything was attached to her and couldn't be snatched away, she leaned toward them and held out her hand. "Naughty boys. What noisy gorillas you are."

They approached and then fled, as if challenging each other to ever-greater recklessness, and Dana was ecstatic. She was so engrossed in the game she was slow to notice that Amahoro had risen, babe in arms, and also wandered closer, perhaps out of curiosity for the pale ape who had long dark fur only on her head.

Amahoro sat now with her suckling infant, serenity itself, scarcely twenty feet away. Senweke had told her not to stare, but Dana couldn't help herself. Like a high-school girl who'd caught the eye of a star athlete, she gazed, love-struck, into the warm chocolate eyes of Amahoro. She saw past the huge nostrils and the heavy brow, and sensed a tranquil, loving mother who wanted only to care for her infant. "How beautiful you are, Amahoro, and your baby is, too." She reached out, longing to touch them.

At that moment, the silverback leapt from his branch and lunged toward her with a deafening roar. In shock, Dana started to turn, then fell back, paralyzed by fear. The huge male shoved away the mother gorilla with the back of his massive hand and stopped just short of Dana's feet, snorting. He growled once, then turned and scampered off, leading the rest of the troupe into the underbrush.

Dana lay stunned for a moment, then caught her breath. She'd ignored all the rules. "I'm sorry. I got too close, didn't I?"

Senweke shrugged. "Next time you will know."

Chagrined, she dropped her glance. "All right. I promise to be more careful." She gathered her things and followed him back through the passageway he'd hacked for them. Chastened, but also elated, she chortled softly. "But I think Amahoro and I are gal pals now."

She trailed behind him as they made their way down the mountain but was soon puzzled. She thought she'd been paying attention, but she recognized nothing, and the trail, such as it was, went off in an unexpected direction.

"Am I completely lost, or are we going back a different way?"

"You are not lost. We are making a circle to look for traps. Like this one." He tapped his panga against the base of a tree, and something snapped shut around it. A wire snare. With a sudden jerk, he yanked it away from the tree it was tied to and hacked it to pieces before shoving the tangled mess of wire into his sack.

"I'm going to have to learn how to spot them, aren't I?" He didn't reply, but now that some of the gorillas had names and faces, the thought of their being trapped and mutilated seemed horrifying. A familiar nausea rose in her, and she shook the memory from her mind.

"Yes, teach me about those, too."

Two hours later, after a circuitous route that yielded four more snares, they arrived at Karisoke, and Dana felt victorious. Her first day on the job, and she'd already spent an hour with a family of magnificent free gorillas. Now she carried the sweet memory of glistening dark eyes and a little black pug nose. She *had* to see her again, and perhaps touch her, and watch her grow up. It was a bit like falling in love.

She deposited her sketchbook and notes in her quarters for later typing and hurried toward Kristen's cabin to report. Personal reporting wasn't obligatory, the notes would have sufficed, but she was dying to share her excitement. Kristen would be pleased, and Dana wanted very much to please her.

But when she arrived and was invited in, it was not for the quiet private talk she'd expected.

To start, the disagreeable odor of cigarette smoke filled the cabin, and it came from a swarthy little man sitting at the table. He was probably of average height, but his round shoulders and slight paunch made him appear smaller, and his partial baldness added to his age. She already didn't like him.

"Dana, this is Rudy Lambot, our part-time veterinarian. Rudy, this is Dana Norland, from New York."

When he put his cigarette between his lips and offered his hand, she noted that his fingernails were stained, presumably with nicotine. Dana shook it quickly and resisted wiping her hand on her pant leg afterward. Meanwhile, Kristen had pulled a chair over to the table for her and she sat down.

Lambot tapped the ash of his cigarette onto a saucer. "New York, heh? My brother's there. Teaches biology at Columbia. Married an American."

"Oh, that's nice." She couldn't think of anything else to say.

Kristen filled the teakettle with water from a plastic jerrycan. "Rudy's just been telling me about the unrest in Kigali." She set the kettle on the stove top, and stepping over to the counter, she added a tablespoon of black tea to the familiar rose teapot.

"Unrest?" Dana recalled something about political tensions but assumed they weren't important. After all, the Christmas party had shown her a people in harmony.

"Yeah. I was in a shop buying supplies for the clinic when a Hutu farmer came in. He must have had some kind of quarrel with the owner, a Tutsi, because he smashed his window and threatened to kill him."

"But the Hutu-Tutsi tension makes no sense. How can you have racial tensions between people of the same race? And they're the same religion, too, aren't they?"

He blew smoke out of the side of his mouth. "Race isn't the issue. Tribal loyalty is. The Batwa, Bahutu, and Watutsi all arrived at different times with different ways of surviving—hunters and gatherers, farmers, cattle herders. They got along fairly well until my people came along and tipped the balance."

"*Your* people? You mean white men? Veterinarians?" Dana snickered.

Unamused, he stubbed his cigarette out in the saucer. "I mean the Belgians. During their mandate, they used the Tutsis as administrators, giving them authority over the Hutus. Worse, they put a tribal designation on everyone's identification card. Then tribal affiliation was impossible to conceal, even for the child of a mixed marriage."

"They have kind of a truce now, don't they? I mean at Christmas, everything seemed fine."

"Yeah, things calmed down in '91 when the president signed a power-sharing agreement between Hutus and Tutsis. But it hasn't been ratified, and the tensions are still there. You hear about murders all the time."

The water had boiled, and Kristen came back to the table with the teapot. "Of course, people commit murder for all kinds of reasons. It doesn't have to be political."

Rudy nodded. "That's true. It's probably not much different in Harlem, right?" He directed his attention toward Dana. "People breaking in, killing each other. My brother has stories all the time. Just a couple of weeks ago, there was a double murder not far from Columbia."

Dana froze.

"A gang killing?" Kristen asked.

"They don't think so. The killer ran into one of the buildings of the university and disappeared."

Kristen looked into the distance for a moment. "Wait, I remember that. I was at Columbia giving a lecture when the police came in looking for someone. That was the day Dana signed up to come here. Remember?" She looked at Dana.

Dana crafted an expression of indifference. "Uh, yeah, right. I guess so. I wasn't paying much attention to anything but your presentation and thinking about making the big move."

Kristen took the saucer of cigarette ashes and dumped them into her compost bucket. "Did they ever find the killer?"

Lambot shook his head. "I don't think so." He cleaned one of his nails with the edge of another.

Her heart pumping wildly, Dana changed the subject. "Uh, so, you're part-time. Does that mean you come up only when one of the gorillas is sick?" She hoped he wasn't a regular social visitor.

"Theoretically, yes. But even then, someone's got to catch them before we can treat them, so I don't usually get involved unless it's a serious case."

Kristen drank the last of her tea and poured another cup. "Be great to have a real clinic up here at Karisoke, but we don't have the funds. So, for the time being, we just look at gorillas and hope they stay well. And when we can, we chase away poachers."

Lambot withdrew a crumpled pack of cigarettes from a shirt pocket and tapped out another one. Inserting the filter tip between his lips, he lit it with a small plastic lighter.

"No money, no medicine. That's the way it is up here," he said between puffs, then glanced over at Dana. "Where'd you say you were from in New York? You know anyone at Columbia?"

Dana dropped her eyes. "Oh, I'm not really from New York. I was just there for a short time looking for work." She realized at once the discrepancy between that remark and her presence in a student audience at Kristen's talk, and she felt her face redden. Kristen didn't seem to notice, but it was obvious that talk about New York had dangerous pitfalls, so she stood up from the table, terminating it.

"I just stopped by to say I had a good day with my first gorilla encounter. I'll write it up, of course. I'm really looking forward to going out again tomorrow to meet the others." Without offering her hand to Rudy Lambot, she tilted her head toward him and said, "Nice to meet you."

It wasn't, and she was glad to be away from him.

CHAPTER SEVEN

Dana couldn't sleep. Rudy Lambot and his questions about New York had thrown her off balance, and she was still excited about meeting the gorillas. It didn't help that the fire in her stove had burnt out and she was chilly. But the moonlight shining through her window told her the night was clear and it was something she shouldn't miss. Throwing back her blanket, she drew on her jacket and slid her feet into her boots. Outside, the night air was cool on her pajama-clad legs, but the rest of her was warm, so she leaned against the cabin wall and gazed up at the sky.

The full moon obscured most of the stars, but in the distance, the snow at the tip of one of the volcanoes seemed to glow white. Was it Karisimbi? She couldn't remember.

Across the path in front of her cabin, several hagenia trees were silhouetted black against the cobalt sky, and the mosses that hung from them like ragged sleeves made them slightly sinister.

The cliché was true. The African night was different from night elsewhere. She could hear the calls of wildlife, harmless and deadly, that prowled all around her. Child of the city, who'd grown up with traffic noise and sirens, she wasn't equipped to identify the sounds of animals. Some she could make no sense of at all, a woodpecker *rattatat* where no woodpeckers lived or the coughing, creaking, squeaking of beasts that were outside her experience. The snorts were probably from a buffalo, the hooting from an owl, but the hissing could have come from insects or from the gurgling of the creek on the other side of the meadow. She thought she could even hear an elephant in the distance. Sleepless now, she followed the path from her cabin through the glade away from the buffalo and toward the creek and the high-pitched metallic clicking of cicadas. She passed Kristen's hut, where no light burned, and was careful to tread softly.

Silently she watched the rippling silver of the creek water. She must have disturbed bats from the trees behind the hut, for they fluttered around her, one of them grazing her as it passed. "Shit! Get awaaay!" she called in spontaneous fear and ducked away from them.

A light went on in Kristen's window and a moment later, she emerged. "What's happening? Are you all right?" She approached, a knitted shawl thrown around her shoulders.

"Oh, I'm sorry I woke you." Dana was chagrined. "I was just, well…I couldn't sleep and came out to walk and listen to the sounds. Stupid of me, wasn't it? Looks like I set off the bats. Who knows what else I could have bumped into, right?"

Kristen was at her side now, and the moon illuminated her in bluish light. "Well, it probably wasn't wise. Wildlife sometimes wanders in to drink from the creek, even the occasional elephant or buffalo."

"I didn't think of that. But the sounds are totally new to me. Buffalo snorts instead of car alarms."

"So, you never got to tell me. How was your first visit with the gorillas?"

"It was thrilling. I got to see the new baby. Unfortunately, just as I was having a tender moment with her, the silverback charged us. I was sitting down. Otherwise I'd have run like hell, breaking two rules instead of just one."

"You did right. Most of the charges are for show, but you do have to recognize the rare instance when one's for real."

"Yes, that's what Senweke said. Not very comforting information."

They stood together silently and Dana tried to ignore the chill on her legs. The night encounter had a wonderful intimacy, and she didn't want it to end.

"Um, about Dr. Lambot. Will we be seeing a lot of him?" she asked, keeping her voice neutral.

"Actually, I hope not. Ruhengeri used to have a whole clinic, called the Mountain Gorilla Veterinary Project. But when the civil war started a few years ago, it closed. Now we have only him. He mostly comes up when we have an injured animal, which we hope is rare. On the other hand, he usually brings news of what's happening in Rwandan politics. Things that we don't read in the newspaper or hear officially."

"How does he know those things? Just listening around?"

"More or less. But he's also very assimilated. 'Bushy,' Dian always said. He's been here for years, he speaks Kinyarwanda, and he's married to a Rwandan woman. It's useful to know someone who has his ear to the ground."

A sudden cry broke the soft gurgling of the stream. It started as a squeak, rose to a pig-like squeal, and then sounded like a screaming child.

"Good grief, what's that?"

Kristen chuckled. "Just a hyrax, one of those furry, rabbit-sized critters. They look like rodents, but they're not. You'll get used to hearing them and lots of other beasties day and night. The jungle reminds you that the world is full of animals and they were here first."

"Interesting. A minister in a church in New York said just about the same thing." Dana smiled inwardly, remembering the afternoon of music and zoo, a bright spot in the otherwise worst week of her life. "And he was standing over hundreds of family pets."

"Good for him. City people see so few animals and too often think of them as pets or vermin, or what they have for dinner, and that's what makes some of them cruel. The French are fond of saying, "The more I know about men, the more I love my dog.""

Dana grunted agreement. "Is that what brought you to Karisoke? Being fed up with men? Humans, I mean?"

Kristen took a step toward the footbridge and gazed down at the silvery creek. "Both, in a way. "When I was a child, my mother used to take me downtown—this was back in the time when people shopped downtown rather than at the mall. Anyhow, there was a man with an organ grinder and a monkey on a chain. Everyone thought it was so cute, but I was horrified. I didn't hear the music. I saw only the wretched little monkey, chained by the waist and holding a filthy little cup. It was the one thing that made me study zoology. I thought about being a vet but then became more interested in wildlife and keeping monkeys and other wild creatures out of the hands of people like that."

"That's very touching," Dana said with sincerity. Performing animals always depressed her, too. "So how did that bring you to Africa?"

Kristen stared at the sky, toward the horizon where a few stars were still visible in spite of the bright moon. "I was doing graduate study at Cornell in 1980 and was in a bad marriage at the time. Then Dian Fossey showed up as an adjunct professor, and I took her course in Comparative Primate Behavior. It was like a boat rescuing me from the water and offering me a voyage, and before it was over, I knew I wanted to go to Karisoke."

"Ah, so you followed the master."

"Yes, into a cauldron of turmoil, as it turned out. When I arrived here in autumn 1983, gorilla tourism was beginning, which Dian hated. It wouldn't go away, though, because it was big money for the Rwandans. Of course, they had their political conflicts, too, which bled over into ours. Then some of her own students fell out with her over her methods and priorities. The rifts kept getting bigger until it seemed almost everyone wanted her out. She knew too much, had too many enemies even at Karisoke, and just wouldn't compromise. And then somebody killed her." She drew her shawl tighter around her shoulders.

Dana could think of nothing to reply. She simply glanced over at Kristen, huddled in her shawl, her hair reflecting moonlight like Karisimbi's snow. What had kept her in Rwanda after Dian's murder—for another six years? She felt a sudden urge to embrace her but didn't move. She sensed enough danger all around her, and that would have been suicide.

Back in her cabin, Kristen stirred up the ashes in her stove and added a bit of kindling. When the fire finally radiated heat, she warmed her shawl, then wrapped it around her shoulders again and returned to bed, waiting for the heat to relax her enough to sleep.

Nice person, that Dana. Pretty, too, with her boyish body and long straight hair that always looked tousled. But she was opaque, even secretive. No matter. She genuinely liked the gorillas and was also willing to do the less glamorous work of collecting snares and dung. Would she commit to a longer stay? Time would tell.

How fortunate she was able to leave New York on such notice, just when two other assistants had to depart and Karisoke most needed new talent. But what kind of life did she have that was so easy to leave? What could she so blithely abandon for an indefinite stay in a wild country? A lost job, a breakup with her boyfriend, bad debts?

Well, Dana wouldn't be the first person to come to Africa to start a new life. She'd done that herself, following the glamorous primatologist into the jungle on the same short notice. Of course, it helped that her husband was a bastard and had slapped her one time too many just as Dian Fossey arrived at Cornell.

And here it was, December 26, the anniversary of her murder. Kristen sat up and opened the drawer of her bedside table. Dian's .38 caliber revolver lay there as always, cleaned, oiled, and loaded with the correct ammunition this time. Dian had been too cautious or too trusting, had kept it unloaded, with the cartridges elsewhere, and that's what killed her. She'd been found, butchered, with that same pistol in one hand and the wrong ammunition in the other.

She lifted out the gun and caressed the wooden grip, murmuring.

My dear Dian. How could you be so careless? How could you be...such a mess of contradictions? World-famous primatologist and quasi-invalid, you were dynamic enough to make me want to follow you anywhere, yet so needy I sometimes had to half carry you up the trail. Your bad knees, back pain, flu, and emphysema couldn't stop you, though they ate away at you, like the loneliness and the drinking. I'd have taken care of you, you know. In spite of our age difference, I would have loved you if you'd let me. But all you wanted was a faithful assistant who stayed out of your emotions, which I did, while the men in your life came and went. But none of them helped you that terrible night, did they?

She glanced down at the weapon that was so heavy in her hand.

And neither did your gun.

With a long sigh, she laid the revolver back into the drawer and slid under the covers. She spoke out loud into the darkness. "I promised at your funeral, even if you wouldn't let me care for you, I'll always care for your children, so you can stop haunting me now." Feeling the blankets warm, she turned onto her side and recalled what had wakened her in the first place. Dana Norland, who wandered the camp at night looking at stars.

It would be nice to have a live woman to talk to, a significant improvement over mumbling to a gun.

CHAPTER EIGHT

By mid-January, Dana had learned a lot. For one, she'd become a fair cook, developing a real inventiveness in combining the odd items available from the Rwandan markets. And all on a wood stove.

She was also developing the knack of tracking gorillas, provided the foliage wasn't too dense. She'd learned the names and faces of three of the main groups that foraged around Visoke in the *Parc National des Volcans*, had a sketchy recognition of two other groups that wandered in and out of Zaire, knew what they ate, and learned that *ngagi* was the Kinyarwanda word for gorilla. She'd traveled on snare patrol with Kristen, and with each of the trackers at one time or another, and brought in dozens of traps.

She'd also made her peace with the steamy, sometimes dreary weather in the Virunga rainforest. All too often she'd set out bravely in the morning drizzle with the tracker of the day, only to have to turn back when the torrential downpours made the ground too slippery to climb and turned the open spaces to walls of water. The gorillas seemed to hate it too and huddled together in the dense vegetation, trying to stay warm. She sympathized with them and realized she used her wood stove as much for drying clothes as for cooking.

The last day of January brought relief, and she set out to check on her favorites in group four. She knew the jungle well now, and because they were so close, she was allowed to go alone. On this bright day, she had no trouble following their nesting sites, large ones for night and small careless ones for day. After only an hour's hike, she came upon them.

When she emerged from the brush lowering her head and making soft grunting noises, Ndengera, the silverback, glanced with gorilla boredom in her direction. Ngabo, the younger male, with just a narrow patch of silver around his midriff, sat stripping wild celery a few meters away. More and more she was convinced he was a younger brother and the kinship prevented a deadly rivalry. Even so, when he matured a bit more, he'd probably have to leave the group and try to start his own harem.

Ah, there they were, the two females Inzozi and Kundu, and the gentle mother Amahoro, whom she had begun to think of as attractive. The adolescents wrestled behind their father and he scratched his chest, ignoring them.

She stood for a while, letting them get used to her arrival, then edged slowly closer to Amahoro. She was taking a slight risk in approaching mother and infant, and in fact, good father and guardian of his family, Ndengera rose up a little and glared at her. But he knew her well. She waited a few moments, then approached within some ten feet of the mother and sat down.

With her head still tilted slightly downward, Dana studied Amahoro and her daughter. The Kinyarwanda name Mwelu, she learned, meant beautiful, and it was quite appropriate, for the one-and-a-half-year-old infant was as appealing as any human toddler Dana had ever seen. Her large brown eyes always seemed to show surprise, though her wild hair now fell slightly to both sides of her head and grew in a tiny widow's peak at her forehead. She puckered her baby lips and hooted softly.

Amahoro blinked and glanced away, perhaps her own way of saying, "Oh, it's only you again." More importantly, she loosened her hold on her baby, and Mwelu slid down onto the ground to land on all fours. Still timid, she wobbled only a few steps, clearly curious about the pale ape-in-clothing.

Dana remained motionless, while the precious face peered up at her with enormous shiny eyes, trying to figure her out. She longed to reach out and draw the adorable fluffy creature into her arms and smooth down her wild hair, but would not make the same mistake twice. Mwelu stood up again on her bowed legs and flopped down again onto her rear with a squeak. She patted the ground and her little mouth twisted sideways.

"You're just too big for your britches," Dana cooed. Mwelu's little gorilla lips puckered and twitched, and she slid a tiny black finger into her mouth, blinking. Then, bending forward, she squeezed out a slip of soft poo behind her and scampered back to her mother.

Dana snorted softly to herself. Poo was also part of her job, for Kristen would want to know if the baby had parasites. She fished inside her jacket for a plastic specimen envelope, then bent forward on one knee to gather a segment of the feces. "We'll run a test on it and call you in the morning," she quipped to the ever-attentive Amahoro, then slid the sealed envelope into her side pocket.

Amahoro took hold of her youngster's arm and swung her onto her back. With a grunt that was presumably gorilla for "That's enough for today," she lumbered leisurely through the brush toward the other females. A few minutes later, the entire troupe moved off.

"Was it something I said?" Dana called after the gorillas, amused at her own humor, then scribbled a few notes and began her way back. She still had a lot of daylight left, so she made a few short trips off on both sides of the trail looking for snares. She'd also grown adept at spotting them, wherever something looked particularly inviting to a hungry animal, and on this day managed to trigger four of them.

All in all, life was good, and as she began the trek down the mountain, she was able to forget for a while that she was a fugitive. And a murderer.

❖

It was always a pleasure to track with Ntampaka, whom his friends simply called Paka. There was something so wonderfully African about his skin, the color of dark chocolate, but with light patches under his eyes that made them seem larger, his glance more penetrating. He could also move through the underbrush like a cat, except for the crackling of twigs as he slashed them in a graceful sweep with his panga.

Today they looked for group four, Ndengera's family, that no one had monitored for several days. They had to travel farther than usual, past the group's normal feeding grounds and toward a valley dangerously near some patches of farmland.

Paka, with his big ears, heard it first, the chest-beating that went on a bit too long. "Something is wrong," he said, and they hurried toward the sound. A moment later they saw the silverback just uphill of the group, and when he spied them, his hooting modulated into a roar.

The adolescents and the blackback Ngabo were huddled close to him, and two of the females were lumbering back and forth, obviously agitated. Was it a buffalo, a poacher? If so, why didn't they flee? Dana's stomach tightened as she realized only one thing could be keeping them all there. One of them was snared.

As she neared, she could make out the faces of the two females. One of them, to her relief, was Amahoro with her infant Mwelu gripping her back. The other one was Inzozi. Where was Kundu?

Paka surveyed the terrain. "Kundu is over there. In a snare. Around her arm." He bounded toward the injured animal, but she turned and snapped at him, and he lurched back out of her reach. "We cannot help her. We must tell Miss Kristen."

"Yes, of course." They both ran full out, slipping and falling sideways on the downhill trail. After what seemed like hours, they reached the camp and Kristen's cabin. Dana knocked once and, without waiting for an answer, shoved open the door. Kristen looked up surprised from her table.

"Group four. Poachers. Kundu is ensnared. But she wouldn't let Paka touch her. The rest of the group is still there but a bit frantic."

Kristen was on her feet at the first three words and shot past them through the door. She sprinted first toward the men's cabin shouting, "Gwehanda!"

The stocky porter emerged as all three of them came to a halt at the men's campfire. "Gwehanda, you're the fastest. Your scooter is down in the car park, isn't it? You know where Dr. Lambot lives. Tell him a gorilla is caught in a snare, and bring him back as fast as you can. Please go right now!"

Gwehanda snatched up a stick and galloped across the meadow toward the woodlands.

Kristen turned to Dana. "What shape is she in?"

"The wire was high on her arm, above her elbow, and below it she seemed very swollen. I think she's been snared at least for a day for it to be that bad. She was passive until Paka tried to touch her."

Kristen winced and rubbed her own upper arm. "Poor creature. They have no idea what's happening, only that they have to break free, and their thrashing just increases the pain." She shook her head. "Unbearable. And it will take Gwehanda over two hours to get to Dr. Lambot, assuming he's even home, and another two hours to bring him back, so all we can do is wait."

"Is there any chance she can break the snare and run away with the wire still around her?"

Kristen laid her forehead in her hand. "Unfortunately, a good chance. That's happened twice before, and it's hell trying to capture the injured animal. And if we can't, they die over days and weeks from gangrene. That's why we don't want to excite them by showing up again without the right tools. Dr. Lambot has a tranquilizer gun and medications, and when he arrives we can do it right. In the meantime…" She grimaced again. "We try to protect her."

She turned to the tracker. "Paka, would you please go back there now? Keep a distance from her, and just make sure no Batwa get to her. Take your panga."

"Yes, Miss Kristen." He took off with a graceful lope toward the mountain trail.

❖

Four-and-a-half hours later, Gwehanda and an obviously winded Rudy Lambot emerged from the woodland to the east of Karisoke. "I hope I didn't hike up here for an animal that's about to die," he said sourly.

"No. When we left her this morning, she wasn't active, but the only damage seems to be to her arm. The silverback may be trying to bite the snare off her, but he won't succeed. It's too high. We just have to hope Paka hasn't had to hold off the poachers."

"Let's go then."

Dana, who knew the exact location of the gorillas, set the pace. Desperate concern for Kundu's suffering drove her to go faster, but the uphill path was sometimes steep, and she knew they couldn't last. Kristen followed directly behind her, apparently without effort, but Lambot, carrying his medical bag, was panting noisily.

Gwehanda, the fittest one of them all, brought up the rear to provide another set of hands. The sky had become overcast, and late-afternoon rain threatened. Lost in thought, Dana fretted over the possible problems. How were they going to treat a wounded gorilla in a downpour? Would Ndengera and the others still be there, or would they have moved on? The thought of the family abandoning her seemed terrible, though it would prevent interference, or even attack, while they tried to help.

When they reached the trapped Kundu, her family, in fact, had stayed with her, though at a distance, as if to encourage her to follow. Seeing four people arrive, Ndengera made a mock charge, but all of them knew to drop to their knees and lower their heads. He came to a halt, snatched at a few branches, and then withdrew.

Cautiously, they approached the injured gorilla, who growled and tried to back away. She had obviously been thrashing and tugging on the snare all day, for the wire was now deeply embedded in the flesh of her upper arm. "Poor thing," Kristen said. "She's in such pain. Everything must seem like a threat."

"I have to dart her," Lambot announced, stopping a few yards away. He set his medical kit down on the surface of the crushed foliage and opened it. "She's about 75 kilos, I'd guess," he said to no one in particular. "With ketamine, you don't want to overdose." Squatting over his kit, he measured out a precise amount of liquid from a vial into a spring-loaded syringe with a pink-feathered tail. Setting the dart aside, he screwed together the parts of a strange-looking sort of air rifle. It had a large sight, but its barrel was a simple pipe only a few centimeters in diameter. The grip was rather like a pistol, and the explosive power came from a cylinder of compressed air that screwed into the body of the grip.

With the delivery system assembled, he slid the loaded dart into the nozzle and stood up to take aim.

Ndengera obviously didn't like the gun and least of all seeing it point toward one of his females. With a barking roar, he charged again.

Lambot fell back onto the foliage while Paka and Gwehanda leapt forward between him and the silverback, swinging their sticks and shouting. Dana joined them, imitating the aggressive gorilla barking as well as she could.

Ndengera halted again and stood upright, exposing his enormous chest, then bared his fangs. "You have to get him away," Lambot said. "I can't do anything with him standing over me."

Kristen joined the shouting and stick banging, and finally Ndengera retreated, though only a few yards. It was clear they'd have to stand guard in case he charged again.

Behind them Lambot seized the moment and shot the sedative dart. Kundu shrieked and tried to pull away from the trap, but the wire and her obvious pain prevented her from breaking it. While Lambot disassembled his dart gun and laid it back in his kit bag, she rolled from one side to another, huffing and panting for several minutes until the sedative took effect and she began to relax.

"Okay, first the wire," Lambot said, and, leaving the two Africans to keep an eye on the silverback, he stepped over the brush to Kundu's side. "Christ, it's really cut deep." He pressed the tip of the wire cutter into the open wound, causing blood to seep out on both sides. Wincing, he moved it around, obviously trying to slip it past the wire. Then, with a grunt, he gripped the handles hard, and Dana heard the satisfying snap of the separating wire.

He slid the wire from around the suppurating arm and tossed it aside. "I'm going to wash the wound with iodine, but it won't stay clean long. We have to hope that she licks it clean herself, until new skin can form." He swabbed the arm with gauze patches until he'd removed most of the darkening blood, then trickled the iodine into the wound.

"I don't suppose you can bandage it, can you?" Dana said weakly.

"No, she'd rip it off in a minute. But I'm giving her a shot of amoxiclav."

"What's that?" Dana had never heard of it.

"It's a double antibiotic, a combination of amoxicillin, which they give to people, and clavulanic acid. It's the best I can offer her. He took another syringe from his kit and filled it from a small brown bottle, then injected it into the gorilla's shoulder above the wound.

Ndengera was becoming agitated again and had begun thrashing a broken branch against a tree, all the while roaring and barking. The other family members had come closer and were adding their own shrieks to the cacophony of sound. If Dana hadn't known the individual gorillas, she'd have been terrified. As it was, she crouched low, ready to fling herself into the thick brush if Ndengera got really serious.

"Time to get out of here," Lambot said, filling his last syringe. While the family of distressed gorillas began closing in, he plunged the antidote into Kundu's hip and tossed everything back into his kit.

"Done," he announced, and, without turning their backs and giving the impression of flight, all five of them edged away from the patient. They waited a few yards distant and watched until the injured gorilla showed signs of waking.

After some five minutes, she began to flinch. She sat up and tried to stand. She swayed for a moment, then fell over. She twisted away from the anchor pole of the snare and, realizing she was free, lurched drunkenly away, toppling and crawling toward the other group members, who were screaming and pounding the ground. Finally she righted herself and staggered on three limbs toward Ndengera as the entire group fled up the slope of Visoke.

CHAPTER NINE

It was early evening when they arrived back at Karisoke, and the drizzle that had hindered them in working on Kundu had become a drenching rain. Kristen thanked the trackers for their help before they took off at a run toward their quarters, and she turned toward Dana and Lambot.

"Come in for a drink and a warm-up by the stove. I don't know about you two, but I could do with a shot."

Inside Kristen's cabin, the fire she'd had going three hours before had burned down to ashes, but a bit of stirring uncovered glowing embers. She added kindling, and flames began to flicker again. A judicious placement of larger chunks of wood fueled the fire, and soon warmth spread outward from it.

Chilled and shaken by the near disaster, Dana hovered over the stove. "Do you think we've saved her? I mean, did we get to her in time?"

Lambot set down his medical bag and pulled a chair over to the table. "Hard to say. Infections are difficult and depend on the health of the individual. You'll have to watch her for the next few days and see how she's doing."

"So, no miracle cures, eh?"

In the corner that functioned as her kitchen, Kristen took three small glasses and a tall square bottle from her cupboard. Without asking their preference, she poured a portion of Jack Daniels into each glass and handed them around. "To Kundu," she said, and took a swallow.

"To Kundu," Dana repeated and did the same, choking slightly on the bite of the liquor on her throat, though after it had made it down to her stomach, it generated a pleasant warmth. Dr. Lambot, she noticed, had a much more comfortable relationship with Jack, emptying his glass in two swallows and wiping his lips with the back of his hand.

Dana sipped again cautiously. "You know, I'm pretty proud of us, taking care of Kundu that way."

Lambot snorted. "Don't let it go to your head. It's not going to make a dent in the fate of those gorillas. The Africans are killing them faster than they can reproduce, and all we did today was delay the inevitable for one animal."

"Boy, are *you* a cynic," Dana said, disliking the man more and more, in spite of his skill. "Why do you bother even trying to heal them?"

He shrugged. "I'm a cynic, not a sadist. But you see them up here while they're squatting happily in their nests, munching on greens. I see and hear about the trade that goes on in Ruhengeri."

"What do you mean?" Dana wasn't sure she wanted to hear the answer.

"Last year, twenty-two gorilla heads passed through the town, and I can't count how many hands and feet. Some through the marketplace, offered discreetly to tourists who look like they'd be interested. Others are custom ordered from abroad or simply kept by one or two merchants for future sales. And there are always buyers."

Dana was aghast. "How do they get away with that? I mean, technically, that's all illegal. Rwanda has laws…"

Kristen poured another glass of whiskey for the doctor. "This is Central Africa, Dana. After the misery of colonialism, the people have a deeply ingrained urge for self-preservation. People care about immediate profit, not some distant future value of wildlife to Rwanda. That's the soil for corruption."

"You mean the laws to protect the endangered species are just window dressing?"

Lambot tossed back his second glass of whiskey, then patted his pockets until he found his cigarettes. "In a word, yes." He tapped one out and inserted it between his narrow lips.

Kristen shook her head. "It's not that black-and-white. There are a few good, honest men, but they struggle against enormous odds. And then there are men who are crooked but can be negotiated with. And a third class that wants to preserve wildlife so they can make money from it, if only they can figure out how. All of them are potential allies."

Lambot sucked air through his teeth. "Allies? I don't think so. Rwanda is a jungle, even in its cities, and you can never let down your guard."

"You mean as a white person in a black country?" Dana asked.

"No, in general. Sure, the white man screwed them over during colonialism, and they have reason to be bitter about that, but these days, the Rwandans hate each other. I should know. I have a Tutsi wife, and the Hutus I deal with won't have anything to do with her. They talk only to me, an *umuzungu*." He opened his cigarette lighter with an angry flick and lit his cigarette. A long inhalation seemed to calm him, and he continued in a more conciliatory tone.

"If it were only one set of vicious bastards plotting against another set of vicious bastards, I wouldn't mind. But it's every man for himself, and that's a very dangerous situation." He picked a piece of tobacco off his tongue.

A sudden loud knock at the door caused them all to jump, as if the social unrest had somehow appeared outside their cabin. Kristen stood up and opened it, and all three of them stared for a moment, speechless.

A man stood in the rain, tall, bearded, and with long blond hair drawn back in a ponytail. His red beard ended just above the wide barrel chest of a lumberjack. He was even wearing a plaid shirt, visible under his half open canvas jacket.

"Peter Hewett," the lumberjack said to Kristen's puzzled expression. "The biologist from Ohio?" He offered his hand.

"Oh, right. Um, come in." Recovering, Kristen shook it and stepped back. "I got your letter a few weeks ago but haven't heard from you since. How did you find your way to Karisoke?"

As the door closed behind him, he stood awkwardly by the wall. "I wrote that I was coming, but it looks like you never got the letter. I didn't hear back from you, but I figured it was safe to come ahead anyhow. I got as far as Ruhengeri and then found someone who knew where Karisoke was. Um…I hope I'm not interrupting anything."

"No, no. Welcome. Glad you made it." She gestured toward the table. "This is Dana Norland, another researcher, and Rudy Lambot, our veterinarian."

Dana did a brief assessment of the newcomer. He seemed a colorful mixture of a lumberjack, a California hippie, and a Viking—and she instantly liked him.

Lambot seemed less charmed and apparently found the arrival a good excuse for his own departure. He stood up. "Welcome to Rwanda, and good luck."

Kristen followed him to the door and handed him a spare lantern. "Thanks for coming up, Rudy. No point in trying to negotiate the mountain at night and in the rain. Why don't you stay over in the south cabin? We always have a dry cot there, and you can leave as early as you want."

"Good idea. Don't worry. I can find my way there myself," he said, and with a quick handshake to Peter and Kristen, he was out of the cabin.

Kristen closed the door behind him and turned her attention to the new assistant. As he set down his enormous backpack, she too seemed to do a quick appraisal of his height and musculature. Perhaps every woman did. Her smile suggested she approved.

"Here, come over by the fire to dry out." She led him by the arm. "I'm trying to recall what you wrote. You said you studied biology?"

"No, ma'am. Agriculture and animal husbandry." He unbuttoned his jacket and held his hands over the stove. "I was raised around horses, and I thought for a while I wanted to breed them."

"What made you change your mind and decide for gorillas?"

He rubbed his palms together, then stroked his beard, transferring some of the warmth to his face. "Well, after a little study, I realized that the low end of the market was already saturated with horses. Except for the lucky few who end up with real horse lovers, most of 'em get passed along as they get old, until they end up auctioned off for slaughter."

Dana nodded. "Not much better than what people do with dogs."

"Exactly. I didn't want to be part of the industry that used up animals. I wanted to preserve them. Then it was just a question of would it be tigers, or whales, or gorillas."

Kristen chuckled. "I'm glad you decided for gorillas. Anyhow, it's almost evening, so as soon as you're warm, I'll show you to the guest cabin where you can settle in. It has a wood stove and the basics to set up household, though you may want to supplement from the market at Ruhengeri in the next days."

"I've read a lot about Karisoke, and I had a look at the place before I knocked. If you don't mind, I'd rather take the tent cabin next to the stream."

"Are you sure? It's pretty primitive. We used to fall back on it when we had an overflow of visitors but haven't needed it in ages."

Peter smiled Buddha-like and stroked his beard again. "Please don't worry about me. I came up here to live in the jungle. I don't want to feel like I'm living in a house in town. Besides," he added, clinching his argument, "Dian Fossey lived in a tent for months before she had a hut built. It's my tribute to her."

"I guess that settles it, then." Kristen glanced through the window onto the porch. "It looks like the rain has let up, so let's go now. I'll show you the way."

"Lead on," he said, hauling his huge backpack up onto his shoulders again. Intrigued by the newcomer, Dana followed them out.

The tent cabin, with its corrugated roof and four canvas walls, stood between two hagenia trees and close to the bank of the creek. A bend in the creek separated the tent from Kristen's cabin, so the two weren't in sight of each other, a fact that Dana found a relief, though she couldn't have said why she cared.

"This is great," he said, throwing back the tent flap and revealing the interior. The furnishings were spare in the extreme and consisted of a folding bed with a rolled-up mattress, a table, a set of shelves with a teakettle and pots, and the ubiquitous wood stove at the rear. A kerosene pressure lamp, similar to Dana's, stood on the table.

"It won't take me long to unload," he said, setting his backpack on the ground. "Then I'll go chop some wood for the fire and start setting up household."

Kristen laughed. "Kudos for your energy, but we pay a man to collect and cut wood for us. The woodpile is over by the men's house, and you can just help yourself. I'm guessing an outdoorsman like yourself knows how to build a fire in a stove."

"Yes, ma'am. Done it a hundred times at my granny's."

"A very good start. But at least this evening, you don't have to worry about cooking supper. Since you've just arrived, you're invited, along with Dana, to my cabin for the usual bean soup. About seven."

He grinned, an expression greatly enhanced by the red-blond beard encircling it. "All right, then. I'll stop by. Sorry I can't offer to bring wine."

"Quite all right. We'll overlook that social error for now." They both laughed, and Dana forced a chuckle as well, though she was growing a little tired of all the cheerful banter. A handsome, virile man was charming the socks off a beautiful woman, and the waves of flirtation between them were bypassing Dana completely.

It wasn't a nice feeling.

To Dana's pleasant surprise, the supper *à trois* was actually a pleasant affair. It was, in fact, the first uninhibited social occasion she'd enjoyed since the "event," as she'd come to think of it. The dinners she'd shared with Tony and Emily afterward, while she waited for her visa, couldn't count, since she'd been quietly desperate, numbed by sorrow, and terrified of capture.

But Peter was engaging in every way: ebullient, passionate about animals, and full of anecdotes that he managed to tell without dominating the conversation. The only drawback to his charm was the fact that Kristen seemed swept away by it and couldn't seem to take her eyes off the man.

Dana stifled her pangs of jealousy and almost managed to forget them, for the next day Peter continued to be warm, even deferential, to her. To her surprise, he hugged her before setting off with one of the trackers for his own gorilla introduction. It was to group six, she learned, which browsed far to the west of her beloved group four. Good, she thought. Let him have his own favorites. She presumed that he, too, would be tasked with dung collection but already knew it wouldn't dent his unflagging good cheer.

She herself had tracked northeast with Paka to check on groups two and three. No babies to coo over, but the juveniles were always entertaining, and she'd seen the females mating with the silverbacks, so perhaps a tiny gorilla or two might be gestating. Then, as always, they'd spent time looking for snares.

In the evening she typed her notes, as always, and was just sliding them into their folder when she heard the knock. It was Peter, exuberant and wanting to share his experience.

"I can't believe how beautiful they are," he said, drawing up a stool next to the stove.

Dana sat next to him on the only chair. "Group six has four females and a lot of young blackbacks, right?"

"Yes, and the silverback…magnificent. As soon as he spotted me, he stood up on his hind legs and gave me the once-over. I could see he was sizing me up and wondering who the hell was the yellow gorilla." He leaned forward, elbows on his knees, and looked wistful. "You can just *sense* their souls, can't you?"

Dana nodded faintly. "I wouldn't call it soul, but yes, I do see a certain intelligence in their expression. Unlike, say, in a lion. You really feel them looking back at you."

He shook his head. "I'd rather not use a human-centric word like intelligence. That measures them against us and they always come out with less. I'd say there's a radiance, a divinity, a truth in all of them, and you *connect* with that truth when you look into their faces. All animals have this truth in them, and if we don't get it, that's our lack, not theirs."

"Hmm. I'm not sure what you mean by 'truth.'"

"I mean that we're all one thing. Have you read Khalil Gibran?"

"No, sorry. He was one of those mystic writers of the sixties, right?" She forced herself not to frown. Mystics, like religion in general, had no appeal for her.

"Yes, a Lebanese poet. Anyhow, he wrote about the oneness of the universe." He held up a hand as if in benediction and seemed to read words from the air.

All things in this creation exist within you, and all things in you exist in creation.

Dana's frown escaped. "I'm afraid I don't know what that means."

"It means that Nature's oneness reaches out to us through animals. When we connect with that oneness, we come a little closer to grasping the living truth, to being one with God."

He tilted his handsome head and smiled so gently, she felt guilty wondering if the "all animals" thing included parasitical worms and malaria mosquitos. That kind of romanticism always sounded silly to her. But romantic people were often very kind, and he certainly seemed to be that. Besides, he loved the gorillas, and that's what counted.

He stood up, virility incarnate, and held out his wide paw. "Just wanted to say it's nice to be working with you." Then he let himself out.

Wow, she thought, looking at the door that had closed behind him. Except for his religious mysticism, the man was irresistible. What straight woman wouldn't fall in love with him in fifteen seconds? Especially a woman who lived alone in the African jungle.

Depression sank over her like a Virunga fog.

CHAPTER TEN

February 1994

Dana had grown to appreciate the rotation system, whereby she observed each gorilla group on a given day, provided they hadn't wandered outside of range. The system generally gave her exposure to all seven groups, and occasionally she spotted the bachelor males who wandered singly or in pairs among the families.

Her favorite workday was Tuesday, when she tracked group four, Ndengera's family, and she always felt privileged to watch them. The females had all grown familiar with her and paid no attention to her, and on her last visit, she noted that Kundu was healing well, though she tended to walk on three limbs and hold the injured arm to her chest. The rambunctious adolescents now found it amusing to snatch her pencil, or glove, or anything not attached to her body. And Mwelu was always irresistible.

But from the human standpoint, Saturdays were the best of all, when she took her report to Kristen and they discussed it over a shared supper.

For weeks, the reporting suppers had been informal and cozy, and they covered any matters relevant to the gorillas: their health, infighting, signs of poachers. They'd never discussed anything personal, had never talked about old relationships other than Kristen's single reference to a bad marriage. But the quiet evenings by lantern light had an intimate feeling that seemed to bring them closer. And she wanted to be close to Kristen Wolfe.

But now three people sat at the table and the atmosphere changed. The reporting suppers were shorter, more businesslike, and the opportunity to get close to Kristen was lost.

She recalled the quiet midnight conversation they'd had her first night at Karisoke. Could she recapture it? Could she get away with another walk in the moonlight toward the romantic footbridge?

She glanced out the window. Early February meant cold nights in the Virungas. They'd been enjoying 80-some degree weather during the day, when it wasn't raining, but nighttime temperatures always dropped precipitously. Still, the air was dry and the moon was nearly full.

Hell, what was the worst that could happen? Meet a buffalo at the creek? More likely she'd just walk around in the dark like an idiot and come back even more depressed. She grabbed her jacket and crept out onto her porch, gathering courage.

But before she could take a step out onto the path, she came to an abrupt halt. A figure was coming around the thicket in the direction of Kristen's cabin, and even from a distance his blond Viking hair was visible in the moonlight.

He strode quickly toward the cabin door where a light still burned. Dana couldn't hear the knock but could faintly make out the opening door and Peter's disappearance inside.

Sick with embarrassment…or was it humiliation…Dana did an about-face and closed the door behind her. Ripping off her jacket, she threw the rest of her kindling into the stove and set the fire burning as brightly as she dared. "You stupid…stupid fool," she muttered, and threw herself onto her bed.

As she stared at the black ceiling, it flashed through her mind. *Don't be a fool. You can never have her anyhow; you're a murderer.* "Fuck!" she called out loud, and it was a cry of pain. Then she turned over and covered her head with her pillow.

The next morning she was sullen, and when she saw Peter emerging from his tent, she felt the faint sensation of a snarl. Obviously he'd returned to sleep there most of the night, preserving appearances. At that moment she hated him, but hated more the social rules that made such connections so easy.

Resigned, she packed a small lunch of cheese and crackers and was about to look for Paka for a day of snare hunting. Paka was a quiet man, and she anticipated a day with little talk. The weather was still holding, and if they managed to free some hapless creature from a trap wire, she'd feel better.

Scarcely had she stepped off her porch and headed toward the men's cabin when Senweke came into sight, running. "Miss Kristen...Miss Kristen!" he called breathlessly. "Poachers. They killed a gorilla."

Her heart sank. This was the horror they all feared, that went on in other zones of the park but not, in over a year, at Karisoke. But now...She ran to join him and they arrived together at Kristen's door.

"Poachers. Killed a gorilla!" he repeated, and a grimace passed across Kristen's face. Snatching up her jacket, she followed them out. Halfway up the trail, Peter, who must have heard the commotion, sprinted after them.

Senweke led them, giving no further explanation, and no one wanted to ask the obvious questions. Which gorilla? Was it only one? She was certain the others felt the same.

As he led them northeastward, Dana gradually guessed the victim was in group four, Ndengera's family, and the realization was almost unbearable. She ran through all their names. Which one was dead?

Driven by distress and outrage, they covered the distance in record time and arrived, breathless, at the scene.

"Ndengera!" The tears that had been gathering inside her now erupted with the calling of his name. The silverback lay on his back, both arms outstretched as if about to embrace them. She knelt beside him sobbing, her hands pressed onto his hairless black chest that she had never touched before. The muscles were cold and hard. Both his hands had been cut off.

Behind her, Kristen spoke with a calm, tight voice. "No spear wounds. No snare." She knelt on the other side of the gorilla and turned his head. "Look. They shot him. Two clean bullets, one to the neck and one to the head. He didn't even fight back."

"And they took only his hands. What does that mean?" Peter asked, but Dana wondered the same thing.

Kristen stood up, obviously shaken. "It means the souvenirs were an afterthought and something interrupted them. I'm afraid it's worse and—"

"Miss Kristen. Over here!" It was Senweke, a few yards away.

Kristen raised her head and her lips trembled. Obviously, she knew, everyone knew, who it would be, and why.

The four of them clambered over the underbrush and stood in a circle around the dark mound.

"Amahoro," Kristen said quietly. "They took her baby." She knelt down now by the female gorilla, who lay on her side, both arms out in front of her, as if she'd held onto her infant with the last bit of life in her. She too had multiple bullet wounds in her neck and one in her shoulder.

Peter's voice was also hoarse. "Who would do this? Who *could* do this? I thought the Batwa used only traps and spears."

"They do when they hunt for themselves. If they did this, and I think they did, it was for an outsider. Somebody with money who would give them a gun."

Kristen glanced up at Senweke. "Arrange for the men to carry them back to camp. We'll do an autopsy later and try to identify the bullets. But right now, I'm going after Munyaro. If he didn't do it, he'll know who did."

"Who's Munyaro?" Dana asked as they hiked back to Karisoke. The name sounded familiar.

"A Batwa hunter. He's been a thorn in my side for years, and as a young man, he was already a menace to Dian. He's caught countless bushbacks and monkeys, which is bad enough, but he's also injured half a dozen gorillas."

"But that's all illegal. Can't you have him arrested?"

"Dian did manage to get him arrested several times, and so did I, but within a few weeks, or sometimes days, he'd be out and back in business. Obviously he has friends who help him or who don't like what we're doing up here."

"Sickening," Dana muttered and knew the others felt the same. "So, what can we do?" she asked helplessly.

"I don't know." Kristen's voice was cold, monotone. "But whoever did this has gone too far."

❖

The Batwa village was a shabby affair. A mix of roughly square mud structures and round, thatched, wattle-and-straw huts stood within shouting distance of each other. The women looked up from where they squatted, and tiny naked children scattered when they marched in. A couple of bony dogs barked at them and backed off, snarling.

The Batwa were dressed for the most part in rags, though Dana couldn't tell whether it was out of poverty or a lack of use for clothing. Dana had seen a few Batwa from a distance in the game park but had never registered their size. Now, as a group, they surprised her with their stature. They were nearly pygmies, though the word seemed ugly and nineteenth century. As hunters and gatherers who lived mostly by the panga and spear, they also seemed an anachronism in the current century.

But they were not there for anthropology; they were looking for a killer.

Senweke seemed to know some of the people, and he walked directly up to one of the women. He spoke in Kinyarwanda, but slowly, and she recalled that it was not the language of the Batwa.

"Where is Munyaro?" he asked simply.

The woman's reply was unintelligible to Dana, but her head-shake was not. The two of them argued for a few moments; then Senweke turned to Kristen and spoke in French. "She says he has gone away. She does not know where. But he is innocent."

"Innocent of what? Does she know why we're here?"

"She did not ask. She only says he is innocent."

"Look inside his hut. If he ran away, maybe he left some object that will tell us something."

Senweke laid the back of his hand against the woman's shoulder and gently but firmly moved her aside. He was in the hut for only a few moments when he emerged holding a rifle. "Under his sleeping straw," he said.

Of course. Where else could you hide something in a mud hut that had no furniture?

He handed over the rifle, and Kristen stared at it as if deep in thought. She glanced to the side toward Dana and spoke in an undertone in English. "Remember what you said about children and animals being equal?"

Dana nodded, sensing what was to come.

Kristen turned toward Senweke. "Do you know which of them are Munyaro's children?" she asked in French.

"That one and that one." He pointed to a boy of about eight and a toddler. "I don't know the others."

"Take the boy, quickly before he understands and runs away. Bring him back to the camp."

Without hesitating, Senweke grabbed hold of the boy by his upper arms, though the bewildered child offered no resistance.

Peter stepped forward and laid a hand on his shoulder. "What are you doing? You can't kidnap a child. It's illegal, and besides it's…it's unscrupulous."

Kristen took ahold of his shirtsleeve. "I'll remind you that this boy's father has just killed two gorillas and kidnapped an infant, endangering its life as well. He's almost certainly responsible for several other gorilla-souvenir operations. Just how many animals are your scruples going to let die before you give up a few of them?"

The question struck home in Dana, who had thrown away scruples in a New York basement and had an idea. She turned to Senweke. "Tell her that we're taking Munyaro's son and that tomorrow we will start to eat him. Piece by piece. Every two hours Munyaro makes us wait, we will eat a piece of him. First his hands and then his feet. And when we're finished, we'll send back his head."

Kristen eyes widened at the savage threat but let it stand, and Senweke dutifully repeated it.

The mother recoiled and ran toward her son, but Senweke had already lifted him off the ground. While he thrashed, Kristen tied a rope around his waist and wrists. When she was done, she stared with cold eyes at the mother. "Tell him," she repeated, then led her kidnapping party out of the village. Behind them, several of the women began wailing.

Once outside the village, Senweke set the boy on his feet but held him by the rope.

"Wow, you really know how to shock," Kristen said in English. "I would never have thought of that."

"Will they believe us?"

"Oh, yes. They're very superstitious. It's too bad we had to terrify his mother that way, but now let's hope his father will be just as affected. We have to jolt him out of hiding, and if that doesn't do it, nothing will."

She turned to Senweke. "Ask him his name. Then make sure he understands we won't hurt him and that he can go home tomorrow. Tell him...I don't know...tell him that we have sweets and he can have anything to eat he wants."

The boy mumbled his name but would not be convinced of his captors' good intentions. Nonetheless, he left off sniveling and marched along with them stoically.

The others were silent as well, and Dana sensed a pall fall over them as they hiked back along the mountain trail. Two gorillas were dead, an infant was in jeopardy, and they were paralyzed until they could flush out the killers. It also didn't help that they were committing a serious crime.

The various anxieties plagued her at every step, but once they returned to Karisoke and locked the child safely in Kristen's cabin, Dana also began to feel guilty. Even if Munyaro was a murdering poacher, it was unfair to terrify his wife and child. What could she do to at least alleviate the boy's fear of them? Perhaps some food, presented by a gentle, unthreatening hand. She opened her sparse larder and patched together a supper of cheese and sausage and her last chocolate bar.

Rather pleased with herself, she carried the package to Kristen's cabin. But when she stepped inside, to her surprise, Kristen, Peter, Senweke, and the little prisoner were sitting at the table eating scrambled eggs. The child had obviously lost all fear, and in between mouthfuls, he was even talking.

Kristen clearly knew how to charm and cajole, and in quiet intervals between offering him tidbits, she posed him questions via Senweke. Where was Munyaro? He didn't know. Where did Munyaro get his rifle? The men who came from Ruhengeri gave it to him. Who were the men? He didn't know. Were they Rwandan or *abazungu*? They were Rwandan. Hutus.

"Hmm. Middlemen," Kristen observed. "Hired by someone higher up to do the dirty work. Animal trafficking is a big business with a whole chain of delivery."

"So what do we do now?" Peter asked, wiping crumbs from his beard.

"Wait until we see what Munyaro does. Me, I'm going to sleep after I've made up a bed for the boy." She glanced up at the food package in Dana's hand.

"Great idea," she said, selecting the brightly wrapped candy bar and passing it to the child. "Chocolate, another weapon in the cause of justice."

❖

Dana thought she was free of the blood dream, but now it came again.

The familiar, terrifying darkness and the awareness of blood. Blood on the floor and on the walls. She knew her way now through the grotesque chamber, though she cringed with every step, groping her way along the sticky stone walls until she stumbled. She knew the creatures that lay at her feet, and she sensed the men creeping in behind her. The metal of their machetes clattered against the stone, punctuating their soft laughter.

She wrenched herself awake and, panting, lit her Coleman lantern. Anything to dispel the darkness. The cabin was cold, but she didn't have the energy to light the stove again, so she huddled in her bed until she dozed again under the light and this time fell into dreamless sleep.

CHAPTER ELEVEN

When Dana awoke, the light from the window told her it was late in the morning and that the camp was in full activity. Someone was chopping wood, probably Kanyara, and someone else was shooing away wildlife, probably from Kristen's chicken coop.

Still grainy-eyed, she extinguished the Coleman and dressed hurriedly, with a sense both of urgency and of helplessness at where to direct it. Kristen had said to wait, but what if Munyaro called their bluff? It was already the third day since the taking of Mwelu. Had she been in a cage the whole time? What must she be suffering in the hands of people who knew nothing about gorillas, who had butchered her mother and ripped her from her arms?

All the rage and anxiety of the previous day returned, and she hurried along the path to Kristen's cabin. Kristen answered immediately, dressed and full of nervous energy.

How did you sleep?" she asked, standing in the doorway. "You look a bit worn."

Dana rubbed her face. "Not well. The gorilla killing's gotten to me. But I'll be fine, once we've found the baby."

"I know what you mean. It's all I've been able to think about, too. If we don't hear anything from Munyaro in the next hour, we'll return to his village, if only to take back the boy. But maybe we can—"

"Miss Kristen!" Someone called out from the path as he ran toward them. "The Batwa have come."

"Thank you, Senweke. Please bring them here to my porch. And ask the other men to join you. We want to make a big show."

A few minutes later, the group stood below them, and when Munyaro stepped forward, Dana was appalled. She expected a virile hunter, but he was as shabby and wretched as his village. If she didn't keep reminding herself of the dead Ndengera and Amahoro, she might have felt sorry for him. He was shockingly small, and though the morning was cool and damp, he wore only a rag that had once been a pair of trouser shorts but now hung in shreds. His shirt, torn at both shoulders, was the same dirt-gray color as the various tiny magic bundles that hung from his neck. He was unarmed, though two of his retinue carried spears.

Clearly aiming for melodrama, Kristen remained above him on the porch with Senweke on one side of her and Dana on the other. Peter stepped behind the three visitors, hands on his hips, and Munyaro's head came only to the middle of his massive chest. It almost seemed unfair.

Calling over her shoulder, Kristen summoned the child from inside the cabin. When he tiptoed outside, she took position behind him and grasped him on both shoulders.

Munyaro's high-pitched exclamation could have been either joy or lament, but his hands held out in front of him showed he was there to negotiate.

The discussion went on in staccato phrases, each one having to be translated into French by Senweke. As she absorbed the gist, Dana was horrified. It was not what she expected. Munyaro wasn't there to negotiate; he was there to beg.

"Please, do not cut off my son's hands as you did my grandfather's."

What? Dana thought she'd misunderstood, but Kristen's reply confirmed she had not.

"I did not cut off your grandfather's hands? I did not know him."

"Your brothers, the *abazungu* in the Congo. They wanted rubber, and when he could not bring it, they took his hand. And then his foot. Please do not cut off my son's feet."

Dana felt sick to her stomach. How could she have been so stupid? As paltry as her education in African history had been, she should have remembered. The Belgian colonists at the turn of the century had murdered and mutilated the Africans in their search for rubber. And if the white men had forgotten that shameful episode, the native inhabitants obviously had not.

"No, I will spare him," Kristen assured him. "But you must tell me the truth. Did you kill the gorillas?"

"Yes. They hired us to catch a baby gorilla, but the big one attacked."

"Us? Who was with you?"

"Men from my village," he replied immediately.

"Where did you get the rifle?"

Munyaro took a step closer to his son. "From the man in Ruhengeri. Simon Bizimana."

Kristen snorted. "That bastard," she muttered in English. "I should have known."

"Where is the baby gorilla now?"

Munyara held out his hands again. "I don't know."

Dana's heart sank. If he was telling the truth, they were almost back where they started.

"How much did he pay you?" Kristen hammered away.

He named a paltry sum.

"You are a fool, Munyaro. He lives like a king and pays you only enough for one sack of grain, and now you will not even enjoy that." She signaled two of the men to seize him. "Your son will go home today with both his hands and feet, but you're going to jail."

The Batwa poacher merely shrugged in resignation, and Dana guessed he expected Rwandan justice to simply release him again. He was probably right. Paka and Mukera led him away to the storage shed, which could be locked and would presumably hold him until he could be escorted into Ruhengeri to the magistrate.

Dana exhaled a sigh of relief. The trick had worked, but they still had to find the orphan gorilla, and it was already day three.

Hours later, while Senweke accompanied the boy back to his village, Kristen ordered Munyaro bound by both hands. To prevent his bolting into the forest that he knew all too well, she also tied a hobble around his ankles, which allowed him to walk in small steps but not to run. The little man was as agile as a gazelle and seemed unhampered by the hobble, so Peter, who towered over him, kept a hand on his upper arm as they descended.

Burdened only by the small rucksack that held the overnight essentials she carried whenever she left Karisoke, Dana held the prisoner by his neck rope, though she was slightly troubled by the realization that three large white people were dragging a small, unarmed black man from his own land. She sighed inwardly. They were in a moral gray area, she understood, but it seemed, on balance, that it was for the greater good. The Batwa way of life could not exist very long in a modern Rwanda, particularly if it did so off the blood of its critically endangered wildlife. If nothing else, at least at Karisoke, the white invaders meant well and had a larger vision for the good of all the creatures of Rwanda, not just of a single Neolithic tribe in the jungle.

However, the prisoner seemed unfazed by his predicament, as he'd been unfazed in his confession, and she suspected he was looking forward to the largesse of the Rwandan penal system for poaching, a crime largely invented by the white men.

In two hours they reached the Parc des Volcans parking field, where Kristen retrieved the camp's Land Rover, and by midday, they arrived in Ruhengeri.

The town had made no impression on Dana when she first arrived, and it made no impression on her now. A typical African provincial capital, it consisted of low one- and two-story public buildings along two main thoroughfares that crossed in the middle of town. It boasted a post office, a couple of dubious hotels, a hospital maintained by the French, and an elementary school, as well as several administration buildings. The houses themselves were built of cement block, a few of them pastel painted but poorly maintained and discolored by the constant rainfall. The street was full of barefoot people, women with babies tied in swaths of cloth against their backs and balancing some load or another on their heads. Men passed them pushing wheelbarrows of wood or bicycles piled high with produce.

The police station in Ruhengeri was a simple concrete building without windows, though its heavy double doors distinguished it from the shops on both sides of it.

As they entered, the officer in charge, who Dana supposed was the equivalent to the desk sergeant in an American station, looked up at them. His glance shifted quickly to the ragged Batwa, and a look of annoyance passed over him. Did he know the prisoner? It seemed likely.

Kristen got right to the point. "We want to press charges against this man for the killing of two gorillas in the Parc des Volcans and the kidnapping of an infant gorilla. He has already confessed to everything."

The officer looked away, and it seemed that he even rolled his eyes, though Dana couldn't tell whether the cause was exasperation at the crime or the arrival of the white accusers to trouble his day.

"Please sit down over there. I will send someone to talk to you when they are free." He turned away to shuffle some papers on a desk and otherwise ignored them.

Kristen shook her head. "I know this place. They're going to take all afternoon, and I don't have time for this. Senweke, please stay with him and talk to the police chief when he finally appears. If necessary, I can come by tomorrow to sign the complaint and encourage the investigation. Just make sure he's locked up."

Senweke nodded solemnly, and Kristen hurried out of the station with Dana and Peter in tow.

"So where is this Bizimana guy?" Peter asked.

"He has a shop just a few streets from here. Ruhengeri's a small town, and commercial buildings are all downtown." She set out ahead of them in long strides. "Here, turn left. It's over there," and in a few minutes they stood in front of a wide shop window. Peter stepped in front of them and opened the door.

The shop, by Rwandan standards, was distinctly high-end. Its sign said EXPORT-IMPORT but gave no hint of what it exported. It seemed to carry mostly an assortment of imported men's clothing, Italian shoes, accessories, and jewelry that few Rwandans could afford. A side counter also displayed foreign cigarettes and cigars. The shop was currently empty, though Dana suspected that in a provincial town like Ruhengeri there couldn't be many customers. A strange enterprise, though not if it was merely a front for other business.

Only one thing didn't fit the attempted elegance of the shop, and when Dana recognized it, she was incensed. The faint smell of gorilla diarrhea.

Simon Bizimana apparently didn't employ a clerk, for he greeted them himself, coming from the rear of the shop. A small man, of delicate features and a well-crafted haircut, he wore a beige suit with a pastel pink shirt open at the collar.

"How can I help you?" he asked in French, laying his manicured hands on the counter. He wore a large opal ring similar to those in his display case. It was surely obvious to him that the three white people who stood before him weren't customers, though that fact did not change his demeanor.

"Where's the gorilla infant?" Kristen's voice was tight with anger. "Munyaro told us you hired him, so there's no point in claiming ignorance."

Bizimana's tone remained velvety, businesslike. "I'm afraid I have no idea what you mean. Do you wish to buy anything? If not, I would ask you to please leave."

"Always the same lines." Kristen scoffed. "Don't you people ever come up with anything new to say?"

"'*You* people?' Do you mean Africans?"

Kristen snorted. "No, I mean lowlife, petty smugglers. I know you, Simon Bizimana. You pay some pathetic little Batwa a pittance to go out and kill or steal whatever animals you want, and then you earn ten times the amount for handing them over to your clients. But this time it's a living creature, and so help me, if she dies, I'll burn down your crappy store."

She pushed past him into the back room before he had a chance to reply. Dana and Peter followed. To her disappointment, it was just an office, small and unpretentious, with a desk and two chairs. A place for business deals. Nothing suspicious. But the odor of gorilla fear was stronger here.

"There's another door," Kristen said, and strode toward it. She tried the handle and found it locked. "Where's the key?" she demanded. "Open it."

"No, no, no. That is private." Bizimana sputtered. "None of your business."

"Peter, would you please open the door?"

Peter hesitated a moment, apparently uncertain what she meant, then threw his shoulder against it. It sprang open, the lock bolt tearing away part of the door frame.

"Wow." Peter murmured as the three of them stood in the doorway. "So that's how they do it."

The back room was a storehouse of contraband. What sprang into view first were four elephant tusks leaning against the rear wall. Blood and pieces of flesh still stained their bottoms. Next to them, a shelf held four large clay pots, and when Peter lifted the lid from one, he recoiled suddenly and dropped it back on. "Shit. There's a snake in there."

"Yes, a spitting cobra," Bizimana said, like a wildlife instructor patiently educating the ignorant. "Very popular with the tourists. Would you like to buy him?"

Peter ignored him while Dana made a circuit of the room, touching the various crates, jars, and containers. A large cage held an African-grey parrot, its frantic climbing suggesting it was recently captured. Smaller cages held other exotic birds, though Dana couldn't identify them, and only a few were labeled: owlet, falcon, barbet.

Standing upright in a crate in the corner were four enormous rhino horns, and in a chest next to it lay a jumble of whip-like objects that closer inspection revealed to be tails: from rhinos, buffalos, elephants, and something furry, probably monkeys. Overhead, two stuffed vultures perched on a high shelf looking a bit ratty.

The three of them stood awestruck for a moment. Then Peter exclaimed, "Ohh, look at this!" and reached for the rifle that leaned against a corner. "What a beauty! Much nicer than the one you found in the Batwa hut. My father used to have one of these at home. I hated his hunting, but the guns were beautiful. And this one…wow. An FN 30-11, bolt action." He inspected it, turning it lovingly in his hands. "Everything a sniper could ask for—a folding bipod for barrel support, adjustable scope, two-section cushioned stock." He drew the bolt to see if it was loaded. "Nice clean internal magazine box. Holds five cartridges at a time, right?"

Obviously unprepared for such a technical question, Bizimana simply nodded, then seemed to realize he was admitting to poaching.

Dana also stood in the middle of the room and pivoted around, noting the wares for sale. "This is how you make your living, eh? Skimming off Rwanda's most precious heritage, its wildlife. You really are scum."

"You can save your rude language. If you object to my inventory, you should take the matter up with the head of the prefecture. Otherwise, you have no right interfering with my business."

Kristen glanced at the rifle, unimpressed, then back at the contraband. "It's against international law, if not Rwandan law, to export these things, but we know already that you've paid off the local police. For the moment, we don't give a damn about your sleazy exports. We just want the gorilla back."

"I'm afraid you're mistaken. I know nothing about a gorilla. Now I must ask you again to leave." He gestured with his hand toward the open door.

"What's that?" Peter pointed toward a wooden crate under the desk on the far side of the room. Without waiting for an answer, he slid it out and opened the lid. It held only straw, but a strong stench of animal diarrhea rose from it, and he recoiled. "I think this was what they carried her in."

Bizimana stepped toward him and slammed the lid shut again. "You have no proof, and you are breaking the law by crashing into my office. Get out of here now or I will summon the police."

Ignoring him, Peter lifted another box off the shelf. Inside was a bundle wrapped in burlap, and he lifted it out. Already its shape and weight were ominous. He set it down and unfolded the layers of burlap. A gorilla hand.

"You bastard," Kristen snarled.

Rapt and horrified, Dana drew close to the revolting souvenir and studied it. The base of the hand where it had been severed from its arm was dark red and sticky. It was a right hand, and the smallest finger was a stub. She said, in a high, tight voice, "It's Ndengera's."

She'd seen enough. Snatching up a pencil from the desk, she grabbed Bizimana by his collar and shoved him up against the wall, then thrust the pencil halfway up his nose. "I know men like you and know what you do. You talk to us or I'll shove this thing into your brain." She pressed harder, and he twitched as a trickle of blood began to flow from the nostril.

He pressed his head back against the wall trying to prevent further penetration, but as he sniffed, he emitted a fine spray of blood. A few droplets fell, staining his suit, but still he wouldn't cower.

"You're too late. It's out of my hands. The animal is being delivered right now. Go and complain to Mr. Zigirazo in Kigali. He's the one who paid for the capture."

"What for? Why does he want a gorilla?"

"He promised the animal as a gift."

"A gift? For whom?" Kristen touched Dana on the shoulder and she released her hold. Bizimana relaxed, taking the handkerchief from his lapel pocket to dab at his bloody nose and then at his jacket.

"A Saudi. A very rich one. You people come here with your 'save the animals' money, and all you do is make us poorer. The Saudi brings in real money. You've lost this one, so just go back to your jungle camp and leave well enough alone."

Kristen was already moving toward the door. "Zigirazo. Of course. It's exactly his style. Let's go."

"Where?" Peter asked.

"To Kigali. It's where all those big shots have offices, and we might still have a chance to stop the sale." She took a step toward the door, and then, as an afterthought, she snatched up the parrot cage and strode from the shop onto the street.

As they drove away from the town center. Dana held the caged parrot on her knees and didn't need to ask what they were going to do with it. The parrots of Rwanda were going to have one of their number back. In a few moments, they passed through the central market and headed south on the Ruhengeri-Kigali road. Some twenty minutes later, they were passing through fields cultivated with plantains and sweet potatoes. As they reached a spit of forest between two villages, Kristen pulled the Land Rover to the side of the road. "Okay, you can release it now."

The parrot perked up when Dana opened the cage and hopped immediately to the rim of the opening. It croaked a parrot sound, which she hoped was a happy one, lifted into the air, and flew without effort to a nearby hagenia tree.

"Will he be okay here, you think?" Dana eyed the bird anxiously.

"He...or she...will probably look for denser jungle, but if he's recently caught, he'll find his way there pretty fast." Just then the parrot took off again and flew with long sweeps of its wings in the direction of the Virunga range.

Waving good-bye, Dana dropped the cage to the ground, and the Land Rover took off again.

❖

It was evening when they arrived in Kigali, and their energy had waned. Moreover, the magnitude of their task quickly became evident. Protais Zigirazo, though a politician and powerbroker known to everyone as Mr Z, no longer held political office and thus had no office at all. The obvious solution was to confront him at his home, though, other than the fact that it was near Kigali, none of them knew where that was.

Kristen pulled over to the side of the street. "All right. We're here, but it's almost dark and I don't think we should pursue this tonight. I'm sure we'll have a much easier time tracking him down tomorrow. After all, he's the brother-in-law of the president, not to mention that the rich love to display. I'm sure half the people in Kigali can point us directly to his house."

Dana understood the logic but didn't like it. "It's excruciating to have to wait another day. I begin to understand how the parents of kidnapped children feel."

"Yes, I know what you mean. Somewhere, that poor orphan is still being confined and probably not fed. And every hour of delay is another hour of its suffering."

Peter was more practical. "So where do we stay? I mean, I can sleep in the Land Rover, but it doesn't have enough space for three."

"Very generous of you to offer, Peter, but there's no need for that. Karisoke Research Center can spring for a couple of rooms in a cheap hotel. I know of one close by that I've stayed in before."

The Afrika Hostel was basic indeed, but its simple wood-paneled walls and functional décor were just fine. Dana had stayed in worse. The cost was modest, so Kristen registered a single room for Peter and a double for herself and Dana. Even better, the hotel offered a simple dining room where one could purchase the menu of the day. They'd been moving since early morning, and in spite of the sense of urgency that drove them, they had to eat.

The meal of the day consisted of potatoes, cabbage, and chopped dried fish. It was probably as good as anything Dana cooked for herself every day, but she had little appetite.

Peter ate ravenously but without speaking, and when he set his fork aside, he leaned back and crossed his arms. Obviously he had something on his mind.

"How far are we going to take this? We're getting sort of deep into Rwandan politics here. If this Mr. Z is as much a big shot as you say, I don't know how smart it is to confront him. He's related to the president, for God's sake. Then there's this whole Hutu and Tutsi feud that I wouldn't like to get in the middle of."

It was the end of a long day of, so far, a wild goose chase, and Dana's patience was wearing thin. "What happened to your philosophy of 'we sense their souls and connect with the divinity and oneness of the universe in them'? What happened to 'nature reaches out to us through the gorillas and we come a little bit closer to God'? Almost your exact words. If they're so precious, why aren't you willing to take a few risks to save them?"

Peter shifted uncomfortably in his chair. "I still feel that way, but we also have to be realistic. What we're doing may be illegal. They could take away our visas and shut the whole center down. And anyhow, I'm wondering how much this has to do with gorilla research."

Kristen was unsympathetic. "It has everything to do with gorilla preservation. If people keep slaughtering them and stealing their babies, we'll have none left to study. Rwandan law says you can't kill gorillas and kidnap their infants, period. This Mr. Z is acting all on his own, so no one's going to take our visas away or shut us down."

Peter shrugged. "All right. I guess I'm in for the duration. Let's just not get killed for this, okay?"

Dana chuckled. "Don't be so grim. No one's going to get killed."

"I suppose that's what Dian Fossey said," he replied, bringing the conversation to an abrupt end.

❖

"What do you think?" Kristen asked as she opened the door to their shared room. "Does it meet your standards?"

The double room was obviously designed for low-budget adventure travelers and hikers. Two cots stood along the walls of the narrow room, with only enough space between them for one person to stand. But the sheets seemed clean, and the toilet and washroom were close by. And the possibility of sleeping within five feet of Kristen Wolfe didn't bother Dana at all.

"Are you kidding? A bathroom with a flush toilet and running water across the corridor? I'm in heaven."

"Yeah, that part is nice. The food wasn't bad either. Why don't you go first to take advantage of hot water and plumbing."

"Plumbing. What a beautiful word. After all those weeks scrubbing down over a bucket, I'm going to enjoy this. I'll even have a shampoo." Dana grabbed hold of the towel folded on her cot and draped it over her shoulder. When she returned to the room, scrubbed clean and in her underwear, she was in good spirits again. Kristen followed, and soon they were both tucked in. Kristen clicked off the single light, and an awkward silence followed while they lay awake in the dark. Finally Dana spoke up.

"I know Peter's a little shocked at how far we're taking this, but I think Dian would do the same thing, don't you?"

"In an instant. In fact, she went to even greater lengths several times to save baby gorillas. Dangerous lengths."

"Really? I wish I'd known her."

"She could be a hard pill to swallow, but her motives were absolutely pure. I never knew anyone so protective of animals. It made her do things people thought were crazy or criminal. She alienated people left and right, and the only person who stayed loyal, other than me, was her friend Rosalind Carver."

"You've mentioned her before. Is she still in Rwanda?"

"I don't know. Last I heard she was raising flowers to sell to the hotels in Gisenyi, but we lost contact with her after Dian's death. A shame, because she was good for Dian and tried to keep her grounded, the way we—her employees—couldn't."

"What do you mean, 'grounded'?"

"Well, she thought Dian was too hard on poachers and indifferent to the native traditions, but of course Rosalind never saw a gorilla dying of gangrene from a poacher's trap. And Dian was basically ungroundable. She had a connection to animals that was stronger than with people. When she wasn't with the gorillas, she had a monkey, a hen and rooster, a tribe of huge rats that she gave individual names to, and the love of her life, her dog Cindy."

Dana looked off into the distance for a moment. "I can understand that. If you're alone, a dog is precious."

"Well, she also considered wild animals equal to humans as deserving life, and she was outraged at their suffering. She once said about those who tortured animals, 'I'd hang them if I could. Or applaud if someone else hanged them.'"

Dana slid her hands under her neck to raise her head, trying to stay awake. "I agree. I think creatures that have understanding have a right to life and happiness as much as humans do."

She heard the rustle of sheets as Kristen turned on her side to face her. "Dian also believed there's no moral difference between wanting the state to punish such people and punishing them yourself. I think it's even braver, in a way."

Suddenly alert, Dana formulated her question as carefully as possible. "If you...let's say...*came across* someone who'd just killed a creature you loved, not for food but out of sadism or for entertainment, could you execute him?"

Kristen was silent for a moment. "Well, in the heat of the moment, yes. But I'd have trouble living with that act afterward. I mean emotionally, not intellectually. Intellectually I could justify it. The regret would come because it's a pretty awful thing to kill someone, don't you think?"

"Yeah..." Dana wanted fervently to pursue the subject. Being a murderer was uncharted territory, and even after four months, she still felt lost.

But Kristen turned over on her other side. "Night," she said, and the moment was gone.

Dana's mind buzzed. It was strange to be lying in the dark so close to an attractive woman. That hadn't happened in two years. She longed for contact, of any sort. A tender word, a touch. But she was a fugitive with nothing to offer a woman, least of all someone as serious and important...as magnificent...as Kristen. And then there was Peter.

Chapter Twelve

Peter was waiting when Kristen and Dana arrived in the dining room for breakfast, and unlike the night before, he seemed cheerful. "I've got some good news," he said, offering them a basket of rolls and biting into one of them himself.

"Do tell." Dana spread a thick layer of butter over hers, thankful for the Tutsi cattle that supplied the dairy industry.

"You were right," he said with his mouth full, then swallowed. "Everyone in town knows who Mr. Z is. I just asked the guy running the hotel. Not only did he know Zigirazo, but he knew where he lived." He shoved the other half of the buttered roll into his mouth.

Kristen's face lit up. "Well done, Peter. Well done. Did he give you an address?"

Peter nodded, masticating the bread as fast as possible. "Uh-hunh." He took a gulp of coffee. "The guy has three houses, believe it or not. His main one is in Gisenyi."

"What!" Dana was aghast. We've wasted an entire day coming to Kigali when Gisenyi is only a couple hours' drive east of Ruhengeri?"

Peter ignored her. "He also has a plantation in the south…"

"Oh, great…" Dana remarked.

"…but he stays in Kigali when he has business."

"Ah." Kristen's eyebrows rose as she seemed to visualize a new plan of action. "And delivering a gorilla infant to a Saudi customer would presumably constitute business."

"Yep. Not to mention that Kigali has a convenient airport for the Saudi to fly into and out of." He started working on a second roll.

"Do you have an exact address?"

"More or less. It's the big house with the palm trees next to the Hotel des Mille Collines. Not only that, assuming we can get our hands on the infant, I bought some milk and bananas."

Kristen gave him a slap on the shoulder. "Good man. That's all we need. All right, everyone. Finish your breakfast. We've got to get this posse on the road."

Posse, Dana thought. She liked the image.

❖

The ostentatious house was easy to spot, and within minutes they were at the door. A male house servant answered, and though he hesitated, a man's voice behind him said to admit the visitors. When the servant stepped back, they could see him.

Protais Zigirazo was a tall beefy man, with a full face and cheeks that blended into his neck. Nearly bald, he had a swath of gray hair across the back of his head and a black mustache. He wore a white shirt that swelled over his belly and tucked neatly into his well-tailored trousers. Dana was briefly intimidated until the familiar odor reached her. The damning odor of gorilla fear. The bastard had Mwelu.

"How can I help you?" he asked, his guarded tone bordering on the hostile. Clearly he sensed his three white visitors meant trouble.

Again, Kristen came right to the point. "We understand you arranged to have an infant gorilla captured. As it turned out, that meant killing two adult gorillas. That's illegal, as you well know, and we're here to claim the infant."

Zigirazo squinted at her, ignoring her announcement. "I know who you are. You're that gorilla woman still living up there in the Virungas. What arrogance, to come to my home and make such ridiculous accusations. Get out at once."

Kristen was a head shorter than he, and probably about half his weight, but stood her ground. "Mr. Zigirazo. We know you have the gorilla, and we know the man who you hired to procure it. So there's no sense in feigning innocence and outrage."

Zigirazo approached them until he stood over them, and his sheer bulk couldn't help but be alarming. Only Peter was bigger, but he stood at the back, useless. "I have hired no one, and I suggest you leave before I have my servant summon the police. I assure you, they'll be here in minutes and it will not go well for you."

Although Kristen had to tilt her head to look up at him, she seemed unfazed. "Yes, we know how important you are, Mr. Zigirazo. Brother-in-law to the president is no small position. That's why I think you would be embarrassed to have it known that you initiated a crime of this sort, in a country that depends so much on gorillas. We have all the proof we need. You might be able to stay out of jail for it, but I daresay, President Habyarimana would not care to have it reported in the international papers that his family was involved in poaching. Do you also sell their heads and hands, or only their infants?"

Zigirazo's mahogany skin seemed to glow slightly purple as rage registered on his face. He spoke slowly and in the monotone of someone certain of his power. "You obviously do not know who you are threatening or what harm can come to you if you cause political problems. Your predecessor discovered that to her misfortune."

"I'm willing to risk that. Are you willing to risk disgracing the president?"

"Your threats are empty. A Batwa poacher who will be jailed for his crime killed the gorillas, and there the matter will rest. Any other people you choose to involve in your claim will not cooperate. Now get out before you have an unfortunate accident falling down my stairs." He glanced toward a doorway to another room, where two other very large men stood. It was a real threat, since the house had no stairs.

They had seconds to get more information. Dana took a step forward. "The Saudi customer. Just tell us, have you handed over the gorilla yet?"

"Get out!" He accompanied the shout with a snapping of his fingers, summoning his two strongmen into the room."

"All right, you win." It was Peter who spoke for the first time, and he already had his hand on the front door. He swung it open, and they hurried out before the two thugs could lay a hand on them.

❖

"Well, that went well," Dana grumbled once they were back in their Land Rover. Peter scratched under his beard, staring out the car window at the house.

Kristen seemed not to hear and sat rubbing her knuckles along her chin, lost in thought. "Maybe we're throwing ourselves into this without really figuring things out."

"What's to figure out?" Peter asked roughly.

"To start, where Mwelu is likely to be. All along, we've arrived too late, and all we could be sure of is that she had been there but was no longer. We have to think forward. What's the likely trajectory?"

Dana replied, "Presumably, at this moment, Mwelu is somewhere between Zigirazo's house and a very rich Saudi."

Kristen drummed her fingers nervously on the steering wheel. "Yes, that's a reasonable assumption. And once she arrives in his hands, how would this very rich Saudi transport her out of Rwanda without passing through customs?"

Peter glanced up at the sky as if perceiving the answer. "He'd fly to Kigali in his own private jet, wouldn't he?"

"I believe he would. But such a transaction involves a certain delay, doesn't it? Even if someone telephoned him and said that they'd captured the animal, they'd still need time to pay people off and move her secretly from place to place."

Dana nodded. "So there'd be a slight time lag, maybe a couple of days, while he waited for his purchase to arrive in Kigali. Then buyer and seller get together and she's handed over." She stared into space, followed the train of logic. "And while he was waiting for the animal to be delivered, he'd stay in the best hotel, wouldn't he?" It seemed obvious now.

"That was my thought, too," Kristen said. "The best hotel would be the Hotel des Mille Collines. Right over there." She pointed across the street. "Admittedly, that's a lot of suppositions, but we do know she's in Kigali, and judging from Zigirazo's behavior, the deal's not yet done. So, all we have to do is find the buyer."

"Can't be too hard," Dana added. "Rwanda's a tiny country. How many Saudis can a Rwandan hotel entertain at any given moment?"

"I think we're on the right track. Let's give it a go." Kristen took charge again. "Peter, you should be the one to ask at the reception.

In the meantime, we'll park down in the hotel garage, just to get off the street. We'll meet you down there. If no Saudis are staying there, we'll move on down to the cheaper hotels."

Peter balked. "Why do I have to be the one to ask for him? I'm not an Arab, and I don't speak any African languages."

"No, but you're a male. A single woman wouldn't dare show up at a hotel and ask about a Saudi man who wasn't her husband."

"Fine. But I need a name to ask for. Something like…Omar Khayyam?"

Kristen snorted. "Someone's a little weak on their Middle Eastern history. Omar Khayyam was a Persian." She thought for a moment. "Try Salah al Din."

"Oh, that sounds authentic."

"It is. He was the Arab general who took Jerusalem back from the Crusaders."

Peter nodded slowly. "Oooookay. I'll go with that." He climbed out of the Land Rover and strode toward the hotel. As his wide back disappeared through the glass door of the entry, Kristen started the motor again and drove them down into the garage. They parked within sight of the elevator door and waited.

"God, I hope this works. I feel like we're grasping at straws." Dana laid her head against the side window and closed her eyes. "This is the fourth day since Mwelu was captured. And those jerks have no idea how to take care of a baby gorilla."

"I think we've got more than just a straw. We managed to trace her to Zigirazo's house. The question is whether we can intervene before they get her out of the country."

The sound of the elevator doors opening caught their attention. Three people emerged, two Japanese who strode toward a sports car and, behind them, Peter.

Kristen waved from the car window and he hurried toward them.

"How'd it go? Did you find out anything?"

"Well, I asked for Salah al Din, and of course the clerk couldn't find him in the register. But he said they did have Mr. Hamza bin Almasi and asked if that was who I meant? Then I said, 'Oh, yes. That's his business partner. Can you tell me what room he's staying in?'"

Peter was almost gleeful. "And the guy gave it to me, just like that. Fifth floor, room 516."

"Well done again, old man. You're really on top of this." Dana play-punched him on the shoulder the way Kristen had done.

Kristen was calculating again. "So far so good. If he's still there, it means he hasn't left yet with the baby. Assuming he's the guy that bought her. So how do we get between him and her? I want you both to think about this as if it were a military strategy. We're three smart people. Surely we can come up with something."

They sat, all staring into space. At that moment, a sleek new Mercedes Benz pulled into the garage and parked on the other side of the elevator column. Only the rear half of the car was visible. Dana glanced idly toward it as the driver and passenger passed by the trunk and headed toward the elevator. She gripped Kristen's arm. "Look."

The men wore red-checkered headscarves and what looked like white shirts that reached to their ankles.

"Saudis," she said unnecessarily.

"Mr. bin Almasi, you think?"

"Or his henchmen. Doesn't look like they've seen us. They're using the other elevator, anyhow."

"All right. Let's wait a few minutes and then go up behind them. See if they go to room 516."

"Then what?"

"I don't know. But we've built this whole plan on the assumption they've got Mwelu. We could still have the wrong guys at the wrong hotel."

"Okay. Here's what I think." Kristen hunched forward, dropping her voice, although no one was in sight who could have heard her. "We two go up to see if we can figure out whether they have her. Maybe listen at the door. Or see if we can smell her. It worked back at Bizimana's. Meanwhile, Peter stays here and watches to see if they bring anything down. If they have her and get past us, he could stall them."

"I don't have anything better to offer, so let's go." Dana was already on her way to the elevator. Once inside and with Kristen next to her, she pressed the button for the fifth floor.

To her exasperation, the elevator stopped at the lobby, where two more guests and their porter stepped in with massive suitcases. Their ride was delayed yet again when the elevator stopped at the fourth floor and they dragged the suitcases out.

Finally, the doors opened on the fifth floor.

But just as they stepped out, the door to a distant room—they couldn't see the number—opened, and the same two men from the garage emerged. They pushed a hotel cart that carried a single large case. It was covered with a white tablecloth, but its shape suggested a pet carrier, of the size that could transport a large dog.

"Mwelu," Dana whispered suddenly. "They're taking her to the car."

The men moved off in the opposite direction toward what seemed to be a freight elevator, and as the doors closed behind them, Dana stepped back into their own elevator and was about to press the button.

"No, the stairs," Kristen commanded, pointing to the emergency-exit door across the corridor. Without waiting for agreement she lunged through the door and took the stairs two at a time. Dana lurched behind her, focusing with every step on not tripping.

As they hoped, the stairs opened to the garage, but they arrived a moment too late. The two Saudis stood before the open trunk of their car. The sound of a gorilla shrieking was unmistakable, but it was muffled as soon as they loaded the carrier into the trunk and slammed down the lid.

Peter had stepped out of the Land Rover but also stood helplessly, apparently waiting for some sort of signal from Kristen.

Dana was sick with impotent rage. The poor creature was obviously terrified, probably starving, and about to be taken out of the country. And they could do nothing to help her. Even if the three of them stormed the men, they couldn't subdue them long enough to transfer the heavy carrier to their own car. It wasn't like in the movies.

Then a miracle happened. One of the men said something and returned to the freight elevator, leaving his companion behind to guard the car. As soon as the elevator door closed behind him, Kristen said "Now," and all knew what she meant.

The ten seconds it took for them to reach the Mercedes seemed endless. As if in slow motion, the man spotted them and started to turn. But Peter was on him and threw him facedown to the ground.

With a deft motion, he wrapped the man's face in his checkered head cloth.

Without speaking, Kristen and Dana raised the lid to the trunk and hauled the carrier up over the edge. The Saudi thrashed, but Peter outweighed him and held him with his arms pinned against his back. After a moment of fumbling for handholds, Kristen and Dana staggered with the carrier toward the Land Rover at the other corner of the garage. Behind them, Dana could hear Peter lift the man and drop him into the trunk before slamming the lid shut.

Mwelu was shrieking again, but they could do nothing to comfort her. All they could do was set her in the back of the vehicle. Once Peter caught up with them, he leapt in next to the carrier, pulled the rear door shut, and they sped out of the garage.

For some minutes, Kristen seemed to drive aimlessly, while the gorilla still shrieked.

"A shame we didn't think of bringing a tranquilizing gun," Dana said, guessing her thoughts. Then, "Look, there's a quiet place. Pull over there for a moment."

Kristen turned into a forlorn lot between two dilapidated buildings where no one seemed to be about at the moment, though they knew that could quickly change.

"We have to quiet her," Kristen explained. "We can't drive down the streets of Kigali with a screaming animal."

"How can you be sure she won't run away?" Peter asked.

"She knows us. She knows me, especially," Dana said. "I'll hold onto her."

Kristen took charge. "Just keep the car doors closed. You climb in the back with Peter and let her out of the carrier. If she panics, she still can't get out, and we'll just keep driving, hoping for the best."

"Good idea." Dana exited the car and went around to the rear door and slid in beside the carrier on the opposite side from Peter. Lifting the tablecloth, she unhooked the door to the carrier. Inside, Mwelu lay on her side with hands and feet tied together. She looked up, her huge brown eyes wide with terror.

"Oh, my God. She must be in terrible pain." Dana took a penknife from her pants pocket and cut through the bindings. Not only did the little gorilla not try to escape, but she cowered at the back of the carrier, her hands hanging limply in front of her.

"Those bastards. They cut off circulation to her hands. She can't even move them." Dana reached into the carrier and stroked the shivering animal. "Come on, darling. You know me, don't you? We played together a dozen times," Dana cooed, but still the infant wouldn't budge.

Mwelu had at least fallen silent, and Kristen focused on the next problem. "Look, we've still got to figure out how to drive back to Ruhengeri without being stopped. Did any of the Saudis see our car? Peter, the guy you knocked down, did he see it?"

"I don't think so. I covered his face as best I could before I dumped him. But it won't make any real difference. Zigirazo knows we've gone after her, so once word gets back to him that we took her they'll know where to look. And I'm pretty sure his houseman saw the Land Rover when we arrived. I'd say it'll take them just a couple of telephone calls and about fifteen minutes to figure it out, and then they'll be after us."

"We have to change vehicles, then," Kristen said.

"How the hell do we do that? What crazy person do you know who's willing to take part in a gorilla rescue from a powerful politician and a rich Saudi?"

"I know only one."

The plan was elegantly simple in the conception but complicated in the execution. While Dana stayed close to Mwelu, trying to soothe her, Kristen drove out of their derelict alley and returned to the rear of the hostel where they'd spent the night. "Be back in a minute," she said.

Mwelu was alarmingly weak and gave no resistance when Dana reached inside the carrier and stroked her arm and swollen hands. She offered little chunks of banana, but the injured infant refused. Finally she slid herself head and shoulders into the front of the carrier and laid her head on Mwelu's shoulder, letting the infant smell her hair. She caressed Mwelu's chest, imitating what she recalled were Amahoro's maternal grunts, and finally a tiny hand tugged at her hair.

With a bit of maneuvering, she got Mwelu out and into her arms and wrapped her in the tablecloth to conceal her from passersby.

"Here, darling. You must be so thirsty." Peter handed her the open milk container, and Dana dribbled a trickle of milk into her mouth. She finally responded, reaching up and encircling Dana's neck.

Dana could have wept. She was the first being who'd offered a protective embrace to the infant since her mother had been butchered in front of her.

In a few minutes, Kristen returned and started the car. "Okay, they let me call Ruhengeri, for a fee, of course. And I got through to him."

"Who, for God's sake?"

"Rudy Lambot. I knew I could depend on him. He's going to meet us where Ruhengeri Road dead-ends at the East-West road into Kigali. There's a wooded area not far away where we can park out of sight. We agreed that one of us would keep watch for him near the intersection. It should take him about three hours to get there. Our job will simply be to hide."

In the three-and-a-half hours they waited, Mwelu had consumed a portion of the milk but still refused the banana. She'd stopped screaming and lay passive and limp in Dana's arms, though she was beginning to feebly move her hands. As she had for all the days of her captivity, she continued to suffer diarrhea, but her empty stomach produced only a thin trickle of fluid, and Dana wiped her clean with a rag torn from the tablecloth. Otherwise, she simply held her close. Had they rescued her too late?

"She's terribly weak," she said to Peter. "How can the man who purchased her be so stupid? He might have paid his thousand dollars for a dead gorilla."

Peter snorted. "The people who buy wildlife for their personal amusement have so much money. He'd have just paid again for another animal."

"Well, he won't be so blasé about having one stolen out from under his nose." Kristen glanced at her watch. "I'm going out again to look for Rudy."

At that moment a convoy of some dozen military vehicles rumbled by on the road leading to Kigali, and Dana covered Mwelu's head with the cloth. The Land Rover was out of the convoy's line of sight, but the spectacle of so much firepower moving into the capital was unnerving. Who were they preparing to fight? No one said anything.

When the convoy had disappeared down the road, Kristen stepped out of the car and started toward the intersection. She hadn't gone more than ten yards when a battered blue Citroën came south from the Ruhengeri Road and bumped overland toward them.

"Hmm. I expected something more imposing," Peter muttered as he climbed out of the Land Rover.

Rudy was all business and in a hurry. "We can talk on the way back. For now, here's the plan. The girls come back with me."

"Women," Dana muttered.

"Right. The women and the gorilla come back with me. Peter waits fifteen minutes, so he's nowhere near us, and drives the Land Rover back."

"Is that all right with you, Peter?" Kristen asked.

Peter blinked, obviously perplexed. "I…uh…wasn't expecting to be on my own in this. What should I do if Zigirazo sends out his men and they stop me?"

Rudy opened the door to the Land Rover, offering Peter the driver's seat. "I don't think they'll do that. They can't arrest you legally. Plus, you won't have the animal or the carrying case. You should be fine, but if you get in trouble, here's my telephone number. Otherwise we'll expect you at my clinic in about three hours. It's a quarter mile south of the main intersection downtown, on the left behind a dairy. "

He strode away, leaving Peter standing forlorn by the Land Rover.

CHAPTER THIRTEEN

The *Clinique Vétérinaire des Virungas* on the Gisenyi Road was less than its long title led one to expect. A single-story cement block house with a faux tile roof and a porch covered with corrugated tin, only the double front door and the sign over it indicated it was a medical facility.

The fenced-in yard held a goat and several dogs, and all seemed in good condition, which was more than Dana could say for dogs she'd seen in the streets of Ruhengeri. The chickens in a smaller pen in the corner of the yard were presumably not patients.

Rudy swung the car around to the rear of the house to a small covered area that served as a car park. It was just becoming dark, and as they pulled up, someone from inside the house flicked on an overhead light. Rudy climbed out and held the car door open while Dana struggled out, the baby gorilla in her arms.

A moment later, a woman met them carrying a baby of her own, and they stood facing each other with their respective infants. The woman's narrow head and long, straight nose identified her as a Tutsi, and her baby, with similar features and much paler skin, looked to be about a year-and-a-half old. She must have known who her visitors were, but she waited silently until Rudy made introductions.

"Kristen, Dana, this is Mary. Mary, this is Dr. Wolfe and her assistant Dana."

Mary smiled but didn't offer her hand, which was just as well, because Dana's were thoroughly soiled.

"My surgery is this way," Rudy said, directing them down a narrow corridor to a small room with a steel table and a sink. He flicked on an overhead light and rolled up his sleeves. "Before we see to the social niceties, let's take a look at the gorilla."

Dana unraveled the feces-stained tablecloth and set Mwelu down on the table, but the still-terrified creature grasped her around the neck. "It's all right, dear. I won't leave you," she murmured, then looked up at Rudy. "Can you examine her this way, or do you have to anesthetize her?"

"It's fine. Just hang onto her while I work." He felt around the animal's ribs and stomach, then peered closely at her teeth and eyes, and finally examined the wounds on her wrists and ankles. He washed his hands at the sink and spoke over his shoulder.

"It's what you'd expect for a young animal kept tied up for several days. She's dehydrated and her stomach's empty. The cuts on her wrists and feet are infected too, so I'll give her an antibiotic, but I don't see any nerve damage to her hands. She's lethargic though, so she needs to eat soon. I'll make up some formula that should appeal to her. And of course, I need to monitor her to make sure she's recovering."

Kristen stroked Mwelu's head. "We'll see to the feeding and to the round-the-clock mothering. A good bath wouldn't hurt either. When she's stronger we'll introduce her into another group, but not right away. She's too traumatized."

"So what's the plan?" Dana asked. "How do we take care of Mwelu without getting caught? By now Zigirazo knows she's been stolen, and since they couldn't stop us on the road, he's bound to send a couple of his thugs up to Karisoke."

"You'll have to hide her." Rudy leaned back against the counter and lit a cigarette.

"But where? In a tent in the forest, a hotel room where you sneak in like an adulterer to check on her? " Dana's frustration made her sarcastic. The victory of the rescue seemed to be evaporating.

"I suppose it has to be here," Rudy said.

Kristen exhaled. "God, I was hoping you'd offer."

"Yeah, well, that's really the only possibility, isn't it? Anyhow, the offer has its limitations. I'll take her, but I can't be an ersatz mom.

Mary can't either. She has her own baby. Someone's got to stay with her and attend to her all the time."

"That will be me," Dana said, brightening. "She knows me the best, and I'm dispensable at Karisoke. Peter can continue tracking and monitoring for both of us until we get past this crisis. Don't you think so, Kristen?"

"That does seem workable, though Peter's not here to give his opinion. I hope he's all right. We sort of abandoned him on the road, didn't we?"

As if on cue, the surgery door opened and Mary stood, placid. "Your friend has arrived." She backed away and Peter stepped past her.

"Oh my God," Kristen exclaimed. "What happened?"

Peter seemed to glare through his one still-open eye. "What do you think happened? They caught me, of course. There was no way they *wouldn't* catch me." The right side of his face was swollen and red, and his right eye was purple and almost shut. The redness seemed to increase with his anger.

Rudy came around the examining table toward him and touched him lightly on the chin, turning his head to scrutinize him. "Hmm. A split lip, but not deep enough to require a stitch." He lifted the discolored eyelid and Peter flinched. "Can you see me? Any double vision or blind spots?"

"I can see fine, but my face hurts like hell."

"I'm sure it does, but I don't see any damage to the eyeball, and it looks like a simple contusion with hematoma around the eye ridge."

Peter pulled his head out of Rudy's grasp and turned to Kristen. "You left me there as a diversion while you got away, didn't you?"

"I'm so sorry, Peter. It seemed the only way to get Mwelu to safety. We hoped they would see the Rover was empty and simply give up, but I guess that was a little naive."

Rudy took hold of his chin again and continued with his examination. "Open your mouth. Any damage to your teeth? No? What about the rest of you?" He indicated Peter's untucked shirt and the blood spots on the front. "What's that?"

"Nosebleed." He lifted his shirt and revealed a wide bruise on his hip and back.

Rudy palpated around the bruised area. "Any pain or nausea other than the bruise?"

"Isn't that enough?"

"What did they do to you?" Kristen asked.

"They slapped me around first. I tried to fight back, but there were three of them, and they knocked me to the ground. Got a few kicks in and then stopped. I guess it was just a warning. They knew about the gorilla, of course, but I didn't tell them anything."

Rudy peered into the damaged eye again. "You're sure you can see normally? No flashes of light?"

"No, nothing, But I'm not sure I'm satisfied with having a veterinarian examine me. No offense."

"None taken. But the rules for trauma are mostly the same. Contusions heal by themselves, and plain aspirin will reduce the swelling and the pain. Internal injuries are something else, but you don't have any symptoms. You can still go to the French hospital if you want, but they'll ask more questions."

"Questions? I'm the one with questions. Those guys threatened my life. How far are we going to go in this?"

"No further than this." Kristen reassured him with a hand on his arm. "Dana will stay here with Mwelu, and you and I will return to Karisoke. With a little luck, Zigirazo will figure out we've outwitted him and we can all go back to work. After all, they can't go to the police. We were undoing their crime."

"We *both* committed crimes. And you mean you're just going to carry on doing business as usual? With this Zigirazo thug breathing down our necks?" Peter's mouth twisted as if he were chewing. "Is Karisoke going to be permanently involved with this guy?"

Kristen shrugged helplessly. "I don't know the answer to that, Peter. Zigirazo is part of the reality here, and so are Rwandan politics. I'm committed to protecting the gorillas, you know that, and I'm truly sorry you had to be brutalized because of it. I promise not to leave you in the line of fire again."

"Thanks," he grumbled. "By the way, they broke one of the windows in the Rover, just to make their point."

Rudy raised both hands to end the conversation. "Look, I know you're all worn out from the whole operation, and no one's really fit to climb up to Karisoke in the dark. We've got a spare room for the two women, and Peter can sleep in the hammock on our porch."

Mary had been standing quietly in the corner behind Peter, but when the discussion seemed to end, she spoke up. "Well, now that all *that's* settled, come in to the dining room for supper. I was expecting you and made beans with cassava. Enough for five." She looked up at Peter, who stood a head taller than everyone in the room. "For six."

The guest room, which obviously was also the storage room, held only a minimum in the way of accommodations. A low platform nailed together from crates held a double mattress that smelled faintly of mold, as did the mattresses at Karisoke, but seemed clean otherwise. The only other furniture was another crate with a small electric lamp and a straight-back wooden chair. Still, comfort was the least of their concerns at the moment.

Kristen and Dana sat side by side, leaning against the rear wall, trying to cajole Mwelu into eating. They offered plantain bits and raisins, but she turned away and simply sucked her two fingers.

"Here, let me take her for a while. You've held her all evening." Kristen drew the baby into her arms and offered her the bottle Rudy had provided. "Ah, look, she's drinking. You see, she was just waiting for Auntie Kristen to be the one." She rocked the little gorilla, who gazed up at her with large, pleading brown eyes and grasped her fingers.

"You know, in the years I've been at Karisoke, I've seen dozens of baby gorillas, had them romping all over me. But I've never held one in my arms this way. It's deeply affecting, isn't it?"

"What are you feeding her? She seems to like it better than the regular milk we tried before." Dana leaned forward to caress the little cheek with her fingertips, enjoying the double pleasure of the baby's soft face and the pressure of Kristen's shoulder.

"Some kind of gorilla formula Rudy made up. Ordinary cow's milk isn't so good for them, anyhow, so it's better she's taking this."

Dana watched Kristen gazing down at the suckling infant with such tenderness. Only her short hair, the rolled-up sleeves of her denim shirt, and perhaps the hiking boots at the foot of the bed were slightly at odds with the serene image. How beautiful she was. Dana felt something she'd almost forgotten about. Longing.

"It suits you, you know. Motherhood."

"Really? Babies are sweet, human or simian, but I don't see the human variety happening in the near future. No sperm donors anywhere in sight."

"Not even Peter? I bet he's got lots of sperm."

"Peter? Not really my type."

"Really? Seems to me he's everyone's type. I thought you two had hit it off. He's always so...attentive...to you."

"I'm sure he's attentive to lots of women," Kristen said neutrally, then changed the subject. "Look, the little cutie's asleep." She gently drew the bottle from the half-open lips and set it on the night table. Slowly and gently, she let Mwelu slide from her embrace onto the mattress between her and Dana. They watched quietly for a few minutes, and when it seemed the sleep was profound, Kristen leaned backward and clicked off the night lamp.

They lay in the darkness for a few moments, and Dana waited for sleep to come. But too much was going on in her head.

"Well, this is awkward," she said.

"What? Sleeping with me or sleeping with a baby gorilla?"

Dana chuckled softly. "The gorilla part. I've never done that one before." There was a moment of silence as she let the implication of the remark set in.

"In fact, I *have*." Kristen kept her voice low. "Slept with gorillas, I mean. The first year I was here when I was working hard to impress Dian, to get my bush creds, so to speak. I camped out with group twelve." Kristen bypassed the flirtatious remark.

"Group twelve? I never heard of them."

"The group disbanded a few years ago when the silverback died. But I wanted them to accept me, you know, to prove to Dian I was a good primatologist. Anyhow, I followed them until they made their night nests, and I curled up in a sleeping bag close by. It was the dry season, obviously. I couldn't have done it in the rain."

Kristen rose in Dana's estimation. "How'd it go?"

"It was awful. Total lunacy. First of all, it was noisy. I heard an elephant in the distance and some snorting closer by, which I'm sure was a buffalo, then all kinds of night creatures whose names I don't know, but half of them would sting you or bite you or eat you from the inside. And on top of it all, gorillas snore and fart like old men. I didn't sleep a wink. I was afraid of snakes, too, although none showed up. Which is just as well, because by dawn, when I finally dozed a little, the whole group had moved on. I woke up all alone in the bush feeling like an idiot."

"What did Dian say?"

"She said I was, in fact, an idiot and if I did it again, she'd fire me. So much for bush creds, eh?"

"She was right, of course, but don't tell Peter you did that. He'll try it himself once his bruises have healed."

"He's welcome to it and could probably pull it off. In spite of his woo-woo notions about sacred nature and communing with God through animals, the guy's pretty tough. I feel terrible letting him get beat up that way, but I'm betting in two days, he'll be back on the trail."

Mwelu rolled on her side without waking and pressed her face against Dana's breast, her tiny black fist curled up against her cheek.

"It's amazing to sleep with an animal, isn't it?" Dana whispered.

"Yes, it is." Kristin leaned in close and cupped her hand around the infant head, her hair lightly brushing Dana's chin. "You feel a sort of primordial comfort, like it's something our ancestors did."

"Two women and a gorilla?" Dana murmured. "Sure. Coulda happened."

Kristen snorted, her breath warm on Dana's neck. "You know what I mean." But she didn't pull away, and Dana bathed in the innocent intimacy.

"It's a shame you have to go back to Karisoke. Be nice to stay here for a week and be cave mothers."

"Mmmm, yeah. But the National Geographic Society pays me for reports, not for rescues. Not to mention Mr. Z, whose thugs are going to show up there soon looking for his gorilla. But at Karisoke, they'll have to deal with me and eight of my men. And I'll take great comfort knowing you're here with our baby."

"Of course. You know we're all in this together, all on the barricades fighting the bad guys. Like in that romantic French painting."

Exhaustion finally was beginning to overtake them both, and Kristen dropped back onto her pillow with a long exhalation. "The Delacroix, you mean. Hmm. Sure. Us on the barricades."

Punchy now with sleep, Dana leaned over Mwelu's warm body toward Kristen. "You can be Liberty with the flag and the bare breasts, and I'll be the boy with the pistols."

"Sure. I don't mind flashing my breasts for freedom."

"You *shouldn't* mind. They're gorgeous."

CHAPTER FOURTEEN

Insensate in the depths of sleep, Kristen and Dana moved about as creatures do, seeking warmth and comfort. At morning light, when Dana awakened, she grasped first that Mwelu was on the floor eating a plantain, and second, that she and Kristen were lying in each other's arms. She savored the pleasure for several long moments, then edged away.

Kristen awoke. "Oh, sorry." She sat up awkwardly and turned away. Dana also turned in the opposite direction, and, perched on opposite sides of the bed, they drew on their respective blue jeans as if nothing had happened.

Obviously delighted that they both were awake, Mwelu scrambled toward Dana and raised her long arms, wanting to be held.

"Good morning, darling." Dana leaned toward her, but as she lifted the little ape into her arms she noticed the pile. "Oh, oh. Night poo," she announced.

Kristen was on her feet now. "Don't worry. Rudy had the foresight to leave us some rags." She came around the bed and knelt to help clean up. "I guess we should be glad she's got enough food in her stomach now to do that."

At that moment, Rudy knocked at the door and, after a polite pause, let himself in. The smell of his morning cigarette was almost welcome, as it slightly diminished the odor of what they had just gathered from the floor.

"Sorry to rush you, but it's seven o'clock and Peter's been up for an hour. Oh, I'll dispose of that." He took the bundle from Dana's hand and turned away. "Mary's made coffee," he said over his shoulder.

"Coffee sounds good," Kristen said, folding the blanket neatly at the foot of the guest bed. "And he's right. We've got to get away from here before anyone spots our Rover or it occurs to Zigirazo that a rescued gorilla might be with the only veterinarian in town."

Dana held Mwelu in her arms again. "I'm sorry you have to go. How long do you think it'll take? I mean to get her out of here and back to the forest?"

Kristen ran her fingers through her hair. "Frankly, I don't know. All I'm really doing is stalling for time. Maybe a couple of weeks, and then we'll try to reintegrate her, either into her own group or another one."

"Is she old enough to make it without milk?"

"I think so. They go through a very long weaning period where they both nurse and eat vegetation. It's almost more important just to have someone nest with her and teach her how to be a gorilla. Once Rudy decides she's healthy, we can smuggle her up to Karisoke and hide her in one of the cabins."

Dana followed her to the door. "Well, I'll nest with her and try to get her to eat her veggies along with the bottle."

"Good. Meanwhile, I'll look after all the others. And Peter, too. Poor guy, he really did go above and beyond. Anyhow, I'll be back in a few days to check on you both, and we'll decide the next step then."

She paused for a moment before opening the door. "All right, then. Mwelu, darling, take good care of Dana." She kissed Mwelu on the top of the head, then brushed her lips lightly across Dana's cheek and stepped through the doorway.

Dana's face warmed. What did *that* mean? A recognition that they were somehow connected by their shared mothering. Or was it a "so long and thanks for everything," as she prepared to head back up the mountain with the magnificent, courageous, and newly martyred Peter Hewlett?

Confused, Dana hugged Mwelu a little tighter and joined the others in the kitchen for the promised coffee.

Within an hour of Kristen and Peter's departure, the household fell into a normal routine. As if nothing special had happened the day before, Rudy left for the Ruhengeri market to purchase iodine and check for packages at the post office. He explained that various medications, especially the veterinary varieties of amoxiclav, butorphanol, and ivermectin had to be special-ordered from Europe. She watched him drive away with the strange words buzzing through her head. They seemed curiously at odds with his primitive clinic and his rough social manner.

After finally giving Mwelu a good wash, Dana returned to join Mary in the kitchen. Standing just outside the door, she realized it was the first time she would have a personal encounter with a Rwandan woman without an intermediary. It was one thing to shake hands with the trackers' wives at a Christmas celebration and quite another to be a guest in a Rwandan home. She wasn't sure how to behave.

The night before, she'd watched the way Mary moved around the kitchen with the same sort of grace that Paka had and studied her fine features, her full African lips, and her large, almost black, eyes. She understood how Rudy could find her attractive. But what did one talk about with an African woman?

Mary stood at the stove, stirring something in a pot, with her child on her hip, and she turned as Dana entered. Abruptly, she laughed.

"Um, may I ask what you find so funny?" Had a smudge of Mwelu's excreta somehow ended up on her face?

"I am not laughing at you but at us, two women with our babies on our hips. If you were Rwandan and we met in the market place, we would both boast about how clever our children are. A little competition, you know? I would say, for example, that my boy is only eleven months and can already say 'Papa' and 'cookie.'"

Dana giggled. "Well, you'd beat me there. My little girl is more than a year old and can only scream. On the other hand, she can already hang by her arms."

"Oh, she wins that one." Mary tickled the tiny gorilla face under the chin. "And she's very cute."

"Yes, but the truth is, what she mostly does all day is poo. I've just washed her but will need to again in an hour. Do you have a wet rag I can use?"

"Yes, of course. Rudy needs rags all the time, too." She reached under the sink and brought out what was obviously once the sleeve of a shirt. "We will wash it each time and hang it to dry so you can use it again, like a diaper. That's also part of my daily schedule."

"I see I'm with an expert. I'm new at this and can use any advice you have." Dana sat down on one of the kitchen chairs and positioned Mwelu on her knees. "Your son's a beautiful boy. What's his name?"

"Landoald," Mary seemed pleased to be asked. "After my father. Landoald Ndasingwa. Do you know him? He's our minister of labor."

"I'm sorry I don't know anything about Rwandan political affairs. I haven't been here very long, and we're pretty isolated up at Karisoke."

Mary sat down next to her and began feeding mashed papaya to her baby. She succeeded in inserting the first spoonful, though half of it dribbled out again. "Probably just as well. Our political affairs are not good. Hostile, really." She scraped the excess papaya from the tiny chin and slid it into his mouth again.

"Yes, I understand there are tensions between Hutus and Tutsis. Rudy explained some of the background to me."

"It is not so much tension as a civil war, and it has been going on for years. When one group controls the government, thousands of the others run away to Uganda or Zaire. Then, when government power changes hands, the refugees come back and the other group runs away. Right now the Hutus are the government, and the Tutsis who ran away to Uganda call themselves the Rwandan Patriotic Front. They attack sometimes from the Ugandan side, though it seldom makes any difference."

"I thought you had a truce and a shared government," Dana said.

"We were supposed to, but that is falling apart. Listen, you can hear it for yourself." She leaned toward the counter and turned on a small transistor radio.

"This is Radio des Mille Collines," she explained. "What most people hear these days. The government runs it, so it is supposed to be fair. But it is not at all. The jokes and the announcements, and the listener calls that come in, are all from Hutus. In the end the Radio des Mille Collines is only for Hutus."

Popular music played for a while, but then an announcer interrupted. He gave a sports rundown and weather report in French, which Dana followed with little effort. Abruptly, he switched to Kinyarwanda.

"I'm afraid I don't understand anything he's saying. I hear only the laughing."

Mary wiped the residue of papaya from the cheeks of her baby and kissed him noisily. "They're rowdy and vulgar jokes, and he is speaking street language, the same as the people who call in. Sometimes they are even drunk. Of course that appeals to people who have no education and no work and are looking for someone to blame. They laugh a lot so they can say they are just joking, but what they say is pretty frightening."

"What *are* they saying?" Dana cuddled her own baby and tickled her stomach. The little mouth opened with the noisy panting that signaled gorilla laughter.

"They are claiming that Tutsis are the ruin of Rwanda. That if the Rwandan Patriotic Front is victorious, they will kill all Hutus. They call us *inyenzi*, cockroaches, and say they have to wipe us out before we do the same to them."

"Do you think it could come to that? I mean real violence?" She stopped tickling Mwelu. It hadn't occurred to her that she might have to face something more than the fury of one corrupt politician cheated of his investment.

"I don't know. Right now, the president is calling for calm. He is a Hutu but a moderate one. We still have a police force and an army, and they will follow him. All we can do is stay close to home and wait."

The opening door drew their attention. Rudy came in with two full straw bags. "I managed to get to the pathetic excuse they have for a pharmacy before they closed. Then I stopped by the market and got food for us and the gorilla." He set down a small bag of boxed items and another larger one filled with cassava, plantains, sweet potatoes, and net bags of several types of beans.

It was an uninspiring inventory, and Dana was touched to realize it was the groceries of a poor family. Moreover, they were going to share it with her without a second thought. She glanced up at Rudy.

"You know, it won't take Zigirazo long to establish that you're our veterinarian. Are we really any safer here than we would be up at camp?"

He began to unload the produce into boxes and drawers. "Only for a while. He'll send his thugs up to Karisoke first. When he finds nothing there and can't scare Kristen into giving him any information, he'll look around for likely hiding places. It should take him a couple of days to work out my connection, but you're right. He'll show up sooner or later. That's why you should sleep in the shed behind the house."

"Shed? I didn't notice any shed."

"That's the whole point. We built it especially so you can't see it from the street or even the house. Come on. I'll show you what I mean."

Still carrying Mwelu, she followed him from the kitchen through the carport and into a thicket of trees and bushes some hundred yards from the house. Covered with brush, the hut was nearly invisible.

He brushed aside the vines hanging over the entryway and tugged the door open. "Go on, take a look. It's not nearly as bad as you think." He shone a flashlight inside onto a space some ten by twelve feet. It was surprisingly clean and had obviously been created as a refuge. On one side was a cot and tiny table, and on the other several shelves with bottles and canned goods. She recognized the pressure lamp, of the same make as those they used at Karisoke. It was in fact a miniature version of her own cabin, minus the wood stove.

"Mary's father had a couple of friends in the RPF who stayed here for a while."

"Rwandan Patriotic Front. You mean the Tutsis from Uganda?"

"I mean the Rwandan Tutsis who fled to Uganda and now are coming back. Yeah, I know, it's hard to keep the players straight. But if you're a Tutsi, you have little choice but to stay on the lookout and have a place to hide. This is ours."

She stepped inside and found it claustrophobic with its single tiny window. "So you think I should stay here?" She shuddered at the thought.

"Only to sleep. Or if strangers approach the house. We're far enough from the street that you have a chance to run here without being seen."

Resigned, Dana scratched Mwelu's neck. "You see, my darling? It looks like we're Tutsis now. Who'd have thought?"

Chapter Fifteen

Three days later, at Karisoke, Kristen sat down to compose a letter to the Leaky Foundation explaining the events of the previous week. Skirting around the facts of the physical attacks on Bizimana and on the Saudi required a certain delicacy, if not evasiveness, and she found it hard to concentrate, for the blustery rain drumming on her corrugated tin roof caused an annoying clatter. A vigorous double rap on the door was the last straw, and she tossed her ballpoint pen on the table.

"Come in!" she called out and the door flew open, bringing a spray of rain with it.

Peter shut the door behind him, but not before a puddle had formed at his feet. She stood up and threw him a rag.

"Sorry." He caught it and slid it in circles with his foot to sop up the water. "I hope this doesn't keep up. It's impossible to get to the gorillas," he groused as he took off his jacket and hung it by the hood on the door hook. He slid the wet rag under it to catch the drips. "I left first thing in the morning, while it was still drizzling, but as soon as I found group three, the skies opened up. They're fine, by the way."

"Well, at least the rain discourages poachers. No sign of Zigirazo's thugs either, even after four days. The monsoon's keeping everyone at home. So, to what do I owe the pleasure? Do you have a report?"

He wiped his damp hands on his thighs and warmed them over the stove. "No, I don't. It takes twice as long to locate the gorillas, and when I do find them, there's just a bunch of them huddled together soaking wet. You can't even see who's who."

"What about snares? Have you come across any?"

"Aside from the fact that you can't even spot them with the dim light, wall of water, and blowing branches, no, I haven't. But I just can't keep this up."

"Well, this *is* the rainy season. If the gorillas have to endure it, so do we. It's part of the deal."

"Yeah, but doing both my work and Dana's wasn't part of the deal."

She leaned back in her chair. "I'm sorry you feel that way. We're all doing extra work for the moment. But you know the reason. Dana is the only thing between Mwelu and her captors. If you can think of a better solution, I'd be glad to hear it."

"Why not just leave the gorilla with Rudy and let Dana come back to work?"

"After all this time, you still don't know about baby gorillas? Mwelu has to have someone with her all the time. I thought you were as concerned about her as we were."

"Yeah, well, we need to talk about that, too. It's not just Dana being away and leaving me her work. That whole kidnapping business has been bothering me, too. It's just not my way to break the law. And then to be beaten up by people I can't even have arrested."

She exhaled noisily, becoming annoyed. This was an old complaint. "I'm sorry about the beating and I've apologized repeatedly. But if the rescue itself overstepped your personal moral code, I think it's your problem. You saw the slaughter those men caused. What would you have proposed we do?"

"That's just it. I don't like these moral dilemmas. I came to Africa to be closer to nature, to some sort of truth."

"Yeah, you told us. That communing-with-God-through-animals thing. Well, they have to be alive before you can see God in them."

"Don't make fun of me. I was looking for something authentic in Africa that was missing at home. But instead, I found gangsters. Gangsters in the government and gangsters that we became ourselves. I did not contract for this." He touched his left cheekbone. The swelling had disappeared, but a dark semicircle remained under his eye, as if he'd been in a boxing match.

She took up the pen again and tapped it on the table. "Then why did you go along with the plan? I don't recall your objecting."

"I did it to impress you."

She stopped tapping. "What? Impress me? Whatever for? A promotion?"

"No, of course not." He twirled a few hairs at the center of his beard, which she noticed he did when he was deliberating. Perhaps conscious of how imposing he was standing over her, he pulled up a chair and sat next to her at the table.

"Look. You're smart, beautiful, single—everything a man could ask for. I thought something might happen between us after a while. You must have figured out by now that I find you attractive. But I can't deal with this…this ruthlessness. I mean, you threatened to chop up that pygmy boy and eat him!"

She sat up, affronted. "Aside from the fact that it was Dana who came up with that bit of whimsy, your job description does not include judging my character. I hired you as a researcher, and that's all I expect and want from you."

Seeing his hurt expression, she softened her tone. "Look. You've been a hard worker and very helpful, and I'm grateful. I really am. And you were quite heroic taking that beating. But I thought you did it out of conviction, not flirtation."

He bent toward her, his elbows on his knees. "I'm not a jerk, and I don't assume every woman I meet is hot for me. But when we met, you couldn't take your eyes off me. You flirted with me first."

"You misread me. You're a handsome, striking man. I'm sure everyone looks at you like that when they meet you. It was admiration, not flirtation."

"Handsome, eh? Well, I think you're gorgeous. Come on now, admit you're lonely up here. You'd have to be. I have a lot to offer you." He laid his large hand over hers.

She slid it away from him. "Don't, Peter. You're making a mistake here, and if you just take your jacket and leave, we can forget we ever had this conversation."

He moved closer to her until their knees touched, and he bent forward again. His gold beard, still wet from the rain, glistened in the light from the table lamp. "I don't believe you. Whenever we're together, the air is electric. I know you've felt it, too."

He rested his hand on her shoulder and let his fingers creep around the back of her neck.

"Don't, Peter."

He drew her gently toward him.

The sudden slap stung her hand and made him recoil, his eyes wide with astonishment. She stood up, outraged, and marched toward the door, where she took his jacket from the hook. She held it out to him and opened the door.

Outside in the pouring rain, Gwehanda stood on the porch. One arm encircled a box braced on his hip, and his other hand was raised, about to knock. "Miss Kristen, I am sorry to disturb. I come with the mail and the groceries you ordered."

"Gwehanda, so happy to see you. Come in out of the rain."

The courier stepped in just as Peter snatched up his rain jacket and punched his arm into one of the sleeves. "Yes, do come in. Miss Wolfe is free now." With that, he stormed out into the downpour, and the vigor and speed of his exit told her it was also a resignation.

She sighed, with both relief and powerlessness.

❖

When Kristen woke up the next morning, it still drizzled, but during the rainy season, that counted for her as a sunny day. Showers were intermittent, and between them, the meadows and forest seemed to light up suddenly for a brief period, giving a false hope that the warmth would stay.

She took advantage of the break in the rain to look for gorilla group four to find out what had happened to them after the slaughter and kidnapping. With the death of the silverback Ndengera, she feared they would fall apart completely. To her dismay, she found no sign of them near their usual nesting place, and so she returned, discouraged, to the camp.

Before she'd even reached her cabin, Mukera hurried toward her, obviously agitated. "Three men are coming up from the car park."

"Who are they? Were they Rwandan or *abazungu*? Batwa or farmers?"

"Rwandan, Miss. Hutu. With spears. One of them wears a suit and carries a big gun."

Bizimana. It had to be. "Mukera, would you call the men together at my cabin? Thank you."

Scarcely ten minutes later, the three strangers appeared marching toward her. She was careful to remain on her porch, slightly above them as they approached. The added height had worked when she interrogated Munyaro but might not be so intimidating for a city man with a rifle. Behind the visitors, she could see her own men drifting toward them to form her backup, though Bizimana didn't seem to have noticed yet.

He halted a few feet from the porch. "Mr. Zigirazo has asked me to fetch his gorilla," he said. His rifle was pointed at the ground, but the threat was clear. She wondered why he brought spear carriers if he had a rifle, then realized it was primarily a show of power. He could hardly murder her in front of her entire staff, but he had a sense of drama, she had to admit.

"She's not Mr. Zigirazo's gorilla. She's nobody's gorilla, and I don't have her anyhow." She smiled inwardly, realizing they were repeating the scene they'd played in Bizimana's office, only in reverse. After they finished speaking their lines, would his detective skills be a good as hers had been?

The little man puffed out his chest and raised the rifle barrel until it was pointed at her feet. "He knows you attacked the men who bought her and then stole her from them. Mr. Zigirazo is very angry about this, and when he is angry, terrible things can happen. Your predecessor found that out."

She'd expected the threat but was surprised at hearing, once again, a near-confession of responsibility for Dian's murder. Once the issue of the baby gorilla was settled—if they managed to settle it—that remark might be useful in a court of law. Or maybe not.

"It will do you no good to threaten me," she said. "If you think I'm guilty of a crime, you should notify the police. But you'll have a hard time making a case against the rescuers of an animal from poachers—or from the people who hired them."

In the meantime, the Rwandan staff had gathered in a semicircle behind Bizimana and his two men, and while the little martinet was too proud to acknowledge them, his thugs kept glancing nervously over their shoulders, no doubt calculating the odds. Even with a rifle, it was nine against three.

Unmoved, Bizimana stood in place and glared at her, unwilling to concede defeat. She was tempted to say "Mexican standoff, eh?" but knew he wouldn't get it.

The tension broke when, to her surprise, Peter came around from behind the cabin and stood directly in front of Bizimana, head and shoulders above him and twice his bulk. He said nothing.

"You are prepared to die for a gorilla?" Bizimana swung the rifle back and forth between Peter's chest and Kristen.

Kristen called his bluff. "You shoot me or my assistant, and my men will tear you apart. They are very loyal, and there are places to bury dead men in the forest where no one can find them."

Bizimana said nothing for a long moment, then lowered the rifle barrel, but he meant to have the last word. "I have only this to say. Mr. Zigirazo wants his gorilla, and if he does not get it, you will not be safe anywhere in Rwanda. He has many friends."

Signaling with his head, he turned and led his little commando unit back along the path out of Karisoke. Mukera and Senweke followed a distance behind them, ensuring they would take the trail leading down the mountain and not turn back.

Peter stepped up onto the porch where Kristen leaned, drained, against the post.

"Thank you for standing up to him," she said. "Does this mean you're still working?"

"No, it doesn't. If I had any doubts, this little confrontation was the last straw. It's pure gangsterism, and I won't be a part of it any longer. I need to work in a legal system I can trust and with a boss who isn't a vigilante. I've already packed and I'm going to start down to Ruhengeri now, while the weather holds up."

"I'm sorry you're going. Really, I am. You've been a great support, all along, but I can't help the way it's turned out. Good luck finding your paradise," she added without sarcasm.

"I'm sorry, too. Good luck with the gorillas." He declined to offer his hand to shake, only held it up in a casual wave and turned away.

She watched him leave, disappointed at *his* disappointment, and slightly angry at what he saw as rectitude but seemed to her to be priggishness. But in the end, she had no real emotion left for him at all. She had too much else on her mind.

Perhaps she'd hear from him in a few days, by way of a polite letter asking for a recommendation. If so, she would give it. He'd been a good worker, and she regretted losing him over a difference in moral codes. Not to mention that now she had no professional help at all. Once again, she was on her own.

Except for Dana. The strange, mysterious woman from New York, whose loyalty never waned. Dana, who could wisecrack one minute and grow solemn and tender the next. And who had admired her breasts.

CHAPTER SIXTEEN

Ironic, Dana thought, staring up at the slightly moldy wooden roof. Her tiny dark shed was a refuge within a refuge, a microcosm of the hideout that Africa already represented for her. In both cases, the crime that caused her to flee was legally wrong, but—she remained convinced—morally just.

The shed was tolerable, but only because she managed to fall asleep quickly in its confinement and escape when she awoke. She had to hide there whenever patients arrived, but that wasn't often. Rwandans, she discovered, were much less willing or able than Americans to spend money on veterinary care. A few professional families made up Rudy's clientele, and otherwise he tended to treat strays. Which explained their modest means and the sad little Citroën that was their family car.

When no outsiders were about, Dana slipped into the main house, careful to keep an escape route to the hiding place in her line of sight.

For all the affection she felt, it was tiring to have an infant on her arm or her back all day long, but Mary's attention to her own child made such constant nurturance seem normal. And in the sunny kitchen, she found it pleasant to help prepare food and have some human conversation.

On this morning, she'd washed Mwelu's rump and, after a hand-scrubbing, finished cleaning the sweet potatoes for the next day. It was near eleven o'clock, and she was restless. The lack of physical exercise was also telling on her.

"Ah, there you are." Rudy appeared in the kitchen. "Someone left an injured dog tied to the front door. Can you come help me with it in the surgery? If you're not squeamish, that is."

"Not squeamish at all. But what should I do with Mwelu?"

"Leave her in the kitchen with Mary and a couple of plantains. That should keep her quiet for half an hour."

"Sure. Glad to help." She handed Mwelu over to Mary, who was momentarily babyless since Landoald napped, and followed Rudy into the medical part of the house.

"Wait here," he said and passed into the adjacent room. While she waited, she studied the room, which had obviously been adapted.

The surgery, with white painted walls and a window that opened to the rear garden, was larger and brighter than she remembered from her arrival a few nights before. Closed cabinets made up one side and open shelves the other, though supplies seemed to be sparse. The open shelves supported wide-mouth jars filled with cotton, steel instruments, and something that looked like a pressure cooker that she guessed substituted for an autoclave. The closed metal cabinets, she supposed, held medications.

The sink in the corner was of the ordinary household variety, and the cabinets along the wall could have come from any kitchen. The sole medical furniture was a steel-top table in the middle of the room with a large industrial droplight on a pulley directly over it. A wooden stool stood in the corner, and a tall sack of newly opened dry dog food rested against it. The dog-food smell mixed disagreeably with that of disinfectant.

A few minutes later, he reappeared leading a large male dog, some sort of mix that would qualify as a pit bull. The animal was covered in lacerations, most notably on its neck and shoulder, and he limped severely.

"What happened to the poor thing? Where did he come from?" she asked as he lifted the dog onto the steel table. She could see now that his back was also covered with scars.

"I found him this morning. People sometimes abandon their dogs here. Saves them the trouble of killing them. This one, judging by the wounds, was used in dog fighting. He probably became too weak and refused to fight."

Dana grimaced in both sympathy and outrage. "Can you help him? Please tell me you can help him."

"I probably can. He's still got plenty of weight. We'll patch the wounds and let him enjoy a few days' rest. But I need you to hold him while I inject the anesthetic. Then, if you don't mind, you can help me wash him." He went to the sink and filled a metal basin with warm water and added some liquid from a bottle.

"Of course I don't mind. The poor beast." She wanted to pet him but his scalp was swollen and lacerated, and she was afraid her touch would hurt him. "Disgusting that people can do this."

"Half my practice is repairing abused and neglected animals. Makes me really hate people. They're cruel to the animals they eat, cruel to the animals they make work for them, and some of them are cruel to animals for amusement. Those are the ones I'd hang if I could. Or applaud if someone else hanged them." The dog whined suddenly as he plunged the syringe with the anesthetic into its rump.

"Funny. That's what Dian Fossey once said, according to Kristen." She stroked the injured animal on a spot that seemed to be undamaged.

"Well, she was right." He held the head of the dog as it collapsed onto the table. "And animals are only a stand-in. They'd butcher each other, if a little bit of civilization didn't keep them in check."

He peered more closely at the wounds, then stepped away and drew something from his pressure cooker. When he turned around, it still steamed as he held it out to her. A safety razor. "You can start by shaving and washing around the wounds, while I prepare the surgical needle. I'll want to check to see if his leg is broken, too, and since I don't have an x-ray, I have to do it by feel." He walked away, and when the razor had cooled, she began to minister to the unconscious dog.

The two large wounds were new and raw, though others around it were old and infected, and she washed and shaved the fur around them as well. She watched the dog breathe the slow breath of sleep, then laid her hand on the side of his chest under his front leg and felt the throb of his pulse. A rush of anguish hit her like a wave.

"Thank you, that's fine." Rudy had returned wearing rubber gloves, and she stepped back to let him do his job. To be helpful, she moved the metal washbasin and razor out of his way and emptied it into the sink, then stood by waiting for other orders. However, he worked with such concentration he no longer seemed to notice her.

Instead, he simply murmured to himself. "No, the bone's not broken. No unusual swelling of stomach or intestines. I think you've got a decent chance, fella." Without looking up, he reached overhead and pulled the lamp a few inches closer to his patient.

Silently, she watched him stitch the wounds closed, growing in admiration for the nicotine-stained little man she'd so misjudged. It was a Sisyphean job, even more so than the care of gorillas, yet he did it year after year. She realized suddenly that the paunchy little doctor was the same kind of curmudgeon that she herself was and that Dian had been. And for all his grumpiness, he loved the creatures in his care.

"Will he have to stay with us until you take the stitches out?"

"The threads will dissolve by themselves, but we'll let him stay for a few days anyhow, fatten him up. Then, I don't know. I can keep only so many. Fetch me the roll of bandages on the counter, will you? And the iodine."

She handed him both objects and watched as he washed the area in the disinfectant and wrapped the leg and shoulder. When he was done, he stroked the dog's jowls, although the unconscious animal couldn't feel it.

"He's a lucky guy. The wounds weren't terribly deep, and the limp is probably from bruises. In a few days we'll take off the bandage, if he doesn't chew it off himself. Now, if you'll wipe down the examination table, I'll take our boy back to a cage to sleep off his anesthetic." He hefted the dog into his arms and carried him out of the surgery.

Satisfied at having been useful, Dana wandered back to the kitchen where Mary was washing beans while Mwelu clung to her leg. Dana lifted the gorilla into her arms, liberating Mary, who would soon have her own toddler hanging on her in the same way. "Can I help?"

"You can sit and keep me company. It's nice to talk to someone other than Rudy. He has only two themes—medicine and politics."

Dana drew up a chair and, with Mwelu on her lap between her arms, she peeled a cassava. "How did you two meet? Or is that question too personal? I'm not sure of the conversation etiquette here."

"It's not too personal at all. We met at university."

Dana felt her eyebrows lift of their own accord. "What? You… you studied in Europe? Rudy never mentioned that."

"No reason he should have. Anyhow, he was studying at the veterinary school at Liege, and I was at the Faculty of Philosophy and Letters. We met at a social event."

Dana chuckled. "You studied philosophy? In Liege? Belgium?"

"Why do you find that so amazing? You think foreign study beyond the capability of a Rwandan woman?" Mary's voice rose slightly in pitch, as if she were about to be affronted.

"Not at all. You struck me right away as intelligent. What surprised me, other than that you could fall for an old grump like Rudy, is that you studied philosophy."

Mary laughed, breaking the tension. "You think he is a grump? That is because you don't know him. He is not so good with people, but he loves his work. We became engaged there, and when he got his degree and needed to find a job, he agreed to come back with me to Rwanda to work. A man who follows his fiancée back to a developing country is a prince, don't you think?"

"A prince indeed. But that still leaves open the question of why you studied philosophy."

"Why not? I always found it unfortunate that Western thought came to Africa only through colonialism. It was time someone studied it from its roots." She set the pot of beans on the stove. "What about you? You cannot have been interested in gorillas all your life."

Dana studied the woman who impressed her more every day. "Uh, no. I wasn't. In fact, I studied classics. Not a gorilla in sight."

"Classics?! Now I'm the one who is astonished. I had a minor in Greek philosophy. It put a fatal dent in my religion, I can tell you, and made it possible for me to fall in love with a cynic like Rudy."

Dana carved out a chunk of cassava for Mwelu, who was thrilled. "I know what you mean. Do you remember the Dialogues?"

"Heavens, yes. We spent a whole week on Plato. Particularly the dialogue that asks whether a man who kills a murderer is evil, or 'impious,' as Plato called it. He never did answer the question."

Dana threw her head back. "Wow. I never thought I'd hear the word Plato in Rwanda. Not to mention meet someone who remembers the ethical issues. I recall only that they failed to come up with a definition of evil."

"Quite right. And if the Greek philosophers could not come up with one, what's a poor Rwandan to do?"

"Or an American. So, why aren't you a schoolteacher?"

"I thought perhaps to have a career in politics. Our prime minister is a woman, you know, so some avenues are open. But then the baby came along. I still want to be in government, but right now things are quite dangerous, and both Rudy and my father have counseled me to wait."

"I hope you don't have to wait too long. It would be a real coup, I think, for a philosopher to be in public office. Plato would be proud."

The door swung open and Rudy's head poked through. "Dana, take the gorilla and go into the shed. Right now. Go!"

Dana was already holding Mwelu, so it took only a few seconds for her to thread her way to the rear of the house to her hiding place in the brush. Closing the door behind her, she peered out the window through the foliage covering it, trying to make sense of what was happening. Apparently a lone visitor had arrived.

Even though his face was turned away, the pastel-colored suit revealed it was Simon Bizimana. Zigirazo and his agents had finally tracked them down.

She couldn't hear any of the words but didn't need to. Rudy's vehement gestures told her that Bizimana was accusing him of aiding the kidnapping in some manner.

Rudy conspicuously declined to invite the visitor into his house, so the confrontation remained at the door. They disputed loudly for some fifteen minutes, with Rudy gesticulating wildly. It was a good show of outrage, but she wondered if Bizimana bought it.

Mwelu clambered on her back, grasping her shirt and hair, no doubt wondering why they were in their nest so early in the day. Dana cuddled her, trying to keep her from making any noise, which would have meant her doom.

Finally she heard a car door slam and a motor start. Curious, that he bothered to drive. Bizimana's shop was scarcely a quarter of a mile away, but she supposed prosperity and the desire to display it required him to go everywhere by car. At least the car motor had warned Rudy of his arrival.

She sat on her bed, fretting, with an increasingly agitated Mwelu, who obviously didn't like the dark.

Finally Rudy arrived and stepped inside, closing the door behind him. He was uncomfortably close, and she could smell the cigarette smoke on his clothing and breath.

"What did he say?" she asked.

He leaned against the opposite wall with crossed arms. "You can imagine. They accused me of helping you. I told them they were crazy, that I never got involved in poaching matters. Of course he didn't believe me, and we went back and forth for a while. He wanted to come in and look around, but I told him Mary and the baby were sleeping."

"Did he threaten you?"

"Of course he did. Those are violent men. He said he'd be back with the police to search the house."

"I see. Does that mean we have to leave?"

He glanced toward the window, as if the threat still lurked outside. "I think so, unless you're willing to stay out here all the time. Even then, they might notice the trees and come out to investigate."

She glanced around at the tiny space in horror. It was bad enough to have to sleep here, but confinement during the day would be intolerable. "I don't think I can," she said softly. "And even if I could hold out, Mwelu wouldn't tolerate it. She needs activity and wouldn't understand being caged."

He rubbed his forehead. "Okay. I'll send word up to Kristen tomorrow morning that she needs to hide the gorilla at Karisoke. I'm sorry I couldn't offer you more. It took Zigirazo four days to get here, so at least I could treat her infections and get her stabilized. She's pretty healthy now and doesn't need a vet any longer."

He leaned against the window frame, peering through the heavy growth back at his house. "There was something else, too. Not just about the gorillas."

"What do you mean?"

"He said 'you will pay, all of you. For the kidnapping and a lot more. Just wait.' Then he walked away. It sent shivers up my spine."

"He's a big talker, you know that. It was all just bluff."

"Maybe." Rudy bent toward the door and took hold of the handle. "Anyhow, it's unlikely he'll return this evening, so as long as we keep an eye out, it should be safe for you to come back to the house for supper. And then tomorrow we'll figure a way to get you back up to Karisoke."

He let himself out, leaving Dana behind on her cot, feeling more helpless than ever. Mwelu gazed up at her, sucking on two fingers, as if to ask "what now?"

"I don't know, my darling," she answered. "God help me, I don't know."

❖

The beans Mary had been cooking were for dinner, and though she had enlivened them considerably with vegetables and spices, Dana had little appetite. All three of them were nervous, fearing that Bizimana could reappear at the door again at any moment, and it was clear this was to be their last meal together.

Mary served her a large portion, as if to compensate for the diminishing hospitality, and tried to make conversation. "Do you think you can reintegrate Mwelu into her original group, even without her mother?"

Dana shrugged. "We have no idea whether the family survived as a group after both the silverback and the primary female were killed. With no silverback, the other females are likely to migrate to other groups."

"I see. There were no other grown males in that family?"

"Yes, Ndengera, the silverback who was killed, has a younger brother, Ngabo. But we can't know until we go and look whether he was mature enough to take over. Gorilla groups have an interesting dynamic, in which the females can choose who they'll mate with. Their situation becomes precarious only when they have infants, and then they have to stay close to the father because an outside male will kill them to bring her into estrus again."

"How does poor Mwelu fit into that scenario?" Mary asked. "Wouldn't the female adopting her, in theory, still be sexually available?"

"Theoretically, yes. In any case, all will depend on whether the young male, Ngabo, has held things together. For Mwelu, that would be the best of all possible worlds, but even then, we don't know which of her two aunts would accept her and, even if one of them does, whether she's old enough to survive without milk."

His dinner eaten, Rudy slid back from the table. "Well, biologically, she should be. But I'll send enough formula with you for another two weeks, so you can gradually acclimate her to an adult diet. You just have to figure out how to keep her out of the hands of Bizimana's poachers." He pulled his ever-present crumpled pack of cigarettes from his shirt pocket. "Now, if you'll excuse me, I'll go have a smoke."

That was the signal for her and Mary to collect the dishes. While they cleaned up, with both human and simian babies playing underfoot, Dana heard him turn on the radio in the living room. It was a popular song, Western style, though sung by Rwandan singers and, to her taste, dreadful.

"I'm going to miss our evenings in the kitchen. The mornings too, come to think of it. I wish now we had more time to talk."

"Well, it does not have to be the end of our friendship. Once you have your gorilla settled, you can come to visit. We are always here."

"Yes, that's true and—"

Rudy emerged from the other room. "Both of you, come listen to the radio."

"What's going on?" Mary picked up her baby from the floor.

"It's Radio des Mille Collines," he said, and led them into the living room, where they sat down, puzzled.

It seemed to be a news loop, a brief, ominous message that the announcer repeated between short intervals of popular music.

One hour ago, the plane carrying President Habyarimana and Burundian president Cyprien Ntaryamira was shot down as it approached Kigali airport. All persons aboard were killed. The government is viewing this as an assassination. All air traffic has been suspended, and all main roads are blocked in the search for the assassins.

Mary grasped her baby as if to protect him. "This is what they've been waiting for."

"Who's been waiting? Who do you think shot them down? The Tutsi rebels?" Dana tried to think in terms of Rwandan politics, but none of it made sense.

"Could have been," Rudy said. "But why? The president was a moderate and had already made a lot of compromises. Basically he'd given them what they wanted."

"The Hutu gangsters, then?"

"That would also be strange. He was one of them, though a bit more reasonable. Unless they wanted to make a useful martyr out of him. But whoever did it is going to set this country on fire."

"What does that mean for you? And for me?"

"It means we have to hope the police and the army will still function. If not..." He strode toward a desk and fished a key from his pocket. In a moment, he'd unlocked and opened a drawer and held up a .22 pistol. "It's not much, God knows. But at least we have something. And for you, it means you shouldn't risk leaving. We have no way of knowing what Zigirazo's role will be. Maybe nothing at all. But for the time being, think of him as a danger and stay in your little hut. I have an uneasy feeling things will become very violent tomorrow."

He seemed to deliberate for a moment. "Probably nothing will happen tonight, but if worse comes to worst, I'll hide the car key here." He reached over and pulled open the back of his baby's diaper. "That way, you might be able to escape.'

"Escape? Worse comes to worst? What do you mean?" She could hear the growing panic in her voice when he didn't answer. He didn't need to. She knew he meant, *if we're dead.*

"It's that bad? Suddenly?"

"I don't know how bad it is. And maybe they'll find some scapegoats to shoot and it will be over in a few days. In any case, it'll take them awhile to focus their rage, so I don't think they'll do anything until morning. Go back to your hiding place, but take water and some extra food."

Mary set her baby in his high chair and busied herself among the cupboards. She returned with a plastic bottle of water and a sack of plantains.

"Stay there and be quiet until one of us comes out to get you," Rudy ordered and led her from the kitchen toward the wooded area. "If you have to use the lamp, make sure the window's covered so no one can see the light from outside. But it's better if you stay in the dark and just use this." He handed her a pocket flashlight.

"So, I should just sit and wait?" It sounded like a horrendous way to spend a night.

"Yes. Try to sleep. And try to keep the gorilla quiet, too."

❖

She lay awake for hours, afraid of Bizimana, afraid of the authorities, afraid of the nightmare. She could relax only by holding Mwelu close to her and imagining both of them lying in Kristen's arms. Could that ever happen? It seemed crass to fantasize such tenderness when they were all in so much danger, but it soothed her and finally she fell asleep.

Gunshots awakened her.

She lurched from the bed and, quaking, listened with her ear against the door. No more shots, but she heard a more terrifying sound. The smashing of glass, of wood, screams, and finally men shouting drunkenly in Kinyarwanda. The chaos went on for some twenty minutes before their triumphant voices became fainter and finally disappeared altogether.

She cowered in silence, paralyzed with uncertainty, waiting for Rudy to come and reassure her. But after half an hour, she knew he wouldn't. What should she do? She could remain crouched on her bed until dawn with Mwelu clutching her neck. But Mwelu's terror was as great as hers, and she had soiled the bed.

Not knowing became intolerable, so she peeked through the door. It was not yet dawn, and the marauding mobs, if that's what they were, would probably still be sparse. If it was rage over the death of the president, things would surely get worse with daylight.

Stepping outside of her shelter, she closed the door temporarily on the whimpering gorilla and tiptoed forward. All was silent but for a few bats that fluttered over her head. The house was still not visible behind the row of bushes, so she crept around them.

The porch light was on, sending a false reassurance of calm. She glanced down at her watch. Four thirty. She harbored a faint desperate hope the noise had been from drunken rowdies passing through and everyone was safe and asleep. Then she saw the smashed windows and the bodies.

The first was an African, on his back with outspread arms. The dark pool in the middle of his chest indicated a clean chest shot that probably killed him quickly. But a few feet farther on, Rudy lay on his side, his arms and head at an unnatural angle. It took only a second to recognize what a machete had done to him, and she looked away.

Should she go into the house? She knew what she would probably find but had to see if anyone, or anything, was still alive.

She crept soundlessly into the kitchen, her mouth dry with dread. She didn't have to go far. Mary lay on her back by the door, a deep slash running diagonally across her ruined face. Like Dian Fossey, Dana thought.

Then, worst of all, on the other side of the kitchen floor was a small mass of bloodied fabric and flesh, as if someone had ripped the child from her arms and thrown him against the wall. Murdered for the sin of being a Tutsi child. Worse, half Belgian and half Tutsi.

The mob had vented its rage on the family but seemed to have lost interest quickly in the rest of the house, for the dogs barking in the yard told her they'd been spared.

She heard a whimpering from the back room and ran to check, fearing to find a wounded and suffering creature she'd have to finish off. But it was the pit bull they'd worked on the previous evening. He must have still been so stupefied by the anesthetic that he hadn't barked at the intruders, and his silence had probably saved his life.

She opened the cage and surveyed the room, wondering what to do with the still-weak animal. As a last resort, she dragged in the sack of dry food and overturned it onto the floor. For water, she laid out as many full basins of it as she could find. To accommodate the dogs in the yard, she left open both the house door and the gate to the street. If no one came rampaging in the next few days, the injured dog could recover in peace, and the others could come and go as they wished. They were strays anyhow, and she was giving them a good chance.

But now she had to see to her own survival. She scurried back to the hidden shack, noting that the mob, in their savagery, had neglected the car. No, she realized on second thought. The smashed side window and dented roof suggested their frustration at not finding the car key.

She knelt on one knee over the mutilated infant, breaking into tears. But she forced herself to feel around inside the blood-and-feces-soaked diaper. Her fingers touched something small, metallic.

She wiped the key dry on her pants and looked around, wondering if anything might be useful in her escape. Antibiotics might be helpful at Karisoke, but she had no time to collect them and wasn't even sure what they looked like.

But it would be insane to venture outside unarmed. Could she find something to use to defend herself? Rudy's gun was gone, almost certainly taken by the men who killed him. What else?

A kitchen knife. She rummaged through the drawers until she found one large enough to look threatening and slid it carefully into her belt. She felt slightly better, though she knew it would be easy for them to snatch it from her. Was there anything else?

Scalpels. Didn't all doctors have scalpels? She rushed back into the surgery and rampaged through the cupboards. Nothing but bottles and boxes. The metal pot on the counter caught her eye, and she inspected it. She was right. It was for sterilizing instruments, but all she found were surgical clamps and scissors. How could he work without scalpels?

She gave the cupboards another try, tearing open some of the boxes. One of them held half a dozen packages that looked like flat toothbrushes sealed in thin paper. She fished one out and ripped open the paper covering. Something in gray plastic, but the tip was metal. Of course. Even in Africa they used disposable scalpels.

She stuffed three of them into her side pocket.

She fetched Mwelu, who was beginning to shriek, and climbed into the Citroën. The gorilla insisted on staying on her lap clutching her shirtfront, and she had to reach around her to try the ignition key. Her last fear was that the car might not start, but the motor caught at the first turn. Taking a breath, she edged out of the carport and turned left, more or less in the direction of the Virunga car park.

A white woman alone in a car was conspicuous, she knew, but the number of people on the rampage still seemed small, and if she could avoid crowds or a roadblock, she might get far.

She drove unimpeded a few blocks north, then accelerated in the direction of the airport, orienting herself toward the dull outline of the Virunga Mountains. An orange spot appeared in the distance, a warm, welcoming glow in the predawn darkness. A bonfire, but she soon realized it was a deadly one, for it illuminated a roadblock. She stopped, reversed, and doubled back along narrow dirt roads, trying to find an alternate approach to the Parc des Volcans. No good. Everywhere were bonfires. Cursing, she turned back into Ruhengeri.

Mwelu seemed to sense her agitation, for she clambered onto her lap and clutched at her neck, making it difficult to drive. Worse, she'd begun hooting, a prelude to what soon would become shrieks of panic. Foolish to have thought she'd sit, docile as a family dog, on the passenger seat, and now it was too late to cage or drug her.

Dana sensed her own panic encroaching. Running again, and this time she couldn't hide. Or could she? Just ahead she spotted a ruined stable, some wreck of wood and plaster that had succumbed to Rwandan rain. One wall had disintegrated and the roof had partially collapsed, forming a triangular hollow.

She stopped the car, lurched across the rubble-strewn ground to the open double doors, and peered inside. It would do. Leaping into the car again, she backed into the hollow space, hoping the tires wouldn't meet any sharp objects or the shock of entry wouldn't bring down the rest of the roof.

Random filth rained down on the hood of the car but nothing more. Once the air had cleared, Dana ran out again and dragged the one moveable door closed.

Mwelu wimpered as if she had absorbed the desperation that Dana was now relieved of. Dana took her into her arms, stroked her head, and murmured comfort. "We're safe now, darling, at least for a while," Dana whispered into her ear. "Though if you have any suggestions as to what to do next, I'd be grateful to hear them."

Mwelu had none and simply pressed against her, sucking two fingers.

"All right, then. I'll do the planning." She took a breath. "First, we'll rest and calm down. That's what they tell you in all those survival lessons, right? Not to panic. Fine. No panic here. Second…"

She couldn't think of a second step. Only the calm-down part seemed useful, since the horror of Rudy and Mary's death, and the terror of flight had left her exhausted. But her mind was empty, and all it was good for was to sense Mwelu's warmth on her chest. Slowly, as if the rational part of her had simply surrendered, she dozed off.

❖

She awoke dry-mouthed with a start and another surge of fear. Her watch said eight. Now what? She flicked on the car radio, trying to get some news. State of emergency. Hutu outrage everywhere. No one permitted to move without identification. Incitement to vengeance against the *inyenzi* roaches. She flicked the radio off and assessed her situation.

It was desperate. No different from the night before. The roadblock was certainly still on the road to the Parc des Volcans, and she couldn't circumvent it. Her only hope was to crash it. In a flimsy Citroën.

"All right, Mwelu. It's time to face the enemy." She set the gorilla on the passenger side, and, for the moment at least, Mwelu remained quiet.

After dragging the decaying door open again, Dana started the motor and rumbled out of the wrecked barn onto the street. A series of turns brought her onto the main road. She accelerated, gathering speed and courage at the same time.

The roadblock she'd seen at night came into view, and in the light of day she could see it amounted to nothing more than a wooden plank placed across two chairs. Two uniformed men and a gang of others stood guard, though they were too far away for her to see if any had rifles. She slowed to normal speed, so as not to put them on alert, then, some hundred feet away, she floored the gas pedal.

The car lurched forward and struck the plank with full force, knocking it high into the air. She heard one of the headlights smash but continued at full speed, until the sound of bullets hitting the rear of the car caused her to swerve. Her heart pounding wildly, she regained control, kept up her speed, and soon was out of range.

"Well, shit!" she shouted, giddy with relief. "If I'd only known it was that easy!" she said to Mwelu, who had once again climbed onto her lap.

Outside of Ruhengeri she encountered no more roadblocks and was almost joyful when they arrived at the parking field of the Parc des Volcans, the last stop before the trail up to Karisoke. She careened to a halt and clambered out with Mwelu on her hip.

"Hey!" Someone shouted from behind her, and she turned to see a ramshackle truck rumbling over the bumpy ground toward her. Men in the open platform in the rear were leaning over the side and waving.

Snatching up her rucksack, she ran full out toward the trees that marked the beginning of the climb. With the added weight of Mwelu, and the rucksack banging against her shoulder, she had no chance.

The men dropped from the truck to pursue her, and their laughter told her they were already drunk in spite of the early hour. They seemed to be hugely enjoying the chase and in no hurry to catch her. Finally one of them reached her and snatched Mwelu by the arm.

With an ear-piercing shriek, she leapt onto him and bit him on the face. Furious, he flung her to the ground, where she scampered *uh-huhing* into the underbrush. He turned his attention toward Dana and lurched after her.

Dana scrambled upward, digging into the ground with her nails, but he caught hold of her foot, tripped her, and dragged her downward toward him. She groped for the butcher knife at her belt, but he managed to grasp her wrist and shake the blade from her grip.

He was on her now, and they both rolled, sliding downward on the path. In a last desperate move, she slid her free hand into her side pocket and felt the paper packages.

His face was within inches, his breath foul. She tugged one of the packages out, the paper tearing as it rubbed against the cloth of her pocket, and with a sudden wild sweep, she dragged the scalpel blade diagonally across his face. He released her immediately and covered the gash she'd cut across his eye and nose while blood poured between his fingers.

But while he toppled backward, two more of the men clambered past him. She scrambled away from them, but seconds later was caught again. One of them flipped her onto her back, pinning down her scalpel hand with his knee, while the other waved his companions over.

A ring of heads looked down on her laughing, and she shut her eyes.

CHAPTER SEVENTEEN

At Karisoke, Kristen slept badly. The confrontation with Bizimana and Zigirazo's threat of retribution turned in her waking mind and seeped into her dreams. Abruptly she sat up rubbing her face. Something had awakened her though it was barely dawn.

Her rooster crowed. Ah, that's what it must have been. Fair enough. She hadn't fed her chickens the day before, and they were probably tired of scratching for bugs. At least the rooster was out, which meant it wasn't raining. As she slipped into her cargo pants and boots, he crowed again.

"All right, all right!" she called back at him and fetched a can of feed from the cupboard before throwing on a jacket. The fresh morning air cheered her a little as she stepped off the porch and strolled around to the chicken pen. A few handfuls of feed brought the rooster and his harem of three hens fluttering toward her. She watched, slightly amused by the jerky energy they expended locating and devouring each grain, especially Lucy, her favorite hen. She should never have named them, for she could still collect eggs, but now killing them for the pot was out of the question.

The spectacle of chickens pecking in the dirt could hold her attention only so long, but she was reluctant to return to the cabin. As she gazed around at the forest, a hyrax appeared some distance away and scurried up the slope toward the gorilla graveyard. On a whim, she followed it.

There they were, all the gorillas Dian had loved. And next to them lay the mounds of fresh dirt covering Ndengera and Amahoro. She wandered among them, as among family members, touching their name plates as she passed. And next to them, belonging to them, was Dian's grave.

For the first time in more than a year, she found herself standing before the metal grave marker. "Nyiramachabelli," she said out loud, pronouncing the long Kinyarwanda title as if it were an incantation. The woman who lives alone in the forest.

"Sorry I haven't visited in a while. I suppose I should have kept you up to date on events directly rather than talking to your gun." She touched one of the stones in the circle with her toe, then sat down on the ground near the grave marker.

"Well, I've got a lot of the same problems you had. *Plus ça change*, eh? Just like you, I've got to write to National Geographic and the Leaky Foundation to ask for more money. Worse, I have to explain the deaths of two of our gorillas and the kidnapping of the baby, while glossing over the way we got her back. I know *you'd* approve of our rescue. It was right up your alley. But I couldn't have done it without Peter and Dana."

She thought for a moment. "You'd have liked Peter, the kind of soft-hearted man every woman goes for. Like a Nordic god, and he loved animals, but he didn't have the guts for this business. More the flower-power type, he helped in the rescue of Mwelu but then called Dana and me gangsters for doing it."

She smiled to herself. "Well, there might be an element of truth in that, but Zigirazo, that same old bastard who probably killed you, is menacing us now, and 'gangster' is all he knows. Without Dana I wouldn't be able to stand up to him."

Her knee dislodged one of the stones from the circle and she replaced it. "You'd like her too, Dian. And you'd have loved seeing her rough up Bizimana on his own turf. Thus the gangster accusation, I suppose. But she's uncompromising and a little mysterious, and both those things are exciting. I've begun to imagine being physical with her, and God knows, it's been long enough since I've had any of that. Did I mention she's quite attractive? Long hair, chestnut. Brown eyes, and her mouth sort of turns up at the corners, like she's just about to smile, though she doesn't do that much. Oh, and she admired my breasts. What do you think? I mean, when a woman likes your breasts, that has to count for something, right?"

"Miss Kristen! Miss Kristen!" Someone called her from below the slope and she got to her feet.

"I'm up here, Senweke. What is it?" she called out as she clambered down the slope toward her cabin. She met him on the porch and was shocked by the terror in his eyes.

"Oh, miss. The news is very bad. We just turn on the radio and we hear it, President Habyarimana killed."

"What? How? When?" She heard herself stammer.

"In a plane with the president of Uganda. The plane shot down near Kigali. During the night. The people are very angry."

She rushed inside her cabin and flicked on her transistor radio. The usual reporting stations were all static, and the only clear frequency was for Radio des Mille Collines. Hutu news would have to do.

The plane had been shot down just before landing, and the announcer described the attack as the beginning of the Tutsi campaign to enslave all Hutus as they had done in the past. "Our people must prepare to face Tutsis everywhere, for they are opening the way for the rebel Rwandan Patriotic Army to sweep down from Uganda."

Kristen was slightly puzzled. "Senweke, he keeps telling people to go to work. What does that mean? Surely he's not just telling people to go back to the fields."

"No, miss. He means go with your pangas and kill Tutsis."

"And foreigners."

"Yes, miss. Mostly Belgians. Because of the old days."

Kristen stood up abruptly. "Oh my God. Dana's hiding at the Lambot house and all of Ruhengeri knows him. We've got to get down there."

She slid Dian's revolver into her pocket and followed Senweke through the door. Mukera was just outside, and when Senweke said they were going down the mountain to save Miss Dana, Mukera fell into step with them.

As they jogged together along the path that led down the mountain, she recalled that Mukera was a Hutu. "Thank you for your loyalty," she said to him, breathlessly. "But you don't have to take this risk. It's not your people they're killing."

"No, miss. Here we are not Tutsi or Hutu. All at Karisoke are my people."

"I'm so glad to hear it, but why are they so angry? Do they really believe the RPA killed the president?"

"It is what they hear every day on the radio. But it is especially the young ones, with no jobs. The leaders tell them to form the *Interahamwe,* the 'ones who fight together,' and save Rwanda by killing Tutsis and also Belgian white men. They were angry before, but crash of the plane gives them a reason."

Unencumbered and descending on dry soil, they made good time. In an hour and a half, they were at the last rise overlooking the parking lot.

Kristen halted. "Look, something's going on down there. Men climbing out of a truck. What's going on?"

"Interahamwe." Senweke said.

She stared for a moment, perplexed, until she saw they were chasing someone.

"Noooo!" she shouted and threw herself down the remainder of the path with the men following. They were in the last tree-covered slope now and could hear the men laughing.

Down, down they plummeted. They slid recklessly, frantically, just to cover ground and all of it was taking too long.

Then, between the trees, she saw the cluster of men, armed with machetes. They stood in a circle over their prey with their blades raised. Without breaking stride, Kristen snatched out her pistol and fired into the air.

The knot of men looked up, startled, then broke apart, and Kristen could see what lay at their feet. It was Dana.

She shot again aimlessly toward the men, hysterical, furious. She slipped and fell, righted herself, and shot a third time, this time winging one of the men, and finally they scattered.

Dana rose on one elbow, and a few long moments later, Kristen reached her and knelt by her side. "Are you hurt? Tell me you're not hurt. I couldn't bear it…"

Dana clutched at her, trembling. "No. I'm all right. Oh, Kristen, they killed Rudy and Mary and…and the baby." She began to sob.

"It's all right. You're safe now. Can you walk? We should get to Karisoke before those guys realize they outnumber us. I'm sure they have guns, too."

"Mwelu!" Dana cried in anguish. "They tried to take her but she ran away. She can't stay alone in the jungle. We have to find her."

Kristen and Senweke lifted her to her feet. "We'll look for her tomorrow. But we've got to get out of here."

Dana tried to walk but staggered. "I slashed one of them in the face. I'm sure he'll be back for me. But I don't want to leave Mwelu."

Kristen urged her on, glancing over her shoulder. "I know. But we can find her tomorrow. I'll send all the trackers out for her, and we'll go, too. I promise."

Placated, Dana began the climb. "It all happened so fast. We heard the news of the crash but had no idea people would go crazy. I went to bed, and in the middle of the night I woke up." Her voice began to quaver again. "I heard them killing Rudy and Mary."

Kristen slid her arm around Dana's back. "I was afraid of that. It's why we came down to get you."

Dana followed, docile, but couldn't stop rambling. "Rudy had scalpels. The disposable kind, not like the ones in the movies. Much lighter, plastic. Really sharp. I used one to cut the guy. He wasn't expecting *that*. I hope I cut off his nose, the bastard."

"Yes, you slowed him down, gave us time to get here. But you're right. He'll be back. Come on, try to climb faster. You'll be safe at Karisoke."

"Yes, Karisoke," Dana muttered. "Mwelu, Mwelu…"

In less than two hours they were back at the camp. Fueled by fear, Dana had made the entire climb, but once they stepped out from the forest onto the grounds of Karisoke, she could only stagger. "I'm sorry. I don't think I have anything left."

Kristen guided her along, keeping a hand on her back. "Don't worry, we're here now, and safe. Thank you, Senweke, Mukera. Will you ask the men to post guards at the top of the path? Tonight, too. There are enough of you, so two hours at a time shouldn't be a hardship."

"Yes, miss. I was thinking the same thing," Senweke said. "But also…"

"What is it, Senweke? Is there another problem? Tell me."

"Our families. Not only Tutsis. The Interahamwe hate all who are friends with Tutsi and work with Tutsi."

Kristen paled. "You mean you all have to leave Karisoke to protect them?"

"No, miss. We want to bring them here. It is safer than in Ruhengeri or in the villages."

"Yes, of course, Senweke. I'm ashamed I didn't think of it myself. Bring them up right away. They can stay in the two empty cabins, even Miss Fossey's cabin, and in the guest tent. Can I leave you to decide who stays where?"

Senweke bowed his head, but only slightly. Groveling was not his style. But his smile of gratitude was genuine and touching. "Thank you, Miss Kristen. I will send the men home right away, and they can bring everyone up this evening. They will be very glad."

"Yes, miss, thank you," Mukera repeated, and both men took off in a jog toward the men's house.

"So, we're to be a fortress," Dana said quietly.

"It seems that way. Anyhow, with the men gone, I'd prefer that you stay with me. I have the gun. I'll put a mattress on the floor by the stove tonight." Kristen led her the rest of the way to her cabin and unlocked the door.

Before stepping inside, Dana glanced up at the dismal sky. "It can't even be noon yet, but you can't tell by the light, can you? Anyhow, I'm no good for anything but crashing right now." She limped toward the table and dropped onto a chair.

"Don't worry. You don't have to do anything but listen to me complain and maybe eat some of my cooking later. Come on. I'll make a fire and warm the place up." Kristen knelt in front of the stove and began to pile in kindling. Just then a clap of thunder struck and Dana flinched. "Thunderstorm," she muttered. "All we need."

Kristen scratched a match against the stove door and lit the kindling. It flickered for a moment, and then the flames crept along the wood surfaces. "Actually, it's a blessing. The Interahamwe aren't likely to climb up here in a driving rain, and when it's dark, even less so. If it rains all afternoon, we should be safe until tomorrow, and maybe the trek up here will prove to be too inconvenient for them altogether."

"Let's hope so. But it's going to be just as difficult in the rain for our men and their families."

"Don't worry. They've all made the trek a hundred times. They know every trail, and the Virunga weather patterns as well. If they sense the slightest break in the weather, they'll start up." She added a few small logs and warmed her hands in front of the grating, then noticed Dana drooping at the table.

"You poor thing. You must be completely spent." Brushing sawdust from her hands, she approached the table and touched Dana on the shoulder. "Look. I'll go talk to Senweke about sending out a team to search for Mwelu. In the meantime, you should take a nap. Go ahead and sleep on my bed."

"Thanks. I think I need that," Dana muttered, drowsily slipping off her boots and shuffling toward the bed in her stocking feet. Her trousers were caked with mud, and she stripped them off, then lay back in her wrinkled shirt in the luxury of the horizontal. She was barely aware of Kristen draping an extra blanket over her and leaving. Her last thought before dozing off was the irony of being invited to Kristen's bed only after nearly being killed. Apparently, that's what it took.

Dana awoke to a touch on her shoulder. "Wake up, dear. It's six o'clock. If you keep sleeping, you'll wake up at two in the morning."

"Oh, right." Dana sat up and ran a hand through her hair. "Six o'clock? Sorry. Did anything happen while I was out? Did you find Mwelu?"

Kristen sat down on the edge of the bed. "Not yet, but we will, and a lot of things are happening in Kigali. We have only Radio des Mille Collines to listen to, but there's no reason to doubt them in this case. The prime minister fled with her children to the home of a UN aid worker for shelter, but the Interahamwe broke in and killed her, in front of the children. So at the moment, Rwanda has no government at all."

"Dear God. It's anarchy now."

"Even worse. Apparently the army, or a good part of it, is still functioning, but it's working with the Interahamwe. They've set up roadblocks everywhere and are checking passports for tribal identity. You can imagine how that ends."

"Yes, I saw the first roadblocks when I left Rudy's, even managed to crash through one. What about your staff? Have they come back yet?"

"Yes, they're all here, and now that the rain's let up, they've built a big fire near the men's house. Senweke, bless him, has decreed that the boys and young men will stay with the staff in the men's house and in the tent, and the women and children will have the two spare cabins. Since nothing has happened up here, the atmosphere is almost cheerful, at least for the children, who have no idea what's going on. The men are even out playing their drums."

She stood up from the bed. "Come on. I've heated some sweet potatoes. The cook made tons of it and brought us a pot."

Dana drew on her trousers, which had been muddy when she took them off but now were dry and crusty. She tiptoed toward the door and stood in the opening to brush off as much dirt as possible. Glancing toward the men's house, she could see the flickering of the bonfire and hear the low murmur of people talking as if at a spring picnic. If only it could last.

"Come eat before it gets cold," Kristen ordered, and Dana obeyed, taking a fork full of the fragrant sweet potatoes. They had a taste she was beginning to like. "Pretty good. Better than their beer."

Kristen smiled. "How are you feeling?"

Dana put down her spoon. "Still in disbelief that everything fell apart so fast. I went to bed, and when I woke up, Rudy and Mary were dead. And the baby, too. How can they kill a baby? An innocent creature who never wanted anything but love."

Kristen stared into space for a moment. "Strange how that is, how one murder incites the next. I think of myself as non-violent, but knowing what those men did, I could kill the murderers. Couldn't you?"

The image of two men lying in a pool of blood in a corridor flashed through Dana's memory.

"Yes. Easily. And without regret. At least not for the killing. Only for the fact that I'd have to run away. That's the hard part. I mean, that *would be* the hard part," she corrected herself, then changed the subject. "Do you think the Interahamwe will come all the way up here?"

"I doubt it. They must realize there's almost nobody they hate up here in the mountains. No Belgians, two Americans, only a few Tutsis. Why should they hike all the way up here just for a few heads? Besides, I've got Dian's gun, remember?"

"The gun." Dana shook her head. "I volunteered for Karisoke to get away from guns, and now we have to sleep with one."

"What guns did you have to get away from?" Kristen chuckled. "Is street crime all that bad where you lived in New York City?"

"No, nothing like that. It was simply a turn of phrase. But anyhow, if those murderers do hike up here, your men can't protect us. All they have are their pangas, and it would be eight men against God knows how many. Shouldn't we have another strategy?"

"Way ahead of you, my sleeping beauty. I have a pup tent right over there." Kristen pointed to the corner of the room, where a bulky sack leaned against the wall. "I used it once, so I know it's waterproof. We can pack some blankets and food and go into the jungle for a few days while our men disperse in all directions. They know the terrain up here and can hold out until the bloodlust dies down."

Dana nodded. "I can see doing that. We could look for Mwelu at the same time. I'm just shattered that we've lost her after all our work to save her."

Kristen touched her hand. "Try not to worry about her. Remember, she's a wild animal. She'll be lonely, but she knows how to climb trees and eat leaves. We'll find her again, I'm sure." She stood up and took their dishes to the sink.

Dana added wood to the stove, and for a few minutes, she heard only the clattering of porcelain and the soft crackle of the flames consuming the fresh wood. "I used to like camping. It's fun with a friend, and when no one's trying to murder you." She stood up and brushed soot off her hands.

"It is. And since we're safe right now, and have an emergency plan for when we're not, how about a whiskey?"

"Whiskey? Oh, that's right. Kundu's whiskey. Glad you kept some for later."

Kristen reached up to a top shelf and brought down a nearly full bottle of Jack Daniels. "I was saving the rest for wars and insurrections," she said and poured out two small glasses of the amber liquid.

Dana sniffed the glass, letting the strong aroma tickle her nostrils. She took a good mouthful, let it burn deliciously around her teeth, and swallowed slowly. The cough was inevitable. "You know, I drink this stuff so rarely, it's always a shock. But a good one."

"It should help us get a good night's sleep instead of lying awake waiting for the chop shop to arrive. Though, given the geography, Karisoke may be the safest place in Rwanda."

Dana ventured another drink and already felt the fear and anxiety melt away. She'd take them both up again the next day. Now she was, as her New Agey friends liked to say, mellowed out. "So I guess we should lay out that mattress now. I'll take off these filthy pants again and wrap up in a blanket."

Kristen took another sip from her drink and seemed to be deep in thought for a moment. "Yes, get rid of the filthy pants. But sleep with me."

The remark hung rich in the air, like the silence after birdsong. Finally Dana replied. "Sure, if you like. After all, you saved my life. That sort of makes me yours."

"Mine? Really? I wish you'd mentioned it earlier. I'd have made you do the dishes."

Dana snickered nervously. The whiskey, as intended, had taken the edge off her fear, and now she sensed the hint of desire. Did Kristen feel it too and was protecting herself with wisecracks? In the five seconds it took for her to slide off her trousers, a series of thoughts buzzed through her mind.

Kristen had said she was in a bad marriage. With a man. What about now? Had she decided by default for women? There was still the horrible possibility that she really was simply sharing her bed for safety and convenience. She sat down again on Kristen's bed, knees pressed together like a schoolgirl at a dance, but mentally she tottered on a high wire. Devoid of repartee, she changed the subject.

"I see now how courageous you've been to stay here. Not only the hardship of jungle camping, but living alone in a country so politically unstable."

Unfazed, Kristen went with the new topic while she removed her own jeans, shirt, and brassiere. God, what beautiful breasts she had. "It's mostly peaceful up here. Remember the night we stood at the bridge and listened to the jungle sounds? Those are what keep me here." From a hook on the wall, she took down two flannel shirts and held one out to Dana.

Obediently, Dana tugged her soiled shirt off and felt her face warm. She unhooked her bra as well and drew on the flannel shirt that smelled deliciously of soap and Kristen. With an awkward backward roll, she slipped under the covers.

Turning off all but a single pressure lamp on the table, Kristen slid in beside her. She lay on her side, her head resting on her bent arm, her chin almost touching Dana's shoulder. "How long does this I-belong-to-you-because-you-saved-my-life agreement last?"

Dana turned on her side as well. "Forever, I think. Unless prohibited by state or local law."

"Good. Then come here." Kristen's hand came to rest on her waist, warming her through the flannel.

Dana covered her nervousness with banter. "Here? I'm already here. Can I be more here?" But Kristen ended the game by taking Dana's face in her hand. She hesitated for a moment, as if to grow familiar with Dana's jaw, then drew her forward.

Though she'd longed for this, Dana was suddenly timid, and all the doubts she'd harbored emerged again. The flirtations and the drunken, giggling gropes at Amherst had taught her nothing about this. She'd bedded a woman, several in fact, but had never loved one. And Kristen had belonged to a man. How did she want to be touched? What did she expect?

Kristen pulled her the final distance, and the touching of their bodies, so warm in the cool damp room, opened the way.

And oh, the joy of the first kiss, the first reaching across the abyss to the other that dispelled the terror of rejection. But after that, what? How far, how fast, how rough or tender? No one had schooled her.

While animal desire simmered in the delicious tightening of her sex, she ventured cautiously on the way to knowing Kristen. Each tentative touch—lip to mouth, palm to cheek, fingers to hair—was another asking. "Can I do this? Is this allowed?" And each wordless answer was, "Yes, touch me this way. Yes, this is what I want."

If Dana was reticent, Kristen was not, and her kiss grew from gentle to fervent. The hand that caressed her face slid around to embrace her ardently. The dull drumbeat that throbbed through the camp echoed the pulsing of her heart that increased along with her desire. It was the sound of the jungle, but it also reminded her of the coming storm and seemed to hurry them on.

Outside the camp a murderous wave was rising toward them, but inside their hut was animal warmth, and their coupling was a carpe diem and a defiance. Kristen's caresses became more insistent, and Dana opened up to them. Yet it also seemed a surrender to the gorillas and the wildlife, the hagenia trees, the mist and the moss, and the very vibrancy of Karisoke.

She wallowed in a warm pool of sensation until Kristen slipped insistent fingers into the wet and welcoming place and urged her toward the pinnacle. Oh, it was good, so good, to climb and climb, then tremble in the final tension and hover in the exquisite bright moment at the top. Oh, and then to shudder when it broke and the waves rippled through her.

Drowsing in Kristen's arms, she murmured, "I want to do that for you," but Kristen whispered back, "Next time," and it was settled. They lay then wordlessly together until the drumbeat across the field finally stopped and sleep captured them both.

❖

The sounds outside the door penetrated Dana's sleep first, and she awoke with a start. "Someone's outside," she whispered, shaking Kristen's shoulder.

Suddenly awake, Kristen threw herself from the bed, snatched up her pistol from the table, and crouched by the doorway. "Who is it? What do you want?" she called through the locked door.

The only reply was a curious whining.

"It might be a trap." Dana was fully awake now and came to join her at the entrance. "I'll open the door and you get ready to shoot," she whispered, grasping the handle.

Kristen nodded and shifted position to be able to fire directly through the opening.

Soundlessly Dana turned the handle, and with a sudden yank, she tore the door open while Kristen pointed the pistol at the place where a man's chest would have been.

There was no chest. And no man. It took several beats for them both to lower their gaze to the black mass of fur that crouched pathetically at their feet, whimpering to be picked up.

"My God! Mwelu! She's found her way to the camp. Oh, my darling!" Dana lifted the damp bundle from the ground and hugged her fervently. "We were so worried!"

Kristen stood, her pistol hanging limp in her hand. "Stupid gorilla," she muttered, with obvious relief. "I bet she followed us all the way up the trail but was frightened by the men and all the noise. Remember, it was Africans who killed her mother and captured her."

"You're probably right. And when the men went to bed, she ventured into camp." She set her pistol down again and came to stroke Mwelu's face. "Sweet baby. Come get warm in our bed again. The mommies will take care of you."

And in a few minutes, they were crowded in again, a curious, interspecies family of three.

CHAPTER EIGHTEEN

Morning brought them back to sobering reality. Only Radio des Mille Collines was broadcasting now. They listened mutely while they fed and examined Mwelu. She was unharmed and particularly happy to feed on plantains, but the news that came over the air was ominous.

At Gikondi, several hundred Tutsis had fled to the Catholic church seeking shelter but were wiped out in a single attack. Only the priest in charge was spared.

"I know that place," Kristen said. It's a missionary church, and the priest is a Hutu. 'Spared?' I don't think so. I bet he was complicit."

"That could be. It's certainly in keeping with some of the drivel they were claiming a few days ago on the radio, that the Hutus were the only real Christians in Rwanda and that the Virgin Mary wanted them to get rid of the nonbelievers."

Dana took her hand, trying to capture some of the solace of the night before. "When I was running away from those men, I still thought the attacks were from isolated thugs running amok and that finally the law would gain control. But now we know it's much worse than that. The murders are official policy."

Kristen entwined her fingers in Dana's but looked anxious. "I have no idea how far this is going to spread, and how long Karisoke will be safe, but if our job is to protect the gorillas, we should at least save this one. We should take her back to the others. Then we'll have one less thing to worry about."

Dana nodded. "You're right. It scared the hell out of me to see one of those drunken savages try to grab her yesterday. But how can we be sure that any of the groups will accept her? We could be handing her over to another kind of death."

"We'll find out after only a couple of hours' hike. I suggest we go now, while the rain is holding off. And before trouble arrives from down below."

"And if we can't find Ndengera's family? If it dissolved after his death?"

"We try with the other families. Group six had a birth a few months ago. Maybe the mother will accept Mwelu. I don't have any other ideas, and time's running out."

"I agree in principle. My point is only, if group four won't take her, are we going to come back here and go out another day, and come back after each failure? We don't have the leisure to do that. Sooner or later we're going to have to face down Zigirazo's men or the Interahamwe—or both."

Kristen stared off into space, as she did when wrestling with an idea, as if an answer were floating somewhere across the room. Dana waited for her to find it.

"Okay. Here's what we'll do," Kristen said finally. "We take the pup tent and some food, and stay in the forest as long as we need to. Or as long as our food holds out. Senweke can look after the camp. With all those people, no one's going to do any work anyhow. Then, when Mwelu's safe, hopefully in a couple of days, we come back here and...well...go from there."

"It's a good plan, which gives us some flexibility and for sure is better than waiting for the machetes to fall."

Kristen let go of her hand and went to the door. Dana could see her wave one of the men toward her, and a moment later, Senweke stepped up onto the porch.

"Dana and I are going to take the baby gorilla back to the forest while we still have time. We hope to do this in a day, but it might take longer, so I'm leaving the camp under your authority. How are the people behaving?"

"Everyone is afraid, miss, so they are very quiet. Of course we cannot go to track the gorillas."

"No, I don't expect you to. Just try to keep the people calm and make sure everyone gets food and a place to sleep." She fell silent for a moment and seemed to sense the precarious nature of all their situations. Senweke's wizened face showed no sign of anxiety or dread, but surely he felt it more than they; he was a Tutsi.

"Thank you, for everything," she added. "And when this is all over one day, we'll have a big feast for everyone, like we did at Christmas."

"Yes, miss. Like Christmas," he said, and turned away.

Kristen stepped back into the cabin and was all business. "The tent and sleeping bags are packed. All we need is a lantern and as much food and water as we can carry. She threw open the cupboard and took down salami, a block of hard cheese, and soda crackers.

"Let's see your backpack."

Dana obeyed, understanding that she would be the food bearer, and handed over her rucksack. Kristen loaded in all the items, pressing them in over the clothes that Dana already carried, then added the fruit from the counter.

"What about a compass and the transistor radio?" Dana asked. "Will we get reception in the forest?"

"I'm not sure. Probably better in some places than others. We'll find out." Kristen hefted the large pack with their tent and sleeping bags onto her shoulders. "Oof. It's going to be fun carrying *this*. So, to start, you get the groceries, the water, and the ape."

Dana was already filling the largest of their plastic bottles and adding it to the food supply. "Do you think we should take Dian's gun?"

"Already packed."

The climb up the slopes toward Karisimbi was arduous, not only because of the heavy packs, but because Mwelu insisted on being carried. After half an hour, Dana set her down and forced her to walk. The little ape seemed to pout and raised her arms repeatedly, but Dana was unmoved.

"Has anyone even seen Ndengera's group since he and Amahoro were killed?" Dana asked. "I feel like we're wandering into a gorilla vacuum."

"Paka thought he saw them from a distance, but it was raining so heavily he simply turned back. It was their usual part of the park, but it could have been another group, too."

"If only they'd stay put. I don't know…start a village or something," Dana groused, trying to remain cheerful. She checked her watch. "I suppose we shouldn't call it Ndengera's group any longer, should we? I mean, if they're still together, someone else will be in charge."

"That would have to be Ngabo, wouldn't it? Let's hope he's found his macho. If not…well, we'll have to hike back to group six on the other side of Karisoke. And you know how risky it is with new silverbacks."

They hiked for several hours in a light rain until they reached a familiar slope. "I'm sure this is the place they used to nest," Dana said. "I've sat here a dozen times and watched them."

"Yeah, I have too, from over there under that tree." Kristen pointed with her chin toward a low hagenia tree. But there's no sign of them. No new nests or droppings."

"Let's give it until tomorrow. I can't really plod any farther in this bloody rain anyhow. I propose we pitch the tent under your tree, feed Mwelu, and settle in for the night."

Kristen sighed and slid the heavy pack from her shoulders. "Yeah, you're right. Staying here is good for Mwelu, too. She might recognize the place."

Dana hiked over to the tree and let her rucksack drop on the soft vegetation at her feet, then eyed the bundle Kristen was about to undo. "So that's the tent, eh? Is this going to be one of those three-dimensional puzzles that takes a degree in engineering?"

"No, it's a simple Timberline for two people. Basic Boy Scout. Look." She held up two of the aluminum support rods and a small plastic link with holes that formed the apex of a triangle. "You just connect this to this, and this to this." She demonstrated as she spoke, grunting slightly as she forced one of the rods into its slot. "And then you do the same for the rear."

"Amazing. If I'd known it was that simple, I might have done more camping. But what's this?" She unfolded a wide rubberized sheet divided at the center by a seam.

"That's the rain fly, which we're obviously going to need. You lay it over the fly rod and anchor it here and here." She connected the sheet to their anchors, a task that also took only two minutes, even with Mwelu attempting to chew on one corner.

Dana held up a folded tarp. "Ah, so this is what keeps out the dampness from the ground. I was wondering." She handed it to Kristen, who spread it out on the floor of the newly erected tent. When they were done, she stood back.

"What a great tent. Ten minutes to set up and waterproof, and with a screen window on one end."

Kristen stayed on her knees and pointed to what was left of her pack. "All we have to do is zip the sleeping bags together and enjoy the comfort of a bed on crushed foliage."

Dana handed her the bags. "We'll be snug as bugs, which of course will be the main thing we'll want to keep *out* of the tent."

It was early evening when they finished laying the last of the brush over the top as camouflage. After the stress of running and climbing, and setting up camp, suddenly they had nothing more to do.

They crawled inside with Mwelu between them, and after examining the corners for insects, Dana stretched out on the ground. "I wish it'd been this nice when I was out patrolling. Now the only thing I miss is a campfire."

"I do, too. But you know we can't risk it. If anyone's looking for us, they'll see the smoke. It might also spook the gorillas."

"I see. All right, then. Crackers and salami it is. And a plantain for Mwelu. Dana opened the canvas sack that functioned as their larder and inventoried their supplies. "We have enough food for… hmm…two days, if we really skimp. As for drinking, we have only about a quart of water, but it shouldn't be too difficult to collect rain."

Chewing on her salami and cheese on a cracker, Dana glanced up as the rain crashed onto the foliage over their shelter. Under the circumstances, she ought to have been in despair, for they'd failed to find group four, and outside the Parc des Volcans, chaos reigned. She searched her feelings but despair wasn't among them. Terrible things had happened to bring the three of them to this moment. Nonetheless, she felt an unmistakable contentment in being in a small warm place with Kristen and the baby they'd lost and found twice.

Mwelu had finished her plantain and now clambered all over her. As soon as Dana could free herself, she packed away the remainder of their food while Kristen zipped the two sleeping bags together. They slipped inside the double bag, but Mwelu found the zipper a fascinating new toy and unzipped it again.

Dana snickered. "Here we are together in this cozy little space, warm and dry. So terribly intimate, and yet, with our little demon there, I don't think we're going to be able to get too romantic."

"Well, the little demon can't stop me from kissing you." Kristen leaned toward her, but at that moment, as if she'd understood the challenge, Mwelu reached up and began to play with Dana's lips.

"Looks like she can. We'll have to wait till she's asleep."

Kristen snickered. "Like a married couple waiting for the kids to go to bed before making love." She slid down into her side of the bag and rested her head on her hand.

Dana rolled onto her side, facing her. "I don't mind, really, if I can just look at you and be happy that fate brought us together."

"Really, it was murder that brought us together."

The remark hung in the air like a thunderclap.

"What...do you mean?" Dana finally managed.

"We've been dogged by murder at every step since we've known each other."

Dana felt a pounding in her chest. Was an announcement coming that would end everything? "I still don't know what you mean."

"In a way, it goes back to the lecture at Columbia."

Dana was silent. *How does she know? How did she find out?*

"I mean, that's where we met, and I wouldn't have been there if Dian hadn't been murdered and I had to replace her to do the fundraising."

"Uh-hunh" was all Dana dared to reply.

"Then you came here, and we would have gone on simply working together if the Batwa hadn't murdered Ndengera and Amahoro and stolen Mwelu. That brought us together in the search to get her back."

Dana began to relax. The conversation was veering into safe territory. "That's true," she replied, waiting to see where it would end.

"Then you hid at Rudy's and would have stayed there if the Interahamwe hadn't murdered Rudy, which made you flee back here to almost be murdered yourself. And I saved you by shooting one of the men about to butcher you. With Dian's gun. That terrible moment made me realize how much I cared for you. So you see, it's almost like Death is our matchmaker."

Dana breathed relief. It was a philosophical discussion, not a condemnation. And it was nonsense. She caressed Kristen's face.

"No, darling. I don't think you should see it in such grim terms. You could just as easily say we both picked up the torch that Dian had dropped and fell in love because we had the same dedication. We're not tainted by murder. We're its antidote. And I'm sure, if Dian were here, she'd agree with me."

Kristen snorted. "If Dian were here, she'd want her pistol back. And then she'd complain that we brought only the salami and cheese and no whiskey or cigarettes."

"Whiskey and cigarettes in the jungle." Dana sniffed in a sort of admiration. "Tougher than Humphrey Bogart, that one."

"Shhhh." Kristen pointed at the bundle between them that had stopped squirming and appeared to be asleep. She dropped her voice to a whisper and leaned across her to kiss Dana.

Their lips touched, and Dana had brought her hand around to grasp Kristen's head when a hairy hand slipped between their mouths. Dana fell back, defeated. "I guess we're going to have to wait awhile before we can make love again."

"You mean when she starts college?"

Dana chuckled. "I was thinking more in terms of tomorrow, when we find a nice gorilla family for her to torment."

"Oh, God. I hope so. Because I want both her happiness and ours." She took Dana's hand and held it to her lips. "You're the best thing that's happened to me in a very long time. Maybe...ever."

Am I? Dana turned out the light in their Coleman lamp. In the darkness, with the thump of raindrops on the tent roof and the baby gorilla settling down between them, Dana wondered at the twisted irony. For it really was murder that had brought them to this moment of happiness.

CHAPTER NINETEEN

The snorting, bleating, whooping, and chest-slapping awoke them all, but Mwelu sprang up first. The zipper tent closure stopped her, and she tumbled back to leap all over them, hooting in her own baby voice.

"Somebody's here," Kristen said unnecessarily and bent to unzip the closure. She crawled out and stood up on the damp foliage, then laughed out loud. "It's the boys!"

Still inside the tent, Dana kept one hand on Mwelu and with the other pulled on her boots. "Boys? What boys?"

"Come out and look."

Still unlaced, Dana scrambled out and got to her feet. "I'll be damned. It's Inzozi's two bad boys. What do you suppose that means?"

"I hope it means the others are around, too." Kristen reached back inside the tent for her boots and slid her feet into them. With Mwelu in tow, they hiked another few yards up the slope through heavy vegetation.

"OhthankGod!" Dana exhaled. "There they are." Mwelu also recognized her extended family and whooped a greeting.

"Oh, yes! There's our boy Ngabo," Kristen exclaimed. "And Inzozi and Kundu are sitting right there next to him. Well done, Ngabo. In spite of the tragedy only a week ago, you rose to the occasion and held the family together."

"So, which one of them should we try to give Mwelu to?" Dana asked.

Kristen stood with hands on her hips, studying the group. Ngabo was on his hind legs and glared back at them but didn't seem threatened. Still, as the new leader, he had to be nervous at any intruder. He thumped his wide black chest but didn't charge.

"I don't know. It looks like Ngabo won't object. He knows Mwelu from before, and he's probably mated with one or both of the females already."

While they stood in quiet discussion, Mwelu had slipped out of Dana's grip and lumbered over to the females, taking the question out of their hands. Inzozi turned and reached for her, but Mwelu slid from her grasp and clambered onto the lap of the older Kundu.

Kundu stared down at the baby without reacting. It was a tense moment.

"What do you suppose she'll do?" Kristen whispered.

"It looks like she's trying to decide whether to give up the freedom of being single," Dana said. "You can't blame her. She has a weak arm from the snare injury anyhow, so how's she going to carry an infant?"

But Mwelu would not be dissuaded from her choice and simply remained seated, sucking on a finger.

Still not acknowledging the invader on her lap, Kundu continued to feed, yanking up a young celery root with her good hand. She stripped away the outer layer with her teeth and exposed the moist core, while Mwelu watched as if it were the most important thing in the world.

Dana held her breath. Would she ignore the baby completely? That was the same as rejection and could be a death sentence for Mwelu. But when Kundu finished her food preparation, she broke off a piece of the core and handed it to the baby with an expression of boredom. Mwelu peered down at it, cross-eyed, and bit into it, looking up at Kundu for approval.

"I think we have an adoption," Dana said.

Kristen breathed a long sigh of relief. "At least one good thing has come out of this horrendous week. We've saved this infant."

They started back toward the tent, and Dana glanced back to see Mwelu climbing onto Kundu's back. "I know it's absurd, but I can't help feeling a little hurt that Mwelu left us so quickly. After all we did for her."

"Yeah, don't you just hate that, when they choose their own species?" Kristen punched her playfully on the shoulder. "You don't need Mwelu to love. You have me now."

"Not the same. I can't cuddle you on my lap and feed you chunks of cassava."

"Sure you can. Sounds like fun. But seriously, Rwanda is more or less on fire, and now we have to make sure Karisoke is secure. I'll follow the troupe for a little while, just to make sure Kundu can travel with a baby. In the meantime, why don't you go back and start dismantling the tent? You saw how easy it was. I'll join you in about twenty minutes."

With mixed feelings, Dana began to pack up the campsite. She'd lost Mwelu, whom she'd come to love the way she'd loved Nikki, but she'd lost her in a much better way. And after all, return to the forest was the whole point of the rescue. Besides, they were going back to face a far graver problem. Some thirty people, counting children, waited for Kristen at Karisoke and would remain more or less in her care during the chaos in the lowland.

How long would it last? Would the Interahamwe, which Kristen had chased off in the parking lot, invade the Parc des Volcans again, or would Karisoke turn out to be the best place to ride out the civil war?

She gave her attention to the task of rolling up the tent into the efficient little bundle Kristen had carried up the mountain. Without Mwelu and the food, at least their packs would be lighter now.

Voices startled her. Men's voices. Was it some of the men from camp? But they'd made no plans for anyone to follow them up. Was there some terrible new emergency?

She rose from her knees and turned just as Simon Bizimana came through the underbrush. Two other men followed.

She bolted, but was no match for the Rwandans, and in just a few minutes, two of them caught up with her and threw her to the ground. While they held her, Bizimana swaggered toward them with his rifle.

He snapped orders at the two men who hauled her to her feet again and held her, while he all but pranced in front of her. His glee was unmistakable.

"Ah, this is my lucky day. I knew it would be worth the climb. Where is your lovely friend?"

Dana remained silent.

"No matter. We will find her soon enough too. But right now, it is time for me to repay you for that nasty little thing you did to me in my own shop. It ruined a good suit and made me much too angry to simply kill you." He paused, no doubt, for effect. "Though I can assure you, you will soon beg me to."

"I don't think so, you shabby little punk."

"Oh, again the rude language. You did not let me finish explaining what we are going to do. You see, you seemed especially upset at finding my gorilla hand. But your hand, the one that stabbed me with that pencil, that will soon have the same fate. Do you think I can sell it to a tourist? There is nothing they won't buy, you know. In fact, I probably could sell both your hands and feet. Yes, we will try that first. White hands and feet should fetch a good price."

Dana twisted from side to side, but the two men were too strong and forced her to her knees.

Bizimana laughed. "Well, I had more to say, but since you are in such a hurry to lose your hand, I will oblige you." He barked another order to the men, and one of them held her around the neck and left shoulder while the other stretched out her right arm. Out of the corner of her eye she could see him raise his machete. She wondered how badly it would hurt or whether she would lose consciousness from the bleeding.

It seemed an eternity as the panga rose, reached its apex, and then began its downward sweep. Instinctively she shut her eyes, waiting for the shattering blow. But instead she heard a gunshot and her hand dropped to her side.

Her eyes flew open in time to see the panga man crash to the ground, clutching his chest. At the same instant, her other captor stepped back in fear, and she realized she was free. She spun around and threw herself into the bushes, scrambling away as Bizimana raised his rifle and shot wildly, first in the direction of the gunshot and again, scarcely aiming, toward her. But she was already flat on her stomach in the underbrush.

Bizimana and his remaining thug stood stupefied for a moment before grasping that they too were under fire, then bolted toward cover.

Meanwhile, from where she lay, Dana could see Kristen's feet, and she crept closer, identifying herself with a whisper. It was clear now that they were in a sort of standoff, invisible to the men who were now also invisible to them. They had to at least get farther up the slope.

Bizimana had also figured out the game and shouted across the distance. "Run away all you want, but I will find you. I will not leave until I do."

Kristen signaled silently and Dana followed her up the hill. Behind them, Bizimana continued shouting but took care to remain hidden. Once they were out of range, Kristen spoke in a low voice. "With that rifle, they have a huge advantage. We have to find a way to ambush them." She exhaled frustration. "Listen to us. We're talking like cowboys. I don't know how to ambush *anyone*." She held up the revolver. "I'd never even shot this thing before yesterday, and now I've killed someone."

"Ambush. Yes, that's it." Dana thought for a moment. "That means that we stay concealed while we get them to cross an open space." She glanced around as they climbed.

"There's a clearing just above us, where the gorillas were earlier. Once we get across it, we look for a place to hide that gives us a view of them coming up the slope. That gives us an edge against that rifle."

Kristen raised a hand. "Wait, the rifle. They had only one, right?" She didn't wait for an answer. "And I'm sure it's the one Bizimana had in his store room. Remember? Peter was so impressed with it."

"Yeah? How does it help us to know that?"

"Because if it's *that* rifle, it carries only five rounds. Then he has to slide in another clip."

"Yeah, sure, but I don't see how that gives us much advantage."

"It does a little. I still have five rounds, and he has three. If we can get him to fire three more times, he'll have to stop for a couple of minutes."

"Or a couple of seconds." Dana grimaced at the thought.

"Enough time to run out and hold a gun in his face."

"How do you propose we make him fire at us? I'm not keen on running in front of him."

"Can you think of anything else? We have a slight advantage in that rifles have to be lifted and aimed. Otherwise the range is meaningless, and you might as well be firing a pistol."

"If you say so." Dana stiffened as she detected motion in the brush below them. "Here's your opportunity. That's them, coming up the hill right now, and they're still pretty far. You want me to wave at them?"

"If you don't mind. Then run, of course."

"This better work." Dana leapt up and ran about twenty feet before diving back into the grass. Bizimana obliged by firing at her.

She crawled back toward Kristen. "Considering it's a sniper rifle, he stinks as a marksman. But now it's your turn."

Kristen snatched up a branch and tossed it into the air before running a similar distance. Again a rifle shot sounded, though whether he aimed at the branch or Kristen was unclear. From a few yards away, Kristen said, "That's four. He's got one shot left. But on the next one, we have to rush him before he slides the new clip in."

Dana shook her head vehemently. "He'll be too far away for us to reach him with a handgun. We have to wait until he's closer."

"But if he's close enough for us to hit him, he's close enough to hit us."

"Yeah, I appreciate the problem," Kristen muttered, but offered no solution.

"Well, when he's close enough, we can try doing what you see in the war movies and hope they don't see a lot of those." She pulled off her jacket and shoved a short branch horizontally under the shoulders.

Crouching together, they peered through the brush, watching the two men advance. When they were some ten yards away, Dana whispered, "That's close enough," and raised her jacket with one arm a few inches over her head.

Bang. The jacket jerked as the bullet passed through it, just grazing her forearm. It hurt like hell. Damn, she'd forgotten about that.

In the same instant, Kristen sprang up and ran toward the two men, her pistol held out in front of her. She stopped just three feet away from Bizimana, who'd dropped his head long enough to yank a clip out of his pocket. When he lifted his gaze, it was to the barrel of Kristen's pistol inches from the bridge of his nose. He stood stupefied as she snatched the still unloaded rifle from his hands. The second man, with his panga raised uselessly, also froze.

Bizimana regained his composure quickly. "Well, it seems we have a draw."

"Draw?" Kristen said contemptuously. "This looks like a victory to me."

"Not when you consider this." He turned and pointed to two other men who had obviously followed unnoticed behind him. They carried no firearms, but they held a young gorilla by her arms. Mwelu.

Kristen wavered. "You bastard. I should blow your head off. You killed even more gorillas to catch her a second time?"

Bizimana smiled. "That wasn't necessary this time, though I could have done it and had one or two more heads to sell. But in this case, we passed them and they ran away at the sound of the guns. The mother just dropped this one. Easiest capture we ever made."

"I won't let you take her." Kristen pointed the rifle at him. "And I have the guns."

"I think you will not shoot me when you know that my men have orders to cut off the gorilla's head if you do."

He gave a final smirk and did an about-face. He'd taken the first steps away from her when an earsplitting roar broke the air, and a gray-and-black mass exploded out of the bush. Bizimana made a half turn with enormous eyes, then toppled backward under the weight of the raging silverback. His men instantly let loose of the baby gorilla and ran.

Freed from their grasp, Mwelu scampered away, squealing as Ngabo sank his canines into Bizimana's shoulder. Keeping a safe distance from the mayhem, the younger males hopped from one foot to another roaring their excitement, then ran in circles while Ngabo gave vent to his aggression. At the periphery, Kundu swept Mwelu into her arms while Inzozi approached, both clearly agitated by the sight of their silverback ripping into a man.

Bizimana squealed now too, his screams competing with the excited vocalizations of the gorillas. "Aiii! Shoot him! Shoot him!" he begged.

Kristen stood implacable, the rifle pointed at the ground.

Bizimana thrashed, but Ngabo's jaws were unrelenting and moved from his shoulder to his neck. Dana could hear the nauseating snap of bones breaking. She watched Kristen, who remained motionless throughout.

Finally it was over, and Bizimana lay on the ground with his arm at a curious angle and blood pouring from his neck. If he still lived, it would clearly not be for long. Without glancing at either of them, Ngabo thumped his chest and lumbered away toward his waiting females.

Quietly, coldly, Kristen bent over the body and snatched a cartridge clip from what was left of his jacket pocket. Then she laid Bizimana's rifle on her shoulder and said, "Pack up the tent and let's get out of here."

They were silent as they made their way down the mountain. After such an event, that was both horrifying yet curiously satisfying, what could they talk about that wouldn't seem banal? What Kristen had said was true. Murder had accompanied them from the beginning, and now they were up to their chins in it.

From time to time they spoke meaninglessly. "Watch out, it's slippery here" or "Do you need me to carry something?" Neither would admit she had no idea how to proceed from that point.

Eventually, they passed an overlook where they could gaze down at the patches of cultivated land and the scattering of brown mushroom caps that were the roofs of farmers' huts. They were too far away to see individual people, and the scene itself was peaceful. That seemed a good sign. It also suggested they were in a direct line for radio reception.

"Why don't you see if you can get a report?" Dana suggested. It also gave them an opportunity to rest for a few minutes.

Kristen withdrew their little transistor radio from her pack and clicked it on. Holding it to her ear, she slowly turned the dial. "The signal's weak, but I can mostly understand it." She listened for a few minutes, covering her other ear to block out the wind and jungle sounds, then shook her head.

"The news is like before. More and more dead. They keep calling it a battle, but as far as I can tell, only one side's doing the killing. No news of the RPF. But if the rebel Tutsis are winning any battles, Radio des Mille Collines isn't reporting it."

"I'm wondering if Bizimana came up with just his personal thugs or whether he led the Interahamwe up to Karisoke. That's what worries me."

Kristen turned off the radio and slid it back into her pack. "We'll find out soon enough," she said quietly.

They hurried now, with a new sense of urgency, taking slight risks and occasionally slipping on the road, but less than an hour later they were at the periphery of the camp.

"It's too quiet," Kristen said under her breath. "I don't like this. We left over thirty people and a dozen children. They can't be that quiet, unless…" She didn't need to speak the rest.

She thought for a moment. "Look, I suggest we leave the heavy packs here under cover. If we discover that everyone's indoors listening to the radio, then fine. We'll just have a little laugh at how nervous we were and come back for them. But if there's trouble, we can run for it."

"Good idea. But let's take the rifle and your pistol, just in case."

"That goes without saying." They backtracked a few hundred yards to where the foliage was denser and cached their packs. Then, at the edge of their nerves, they crept forward on the path that led into camp.

"Oh, God," Kristen murmured as they came within sight of the men's house. Ahead of them lay a dark shape facedown in the grass, and the white hair identified him even from afar. "Senweke." She hurried over to kneel at his side. A machete blow had cut through his shoulder and neck, leaving his head tilted unnaturally far to one side.

Senweke, who had served Karisoke for a decade and seemed as ageless as the forest, gone.

Dana stood over her and knew they both had the same unspoken question. Where were the others? She walked farther along the path and soon, in the tall grass, she saw the rubber boots, the Christmas boots, on Paka. Beyond him lay a woman whose name she hadn't bothered to learn but wished she had, for now the corpse was nameless. And so was the infant in her arms.

Kristen was by her side now. "Have they killed them all?" she asked, then looked toward the men's house, where wooden crates lay overturned. Together they righted two of the crates and climbed up on them to look over the high grass of the camp meadows.

Their worst fears were realized.

The victims lay in groups of three and four like dark creatures that grew up through the grass. Spots of color leapt out at them from the women's dresses. The bright red still visible on the gaping wounds of those nearby told them the slaughter was recent.

Dana's throat tightened. She wanted to walk among them, to touch each one and say their name. Should they…could they…bury them all? Who could they notify? What authorities were left who cared? The unspoken questions already had answers. No, no one, none.

"Look, over there. Someone's alive." Kristen pointed toward her own cabin where a man had just emerged. The distance of some two hundred yards made it impossible to make out whether it was friend or foe. But he lifted something in the air by its feet, and a wing unfolded, revealing it was a dead chicken. Lucy. The figure was joined by another, then a dozen more, and all of them brandished machetes.

Interahamwe, still on the rampage, in such numbers that their guns were useless.

They leapt from their crates and dashed back along the path into the woodland. The killers spotted them and gave chase, but the distance was too great and they escaped into the denser brush.

The marauders soon lost interest in the pursuit; perhaps they were too drunk. Dana was winded, and Kristen, too, slowed to a walk, gulping in air. Neither of them could talk, and they simply dropped onto the ground.

Dana stared up at the gray, indifferent sky, and the full weight of events finally struck her. The murder of Rudy and his family and the radio reports of massacres had all seemed discrete events, individual crimes that could be identified and ultimately punished. The world would go on.

But now Karisoke, her world, had been destroyed. All over Rwanda, the same was happening. No one was burying the dead, and there was no one to notify, for the families of the dead were dead as well.

Finally she had a word for it, and it almost shook her more than the deaths had done. This was genocide, the collapse of a state. And she was trapped in it.

CHAPTER TWENTY

Dana lay for long minutes with closed eyes, catching her breath. Finally she sensed Kristin roll onto her side and take her hand. The look of despair she'd had when they found Senweke had disappeared. In its place was clarity and the concentration of someone who was forming a plan.

"Karisoke's gone, all of it. We have nothing to go back to." She threaded her fingers into Dana's as if to hang on to what was left.

"Yes, I know. Do you think we can get to the embassy? Or to some UN troops? We still have both guns."

"If the Interahamwe has gotten as far as the Virungas, we know they're in control of the lowland. Do you think two white women could get past them alone? We'd have to go down the mountain and travel all the way to Kigali, and our two guns wouldn't be much use against gangs in every town and village. And that's not even taking into consideration that Zigirazo is still hunting us."

Dana nodded acceptance of the grim circumstances. "Only the forest is still safe."

Kristen was staring into space again, obviously still planning. Dana could almost imagine the list she was making. "We'll need to retrieve our packs first. For the tent and the radio."

"Yes, the radio will tell us what the conditions are, and then we can decide whether to risk going down. If we can't, we figure out whether to stay and wait for the UN to negotiate a ceasefire and hope the Leaky Foundation will come rescue us—or that we find an escape route on our own."

"Both possibilities seem far-fetched at the moment. But let's cross those bridges, or burn them, after we get the bigger picture from the radio."

Dana was on her feet again. Like an exhausted mountaineer who focuses on each footstep instead of the mountain, she was glad to at least know which way to point her feet. "That counts as a plan. Let's go."

❖

Panic had simmered at the back of Dana's consciousness, but the mechanical act of setting up the tent soothed her. She could accomplish this task even if the rest of the world was collapsing. Fitting the poles to each other to form the roof and cutting new camouflage took her mind off the unfathomable events of the previous days. Finding out what was still going on in the lowland was Kristen's job, and she'd hiked back to the rocky outcropping where the radio signal was the strongest.

When she finished, she brushed dirt off her hands and glanced around the spot they'd chosen. It wasn't far from their previous location and showed signs of use at one time by group four. They couldn't care for the gorillas any longer, were in fact quite useless to them now, but being near their resting ground gave Dana a certain comfort. Not to mention that they might see Mwelu again.

The sound of footfall over broken branches startled her, but she relaxed when Kristen appeared. "What's the news?"

Kristen dropped onto the ground and stared up at the sky.

"That bad, huh?"

"Yes, in fact. You have to know how to interpret the news from Radio des Mille Collines. They report all the killings as victories in the battle for the true Rwandan way of life, and so far they've done nothing but cheer. I heard no indication that the RPF is advancing anyplace, so if we were hoping for the rebel army to rescue us, we can forget about it."

"All right. Then we stay put for a couple of days. The rampage can't go on forever."

Kristen eyed the tent Dana had set up. "Good job. Thanks for doing that. At least we're protected from the rain. But our little picnic is long gone. We'll have to live off the land."

Dana glanced at the foliage all around them. "I see. Well, do you know what's edible here?"

Kristen didn't reply but merely glanced past Dana and grinned. "No, but *they* do."

Dana turned to see a long, hairy black arm reach out from the nearby underbrush. A second later, the entire gorilla appeared and sat down a few feet away, with her adopted infant on her back. "Kundu, darling. You've come back."

The new mother yawned with her massive jaws, giving, for all the world, the appearance of boredom. Then, as if to show how it's done, she yanked a length of stem from the closest bush, bit it off, and with three swift passes of her teeth, she stripped it of all its bark. With some eight inches of pith exposed, she bit off one end and presented it to Mwelu.

Kristen chuckled. "Show-off."

But the lesson continued. With Mwelu hanging beneath her, she lumbered over and sat down between them. She scratched her throat for a moment, as if waiting for their full attention, and then, with a sudden and efficient movement, she ripped out another stem, stripped it along its full length, and dropped it in front of Dana.

"Isn't that touching?" Kristen said. "The gorillas are saving *us*. It's wild celery. And look around. The ground's covered with it. Okay, it's not the kind you put in your salad at home, but the pith should be edible." She picked up the proffered stem from the ground and studied it.

Dana peered at it suspiciously. "Oh, yummy. You go first."

Unperturbed, Kristen slid a small penknife from her shirt pocket and began slicing away the last layer around Kundu's gift. After a minute of careful shaving, she reached the core, a soda-straw-sized column of pith. "There you go. *Bon appétit.*" She clipped it into halves and handed one to Dana.

The fibrous plant was more bitter than domestic celery, and Dana had to chew longer and more vigorously than she liked, but it could, in a pinch, pass for food. Slightly. "It could use a little salad dressing. And tomatoes, and lettuce, and baco-bits."

"Picky, picky. Here, have another and be glad we're not in the Sahara." Kristen leaned over to cut another length of the plant stem.

"Oh, look," Dana said. "Here come the others." The rowdy young blackbacks came first, followed by Inzozi, and last of all, as if with studied leisure, Ngabo deigned to arrive, taking his good time. In a few minutes, the entire troupe surrounded them chewing on celery stems.

Dana was amused. "It's like a family picnic, isn't it? I hope they don't move off to make their night nests."

"I don't think you'll have to worry about that. Ngabo seems to be settling in."

In fact, the novice leader was as relaxed as Dana had ever seen him. He stripped the wild celery branches but retained the outer scraps, and while he dined with one hand, he used the other to gather the stripped material and other loose foliage into a circle around him.

Inzozi, the female who had arrived before him, now turned back and brushed past him, obviously signaling her availability. Immediately and almost mechanically, he grasped her by the arm and pivoted her into position for mounting.

Their coupling took scarcely more than a minute, and although Inzozi had initiated it, she seemed the model of forbearance during the act, leaning on her elbows and staring up at the sky. When Ngabo released her, she wandered off nonchalantly and began to gather foliage to create a nest for herself.

Kundu had also taken the hint and left off eating long enough to prepare her own bed, and Mwelu wandered over to Dana and Kristen. She climbed over both of them in turn, resisting both their attempts to hug her, then ambled back to Kundu. A good sign, Dana thought, in spite of the rejection. Mwelu knew where she belonged.

In the rapidly falling light, all the gorillas settled down, still feeding intermittently. "Should we light the lantern?" Dana asked.

"I don't think so. If any of the Interahamwe are on the mountain, it would advertise where we are. Come on. Let's get into the tent while we can still find our way in."

"Good idea." They crawled together into their little shelter, and once they were inside, it was pitch-black. Blindly, Dana slid off her trousers and rolled them into a pillow, feeling Kristen next to her doing the same. They slid together into the double sleeping bag and moved automatically into the spoon position.

Dana waited a few minutes until their combined body warmth dissipated the chill of the forest night, then kissed Kristen on her shoulder.

"Everything seems so unreal, doesn't it? I mean, we've just witnessed the massacre of our friends, and we're running for our lives in a country that's descended into anarchy. Yet lying here with my arms around you feels so utterly comforting I can almost forget. At least for a while. Is it crude, or immoral, that with all the horror and destruction around us, I still want to make love to you?"

She felt the sleeping bag rise as Kristen turned toward her, and a moment later a hand caressed her cheek. "No, I don't think so. It's as natural as what Ngabo and Inzozi did."

Dana chuckled softly. "I hope we're a little more romantic than those two were."

"I don't know. You'll have to kiss me to find out."

Dana pulled her close, and it was, in fact, very romantic to kiss in complete darkness and make one's way solely by touch. Dana slid her free hand inside Kristen's shirt, exploring the contour of her warm back. How quickly the rush of excitement came, the tight heat in her groin that demanded release.

Did Inzozi feel the same when she offered herself to Ngabo? If so, perhaps her skyward gaze was gorilla gratitude for nature's exquisite gift.

Kristen's wet mouth that gave and took was delicious, and so was her sweet sex that Dana tasted with her fingers. At that moment, Kristen's hand crept down her belly and invaded her own aching center.

Thus doubly joined, they urged each other forward, as they'd once climbed Karisimbi, and step by aching step they rose toward the explosion of pleasure that came much too soon.

And so it was, that while the killing in the lowland went on through the night, they made love to each other as a sort of proof they were still alive.

"So good," Kristen murmured. "I want us to do this every day and night for the rest of our lives."

"Mmmm," Dana murmured back, drowsily, though a part of her fading consciousness wondered how long that might be.

❖

Hours later, Dana awoke and groped her way out of the tent to relieve herself. Her dark-adapted eyes could make out shapes by the dull ambient light of the night mist. Not only the tent but also the black lumps, large and small, of the gorillas sleeping nearby. One or two shifted position in their sleep, reacting to her or to the other jungle sounds. The others lay unmoving and snored like old men, or snorted, farted, or smacked their lips. Kristen was right. It was as noisy as a night in an army barracks.

As she slipped back into the shared sleeping bag, Kristen stirred and mumbled something.

"Oh, I'm sorry I woke you."

"It's all right. I was wondering why my back was cold. I thought you might have gotten fed up and run away."

"Run away and joined the gorillas, eh? Have you seen the way Ngabo treats his women?"

Kristen turned on her side and tucked her head under Dana's chin. "Yeah, and their cuisine isn't so good either. But seriously, I've been thinking. I'm sorry I lured you into this disaster. You could be back in New York with some safe job if I hadn't refused to accept that Rwanda was a powder keg. I not only got you into this horror of a civil war, but I've also killed two men in front of you."

"You didn't kill Bizimana. Ngabo did."

"I could have shot Ngabo and saved him. You know that, and Bizimana knew it when he died."

"You killed someone vicious who'd killed something innocent. Many times. That seems like justice to me."

"You don't think a human life is worth more than a gorilla's? That, in the end, it's sacred?" Kristen's breath was warm on Dana's chest.

Dana caressed her hair. "I don't even know what the word sacred means. But no, I don't." Dana was intrigued. Where was this conversation going? "What about you?"

Kristen moved her head back slightly, to speak more clearly. "I don't think human beings, all five or so billion of us, are special. We're just another intelligent species. One that causes more harm to itself and to the planet than other intelligent species."

"Yes, that's true. But don't we have a moral obligation to protect our own? Note that I'm playing devil's advocate here."

"Do we as white people have an obligation to protect whites from other races, no matter what?"

"Good point. But then how do you decide which humans to protect and which not, or for that matter, which animals?"

"Do you mean do I have a formula or a doctrine? No, I don't. But neither do most enlightened societies other than an evolving sense of who or what is harmful to the group. I don't think people can even come up with an absolute definition of justified killing versus murder. Whether you're allowed to kill a killer, for example."

"Funny. Mary and I talked about just that the last night of her life. We were recalling Plato's *Dialogues*."

"You discussed Platonic dialogues with Mary?!"

"Yes. She had a degree in philosophy. Didn't you know?"

"I had no idea. What did you decide? About when killing is allowed?"

Dana rose and leaned on her elbow. "We didn't. And neither did Plato, in fact. And then, a few hours later, she and her family were murdered."

"Unbelievable. One minute 'killing' is just an intellectual concept, and the next minute it's in your house, swinging a machete."

Dana needed to move beyond the abstract. "What I'm trying to ask is, do you believe there are circumstances in which one could rightfully kill a human being?"

"We were just in those circumstances. I mean self-defense."

Dana paused for a moment before pressing her point. "What about killing someone who's demonstrably vicious. Sadistic, but no threat to you personally." There, it was on the table.

"I don't know. I'd have to hear the details."

Dana dropped back onto the sleeping bag and stared into the darkness, gathering her courage. "I killed two men. In New York."

Kristen was silent for an excruciatingly long moment. "When was that?"

"The day we met." Another beat. "That's *how* we met. That's *why* we met. I was running away and hid in the auditorium while you were lecturing."

"Dear God. So those policemen…"

"…were chasing me. Yes." Dana imagined the horror that was surely on Kristen's face.

"Who did you kill? Why?"

"That's the crux of it, isn't it? It wasn't a robbery or lover's quarrel, if that's what you mean."

"I don't *mean* anything. Just tell me what happened."

The darkness made talking easier, and Dana spoke into the void as if to a confessor. "Well, I'd just graduated from Amherst and come back to New York to look for work. I was staying with friends of my parents, and all I really had to call my own was my dog. Nikki. A husky-shepherd mix. Beautiful, the light of my life." The pain of remembering him caused her to fall silent a moment.

"Go on, please."

"It was a ground-floor apartment in Harlem, one of the old buildings, and because my friends had a cat, they made me keep him outside in a dog house at night. That was all right in the short term. But one night someone took him, just like that. Cut his chain with metal cutters and stole him."

She paused for breath, searching for ways to summarize, to tell the truth, and not excuse herself. "Luckily, one of those street kids who are out at all hours saw them and the van they took him into. The next day, for a little cash, the kid told me what happened. I suppose I should have reported it to the police, but I knew they wouldn't do anything. Anyhow, the kid described the van so well, I walked around the neighborhood day after day, looking for it, and finally I spotted it a just a few blocks away. I watched it for another couple of days and found out who the owners were, and that they had a basement apartment."

Dana paused, waiting for a reaction, but Kristen just said, "Go on."

"They kept it locked, of course, but it was easy to break a window and get inside one afternoon when they were gone. It was a tiny office, and behind a door, I found a second room of concrete block that must have once been a coal cellar."

"Did you find your dog?"

"Yes. In a freezer."

"Oh, God, I'm so sorry."

"There's more. It wasn't just that they'd killed my dog. They'd killed a bunch of others, and cats, too. They had a whole cabinet of videos, and the titles told what they'd done to them. I won't tell you any of them, but they made my stomach turn. These guys weren't just jerks who liked to hurt animals. Making sadistic animal videos was their business."

"That's despicable. But you're sure they were the ones who made them?"

"Yes, I saw their video equipment, lights, the ropes, the stuff they used. It made me want to vomit."

"So what did you do?" Dana felt the motion of Kristen sitting up.

Dana remained lying down. It seemed easier to talk from a slight distance. "At first, nothing. I was just stunned. Of course I thought of calling the police then, too. The men would be arrested, but so would I, for burglary. And I also knew their penalty would be a fine and maybe a few months in jail. The bastards would just come out and start all over again. I felt this helpless, sickening fury." She paused, trying to speak calmly in spite of the rage and nausea that came over her.

"And then, it was like the universe offered me a chance to do something about it. In one of the drawers I found a couple of guns. Old revolvers. Ammunition, too. So I loaded one of them and waited for the guys to come back." She paused, allowing the hideous memory to flow back, like filthy water, polluting her again.

"I can even tell you what they looked like. One was paunchy, balding, and the other one was swarthy with lots of black hair. Both wore Dockers and dark T-shirts. Ordinary guys. That was kind of the worst part. They'd have been invisible in a crowd."

"And you shot them."

"Yes. Cold, calculated execution. One of the neighbors must have heard the gunshots and called the police. That was New York, and patrol cars are everywhere, so in just a few minutes, they arrived. I barely had time to get up to the street. The police chased me for blocks, onto campus and, finally, into that auditorium. And the rest you know."

Kristen blew out a puff of air. "Wow. That's a hard story to get my head around."

"Good luck with *that*. I haven't got *my* head around it in four months. I feel sick when I think about it. Not because of what I did. I'd do it again. But it's awful to be a fugitive and have to lie to everyone you care about. I thought I could do something useful in Rwanda and that would make up for it. I didn't count on a vengeful black marketer and a civil war."

"And a corrupt politician. Remember, Bizimana was just acting for Zigirazo."

"Yeah, him, too. So here I am, a murderer. I can't go back and I can't stay here."

Kristen's hand felt warm on her cheek.

"You're not any more guilty than I am. We both killed murderers of the innocent. Even Plato would have approved."

Dana covered Kristen's hand with her own. "I'm glad you see it that way, though I doubt the NYPD would."

"Let's not worry about the NYPD. Right now it's more important that we take care of ourselves. Anyhow, I think we've done enough soul-searching for one night. Let's try to sleep a bit more before daylight, and then we can plan what to do from here." Kristen slid back down into their common sleeping bag and draped an arm over Dana's waist.

All the while they'd talked, it had apparently rained gently, but it was only now that Dana noticed the soft patter of rain on the foliage that covered their tent. So much had happened in a single day that she was drained, but now at least the weight of guilt and secrecy was lifted. She buried her head in Kristen's arms and murmured, "Yes, rest for the wicked."

CHAPTER TWENTY-ONE

Kristen woke first, disturbing Dana when she sat up. "Go back to sleep, darling," she said. "There's just enough light for me to hike back to the outcropping that faces Ruhengeri, where I can get the radio news. I'll be back in a little while."

"Mmm. Okay." Dana let herself drift back into sleep, dreaming about gorillas eating pizza. But in just a few minutes, the sun rose high enough to shine through the foliage over the tent roof, and the brightness woke her again.

When she crawled out of the tent shelter, the gorillas had moved on. Disappointed, she pulled on her hiking boots and wandered over to where they'd slept during the night. The hollowed-out depressions that had been their nests lay scattered along the slope just above the tent, and most had little piles of dung, like farewell gifts.

Dana stood over the nest where she'd last seen Kundu and Mwelu as Kristen returned. "What's the news?"

Kristen shook her head. "Not good, I'm afraid. Mille Collines is calling it 'battle victories,' of course, but basically, the Interahamwe is rampaging everywhere between Ruhengeri and Kigali. They're using grenades to blow up crowds inside buildings and churches. Then they finish them off with pangas and clubs. It must be a living hell down there. And they're still going on about the whites siding with the Tutsis."

"Isn't there any mention of UN troops? We saw them patrolling in Kigali."

Kristen shook her head. "After the murder of the prime minister and the Belgian peacekeepers, the Security Council decided the mission was too dangerous and recalled all their troops, except for a couple hundred."

"So the Western countries are abandoning their citizens."

"No, only the Rwandans. Yesterday, troops from France, Belgium, and Italy landed at Kigali airport to round up their respective expatriates and airlift them out."

"What about the Americans? They didn't send anyone?"

"The Americans are also sending several convoys starting from Kigali to round up their embassy staff and whatever business people they can reach. But we obviously can't get to Kigali, or even Ruhengeri. I'm sorry, darling. If you'd stayed hidden at Rudy's house, you might have had a chance."

"Don't even think that. I want to be with you, not to mention that we had to be sure Mwelu was safe." She paused, ordering her thoughts. "Okay, what are our alternatives?"

"Realistically speaking? We have quite a few, but they're all bad." She began counting on her fingers. "One, hike down to the car park in hopes that the car's still there, then make a run for Kigali airport."

"Assuming the planes haven't taken off and we could get there in time, the Interahamwe have roadblocks everywhere, and two white women in a big fat Land Rover might as well have a flashing neon sign saying KILL US." Dana snorted softly. "Doomed by your color. Gives you a whole new understanding of what it was like to be a runaway slave in Georgia, doesn't it?"

Kristen seemed to be barely listening. "Two, hike over to the Congo, except that would pretty much be leaping from the frying pan into the fire. Assuming the border isn't closed, which it often is. And also assuming we don't get lost in the jungle."

"Isn't the Rwandan Patriotic Front fighting back? Those Tutsi rebels they keep talking about on the radio—maybe we could locate them."

"That's alternative three. Hold out until they get here. *If* they get here. But judging from the so-called battle reports, they're still nowhere near. Besides, we have no idea whether they have a chance. Nothing so far indicates they'll win this war."

"Is there a number four?"

"No. Only a three-B. That is, stay put until *any* help comes. The UN, the marines, the rebel army. That basically means just holding out. We can do that, if we live like the gorillas."

Dana turned back to the night nest she'd been standing over. "Live with the gorillas, like Tarzan. Hmm. We'd have to locate them. It's so rude for them to leave without saying good-bye, don't you think?"

Kristen kissed her quickly on the ear. "That's probably what saved them from being hunted to extinction. But look, they left us all this wild celery to eat." She swept her arm in an arc over the entire slope.

Dana winced. "I'm sorry. It was okay for one meal, but if I have to eat only that day after day, you can just shoot me now. Surely we can find other things humans can eat in these mountains."

"Theoretically, we can. The Batwa have lived off the land for centuries. I'm not at the point of wanting to trap a duiker or a hyrax, since I've been destroying traps now for eight years, but I do know the Virunga range has edible flora."

"We're not going to have to eat bark and insects, are we?"

"Not just yet. Africans cultivate any number of things that also grow wild. The oil palm, for example, flourishes all over the Virungas where there's plenty of sunlight. Wild figs supposedly grow here, though I've never looked for them. Merula nuts are our best bet. The Batwa collect them, and if you find a merula tree, you can eat the leaves and flowers as well. I thought I saw a couple of them west of here, near group six's territory. I've also seen a tufted grass called teff, which has edible parts, lower down on the slopes."

"And the nettles? I heard you can make a soup from them."

"Maasi nettle. You can, though of course you need a fire and something to cook them in. But we might luck out and find some safou. We can eat that raw."

"Is that like tofu?"

"Alas, no. It's a tree with fruit that's very nutritious. It looks like a plum tree, and fortunately for us, it blooms at the beginning of the rainy season. If we locate a tree, it might have some fruit already."

"I like the idea of a food search much better than sitting here and stripping wild-celery bark. Can we just head out now?"

"Sure. But I think we should take the tent."

"Why? It's just a big load to carry around. It'll slow us down."

"Yeah, but we could end up very far from here, just searching for food. What are we going to do if there's a downpour? We'd have to hike the whole distance back here, and for what? Just to be near your favorite gorilla?"

Dana sighed. Mwelu really was the reason they'd chosen the spot as their base, but Mwelu no longer needed them. "I see what you mean. All right. Let's pack it up. I get grouchy when I'm hungry."

"Well, if you're going to be in a bad mood until we eat, I'd better carry the rifle."

❖

"I haven't tracked this far west in ages," Kristen said, shading her eyes against the afternoon sun. "The men usually cover the groups on the Karisimbi slopes, so I don't know the trails very well any more. Good thing we have the compass."

Dana gazed out over a slope covered with low bushes and grasses. "This is where group six nested? I don't see any sign of them. No dung, nothing."

"The last person who checked on them was Peter, unfortunately, and I never got a chance to read his report. I hope no one's got to them."

They plodded along watching their feet, and Dana tried to ignore her hunger. "So what does a safou tree look like, anyhow?"

"It's a low tree with a wide crown. Like a plum tree, actually. It also produces fruit like plums, but in clusters. A shame the Batwa hate us so much. They'd know where to find them."

"I see a few trees over there at the bottom of the slope. Should we check?" Without waiting for a reply, Dana set out toward them. She halted suddenly. "Good God! What's that over there on the top of the post?" Some twenty yards away, at the edge of the clearing, a post tilted sideways with something dark and round at its top. "Please, don't let it be a head!" she murmured to no one in particular.

Kristen frowned. "It *can't* be a head. The Batwa don't do that."

"Yeah, but the Interahamwe do." Taking the sniper's rifle from her shoulder and pointing it toward the invisible enemy, Dana scanned the area looking for any sign of men. It would be a damned shame if they'd hiked so far only to run into another band of killers. If they did, she had five bullets and would use all of them.

Kristen marched past her toward the post. When she came within a few feet of it, she stopped and broke into laughter. "Well, I'll be damned. I never thought I'd see that ugly thing again."

Dana caught up with her and stood, puzzled, before what obviously used to be a hollow rubber head. It was shredded at the neck and split in several places, but still unmistakably a Halloween mask, a very ghoulish one. "Good grief. What the hell's that?"

"It's one of Dian's. I guess she put it up here to keep the poachers away from group six, and no one ever bothered to take it away. I'm surprised it's held up this long. Must be nine years now."

"Are you sure it's Dian's mask and not someone else's? She can't be the only person in Rwanda who had ugly masks."

"Yeah, but she had a whole collection. Remember the one in her cabin? She brought them from the States to Rosalind's house to try them out on her servants. They terrified them. I remember this mask with the pop-out eyes in particular because it's the one Rosalind hated the most." She stared into space for a moment, as if witnessing a revelation. "Rosalind. Rosalind Carver," she muttered.

"What about her?"

Kristen was suddenly animated, almost cheerful. "Rosalind was one of Dian's friends. Her only one, really. She had a flower plantation called Mugongo in a little community called Mutera. And other foreigners kept a few farms around the area. I wonder if she's still there."

"You think that someone Dian knew nine years ago is still living in the same place and can help us?"

"It's a long shot, I admit. If she's even there, she might have been evacuated. Or she might be dead. The last time I saw her was at Dian's funeral, and she was seventy-something then. But other foreigners lived at Mutera, too, and we might be able to connect with them."

"How far is it?"

"Eighteen or twenty miles, maybe more." Kristen looked at her watch. "It's already afternoon so we couldn't get there before nightfall. The times we went there we always drove, of course, but I think I remember the route. She stared into the distance and seemed to be visualizing a map. "Rwanda doesn't have that many paved roads anyhow. So, once we leave the Parc des Volcans, we follow the main road leading southwest. It goes through farmland with patches of woods, so we'll have to watch for gangs and stay out of sight."

"Yeah? Then what?"

Kristen stared into space again, apparently plotting their route. "The path crosses a much wider road at a village. I can't remember the name. Maybe it doesn't have one. But that's about halfway along. If we get to the crossroad by nightfall, we can pitch the tent somewhere discreet and sleep a little. Assuming the Interahamwe haven't taken over the local people completely, we might even cajole some food."

"Food would be nice. Okay, so we sleep. Then what?"

"Then we start out before dawn, basically in the same direction, southwest. I remember a narrow dirt road, and where it crosses another wider one, that should be Mutera Road. You can't miss it because foreigners have built a lot of nice houses along it, and some missionaries have a school there. Once we reach the intersection, we head slightly north to the rocky drive that leads up to Mugongo, the plantation."

"You make it sound easy."

"The directions *are* pretty easy. The hard part will be staying out of sight. And being hungry."

Dana hefted the rifle onto her other shoulder. "No problem. I've got some yummy wild celery in my pack. Let's go."

❖

The very unrest they fled proved to be a benefit in concealing them while they traveled, for few farmers were on the land. The continuous rain might also have been a factor. Fortunately, too, at the higher elevations, clusters of trees and bushes marked off border zones between cultivated fields, and they could hurry like pursued wildlife, from one copse to the next.

Kristen's estimate was also accurate, and by early evening, they spotted the row of houses that marked the intersection of the little road with the big road. Here, too, the fields lay untended in the rain, but one or two women were visible carrying baskets on their heads.

Men, they decided, were an automatic hazard, for the farmers were all Hutu. But the women seemed less threatening, and they'd seen no sign of them in the Interahamwe. So when Kristen and Dana happened upon an old woman with a basket of small melons on her head, they eyed her load hungrily and risked engaging her.

As they approached, the old woman halted, nervously eyeing their clothing, backpacks, and, especially, the rifle.

Kristen greeted her in Kinyarwanda, addressing her as *Mama*, which counted as polite, even to a stranger. That seemed to break the ice. The rest of what she said was largely unintelligible, though Dana did recognize the words for melon, hungry, and buy. The transaction was agreed upon, and Kristen handed over what amounted to the last of their cash for four melons the size of coconuts. Only four. Dana's stomach growled.

The discussion continued, perhaps the exchange of courtesies, but Kristen had an expression of serious interest, and when the old woman paused for breath, Kristen summarized its meaning.

"She said the men in the village have made their own Interahamwe and have gathered in the square to listen to the radio and drink beer. So far, they haven't attacked anyone, but the Tutsi shopkeepers have closed their shops and fled."

Dana shivered slightly as the rain found its way into her collar and down her neck. "Then we'd better go find some woods and set up camp."

The old lady had obviously understood by their equipment that they'd been sleeping rough and pointed toward a building where the wide road ended. She spoke a few phrases and Kristen interpreted.

"She said the building's empty. It used to hold grain, but the Tutsi who owned it ran away last year. She thinks he joined the rebels."

Dana took a risk. "You don't like the Tutsis?" She spoke in English and Kristen intermediated again.

The old woman shrugged, and her reply passed through Kristen again. "Nobody likes the Tutsis, she says. But that one, he wasn't so bad. He paid a good price for the farmers' grain and gave them credit in his shop. She's sorry he ran away."

The woman seemed to lose interest in the laborious conversation and, pocketing the money, continued on past the empty granary into the village.

"What do you think?" Dana asked. "Do we dare go there? It'd be nice to be dry for the night. But if we're going to sleep in the jungle again, we'd better get moving. My feet are already soaked."

Kristen peered forlornly in the direction of the village as they stood together in the downpour. "All right. We may regret this, but I don't want to walk any more either. Let's check out that granary. We have two guns in case anyone comes around."

Dana knew—and she knew Kristen knew—that two guns would be of little use against large groups, but the idea of a roof for the night, a dry sleeping bag, and a dinner of something that was not wild celery pith, overrode all caution.

The two-story building seemed to have been a combination warehouse and barn in which the ground floor had housed livestock. The odor suggested goats, or perhaps a donkey, while the scattering of feathers indicated chickens. Very likely both.

The granary upstairs had been stripped of whatever stock it had held, and only a few torn and filthy burlap bags lay scattered around. Dana kicked them out of the way and cleared a spot near the single opening that had once been a window with a view of the street below. From a discreet position, Dana peered toward both sides.

"It's the main street, isn't it? Or the tail end of it. I think over there, where it curves to the left, it leads to the square. I can't really see much, with the darkness and the rain. But it looks like this is the last corner you pass before you leave the village." She withdrew and brushed the rainwater off her hair.

Kristen had spread their tarp over the gritty concrete floor and laid the double sleeping bag over it. "Better stay away from the window, and come have your dinner." She ripped apart the bundle and laid out the melons on the sleeping bag. "Pretend it's a picnic."

"Of course," Dana said, sitting cross-legged in front of her. "Except for the concrete floor and the food and the mortal danger, just like a picnic."

"As long as we stay in the dark, we should be all right. Eat up, dear, and then let's get some rest. At least the weather is keeping the murderers off the street."

❖

The rain had its usual soporific effect, and they slept until roused by the voices outside. It was dawn, and though the interior of the granary was still dark, the dull pre-sunrise light made it possible to look down onto the street. It was their worst fear, the Interahamwe.

Standing off to one side to avoid being seen, they watched as some dozen men laid a tree branch across two chairs to create a roadblock at the end of the street that led out to the fields.

In spite of the very early hour, people were already moving along the street. It became immediately obvious that the roadblock was intended as a checkpoint, for as they watched, a man reached it, showed some kind of folded cardboard, then passed through it.

Following him, two farmers with wheelbarrows rummaged through their pockets to display what was most likely an identity card, and they too were permitted through. But the couple following was not so lucky. The man must have grasped the danger and balked, but it was too late. The very fact of his withholding his identification was enough to condemn him. In a moment, two of the killers set upon him with their clubs, and two others dragged the screaming woman off the street into a narrow passage.

A family of three, parents with a young child, farther up the street saw what had happened and tried to turn back, but could not. Several more men carrying clubs and machetes surrounded them, blocking their retreat. When the father snatched up the child and tried to run, the armed men threw both of them to the ground and hacked them to death. It all happened in a matter of minutes.

"My God. It's plain butchery. And look, they're clearing the bodies away so people coming from around the corner don't see what's waiting. They're capturing any Tutsi who tries to leave."

Dana stood hypnotized by the gruesome spectacle as the drama repeated itself again and again. People strode around the curve with no idea of what awaited them at the end of the street. The ones who continued without pause and showed their IDs without fear were presumably Hutus and knew they were immune. But anyone who tried to flee was assumed to be Tutsi and was chased down and killed.

Over and over, with mechanical regularity, the executions took place and the bodies were moved to the passageway. Soon they were piled one atop the other.

Dana stepped back from the window. "How the hell do we get out of this place?"

A woman's voice behind them caused them to turn in terror. Dana threw herself onto her pack and snatched up the rifle. Next to her, Kristen fumbled for her pistol.

It was their melon farmer, who stood unperturbed at the top of the granary stairs, and beside her was a young man, perhaps her son. Without coming closer, she spoke again to Kristen.

Kristen lowered her pistol and signaled to Dana to back down, too. "She said she wants to help us."

"How do we know we can trust her? She could just as easily be leading us right to those butchers."

"Why would she bother? All she has to do is tell them we're here."

The woman seemed to grow impatient and waved them toward her, scowling. Without waiting to see if they followed, she marched over to the interior wall of the room. Only the young man, no more than sixteen, seemed slightly frightened by the whole scene.

"I think we should trust her," Kristen announced. "We can't stay here, in any case. If it's a trap, we still can shoot a few people." She spoke to the boy, then explained to Dana. "I've told him to wait five minutes while we pack our things." She threaded her arms through her small backpack.

The boy shook his head, and Dana recognized the simple Kinyarwanda: "No, no time!" She balked, not willing to give up what had been their life support while they fled. But then she heard the men's voices and threw a glance out the window. A handful of the killers had broken off and was coming toward their building.

At that moment, Kristen snatched her by the wrist, pulling her toward the boy and his mother. The woman stood by a hinged wooden hatch on the lower part of the wall Dana hadn't noticed before.

The old lady lifted it, revealing a chute. Where did it lead? Fear of being immured alive paralyzed her for a moment, but the boy shoved her into the dark opening and she tumbled downward. Her feet struck another wooden surface, and for a second she panicked, but then it opened under her weight and she rolled out. Kristen came immediately behind her, then the boy, then the old woman.

Dana tried to get her bearings by the scant light that came through the slit at the top of the badly hung door. They were in a narrow space, one of the barn stalls she hadn't seen when they came in the evening before. And the chute they'd come down was obviously for loading the grain onto carts. Through the flimsy wall on one side they could hear the pursuers arguing as they began to climb the stairs. It wouldn't take them long to discover the sleeping bags and to figure out someone had just fled. They had seconds to escape.

The old woman cracked the door and peered outside, and Dana hoped the camping equipment would hold the attention of the men for a few minutes, at least. The alley was clear, so the woman threw the door open and turned sharply to the right, running along the rear of the buildings. She ran astonishingly fast for an old person, and Dana worked hard to keep up with her.

When they'd passed six or seven houses, the woman pointed out toward the fields and hissed a single word, which Dana knew meant "Go!"

Kristen thanked her, also with a single word, and they ran full out across a field. Mercifully, it had a stand of trees at the far side. If the drunken killers stayed three more minutes examining their tent, they could make it.

The practical value of a good tent, two sleeping bags, and a sniper's rifle obviously far exceeded the pleasure of capturing some evasive foreigners, to kill or not kill, to nobody's profit. Perhaps the drunken gang fought over the items, especially the rifle, and so forgot their original purpose. In any case, they didn't emerge from the granary for the fifteen minutes that Kristen and Dana watched from hiding.

"I think we should go," Kristen finally said. "We've got a good head start, and they don't seem so keen to chase us any longer. There's another stand of trees over there." She pointed to a spot of green some quarter of a mile toward the southwest.

"Is that the direction we need to go?"

"Yes, more or less. Mutera is that way." She pointed with a flat hand. "Of course, we'll have to travel parallel to the road, keeping out of sight. Even so, I think we're only a few hours away. Good thing, too. We have nothing to sleep in now."

"No rifle, either. Do you still at least have the pistol?"

"Yes, in my jacket pocket."

Fatalistic at this point, Dana sighed. "All right, then. Let's carry on."

❖

Kristen's estimate had been conservative. With their need to stay out of sight, they had to take numerous detours and then wend their way back to trace the line of the road southwest, and finally, five hours later, weary and footsore, they reached the intersection of "the little road with the big one."

Mutera Road was exactly as Kristen had described it, with fine houses on both sides that gave it the look of a prosperous American suburb.

"What's that?" Dana asked, pointing south toward a cluster of buildings. "It looks like a college campus."

"It is, more or less. It's the missionary college I told you about. This must be Mudende. We're a bit south of where we want to be. Mutera itself is just up that road. Another half hour, maybe.

This time her reckoning was correct, and even with the need to travel invisibly, scuttling from cover to cover, they soon reached a pebbly road where Kristen halted.

"Here it is, Mugongo Flower Plantation." At the end of a rise they could see a house that for all the world could have been an English cottage. "And people are still there!" Dana exclaimed, spotting a van and two cars parked in front.

They were saved.

Spontaneously, they picked up their pace until they came within a hundred feet of the house.

"*Arretez!*" a voice barked behind them, and Dana turned to see two men with rifles pointed at their heads.

Anger was her first response, at being threatened yet again, and Kristen, too, reached for the pistol in her jacket. But they registered at about the same time that the soldiers wore blue helmets with the white letters UN.

"*Nous sommes Américaines,*" she said, raising both hands.

The soldier peered at them in the dim evening light and satisfied himself they were harmless. "*Bon*," he said and turned away.

They looked at each other, giddy with relief, and Dana snorted. "Who did he think we were? The white division of the Interahamwe?"

Kristen shrugged. "I guess everyone's nervous." They marched toward the open doorway of the house, where a small, white-haired woman was explaining something to a Rwandan who held two suitcases.

"Rosalind!" Kristen called out and took off toward her.

The woman turned at the sound of her name. She looked puzzled for a moment, and then her face brightened. "Kristen Wolfe, is that you?" She stepped closer. "My gracious, it is." She gave her a quick hug. "How are you, my dear? Oh, I suppose I shouldn't ask that question. None of us are fine, are we?"

She turned back to the Rwanden and signaled that he should set the suitcases by her side, then continued. "Your appearance here is ominous. Does it mean that Karisoke is evacuated?"

"Worse than that, Rosalind. They massacred my entire staff. We hid in the forest and then made our way here hoping to find you, and of course some way out. I'm so glad you haven't been harmed."

"Oh, I'm terribly sorry, my dear. That's what this is all about." Rosalind swept her hand along the line of vehicles drawn up in front of her house. "The Belgians are evacuating the school at Mudende, and they've let me join. You two also, of course. Who's your friend?" She offered her hand and Dana spoke for herself.

"I'm Dana Norland, Kristen's assistant, since December. Nice to meet you."

"Thank God you both made it out." Focused primarily on her own predicament, Rosalind glanced back and forth from Dana to her houseman to the UN soldiers who were pacing up and down the pathway. "The Belgians are just about to take us to the college at Mudende, where we'll join the school staff. They have a convoy waiting to evacuate us under guard to Gisenyi and then across the border, to Zaire."

She glanced back through the door into her house. "It breaks my heart to leave my Rwandan friends and workers, and my animals, too."

"I understand. I..." Kristen stopped in mid-sentence as one of the Belgian soldiers snatched up the two suitcases and carried them to a van. With a careless swing, he tossed each one in turn up onto the roof rack, then secured them with elastic ropes.

Rosalind stepped back in surprise. "You have no baggage? My Lord, did you have to leave that suddenly?"

"We had camping equipment for the first night but lost everything halfway here when we ran away from the Interahamwe. It's a long story."

"Well then, come on, my dears. Sit with me in the van and tell me the whole tale. We have so much to talk about, don't we?"

It was fully dark when their van pulled away from the cottage. Rosalind dabbed at her eyes with a handkerchief, and no one spoke comfort for there was none. People were weeping all over Rwanda.

Some ten minutes later the van pulled onto the ground of the missionary college and sat waiting behind busses that were already loading students and teachers.

"Forgive me, my dears," Rosalind said, and blew her nose into her handkerchief. "Here I am sniveling over the loss of a home, but you've suffered just as much, and you haven't told me yet how you got away."

Kristen began the narration of their escape. "We were on the mountain taking a gorilla orphan back to her family. We wanted to see if one of the other females would accept her, and that meant camping out for a night with the gorillas."

"Sleeping with the gorillas. Oh, that does sound adventurous." Rosalind cleared her throat, obviously glad to be talking about something other than loss. "Did they accept her?"

"Yes, and we were overjoyed. It had been so difficult to get her back from the traffickers who'd stolen her, and we were afraid it might all be in vain. In fact, on the way back to Karisoke, we met the trafficker who tried to kill us for confiscating her. It took us awhile to...uh...get away from him. Anyhow, when we reached Karisoke, it was a killing field. All our men and their families..." Her voice broke.

Dana finished the story. "We still had our camping things, which made it possible to stay in the forest, because from that moment on, we were on the run."

"And then you thought of me? After so many years?"

"I did." Kristen cleared her throat and resumed talking. "Remember Dian's masks?"

"Oh, yes. They were dreadful. I suppose they worked for her, but they seemed so evil. I know it was play-acting, but it brought out the worst in her."

"Well, one of them saved our lives. Indirectly. We ran across it posted in the forest. The one with the bulging red eyes that you particularly hated. It survived all those years. Of course, it reminded me of you, and we couldn't think of any better solution than to try to reach you."

Rosalind clasped her hands in the prayer position. "Imagine that. Saved by one of Dian's monsters. I bet she'd be pleased to know it was still haunting the Virungas long after she was gone."

Kristen offered a wan smile. "Not just her masks. She left relics and souvenirs all over Karisoke that haunt us. She never rested when she was alive, and I'm certain she's not at peace now."

At the front of the van, two more people climbed in and the driver started the motor.

Rosalind's hands closed into fists at her chin. "No, she surely would not be."

CHAPTER TWENTY-TWO

Dana had never been in Gisenyi, and it made no impression on her now. She knew it bordered on Lake Kivu and boasted a number of luxurious mansions on the lakefront—including that of the corrupt politician Zigirazo—but the town itself seemed little different from Ruhengeri, with nondescript one- and two-story houses separated by wide, dusty streets. And now, at night, while they fled, the town seemed ominous.

On the outskirts, the vehicles from Mungongo and Mudende joined cars and trucks from elsewhere, marked by various European flags. They lined up, one group behind the other, as if preparing for an international parade, then waited.

Finally, when the count of vehicles seemed to satisfy the forces in charge, the convoy moved out and snaked its way through the streets of Gisenyi. Its goal was the international border that separated Gisenyi from Congolese Goma.

As they feared, the Rwandans had thrown up a roadblock. Uniformed soldiers surrounded by gangs of young men with machetes brought the convoy to a halt.

The crowds that gathered on both sides of the street, jeering and cursing at the fleeing foreigners, exacerbated the already tense atmosphere. Outside Dana and Kristen's van, individual men and women rushed forward to pound on the windows.

Dana first thought they were raging at them, but Rosalind called out, "Dear Lord. They're begging us to take them along."

More rushed toward them now, women with wide terrified eyes, holding up their babies to the car windows.

"Why can't we take them?" Rosalind called to the driver in French. "Any of them. Even just the children. Leaving them is a death sentence." She broke into tears again.

"Impossible, madam," he called back over his shoulder. "We have orders to evacuate only our own people."

The convoy started again, edging forward in fits and starts, but each time they stopped, people threw themselves at the vehicles.

It was excruciating, and Dana's tears welled up as well. Half the people on the street wanted to kill them, and the other half was desperate to join them.

When their van finally reached the checkpoint, Dana saw the reason for the delay. Every vehicle was being searched.

The car just ahead of them had obviously tried to smuggle out a Rwandan, perhaps a houseman or an employee. But soldiers hauled him out by his neck and dragged to the side of the street, where a crowd set upon him. Dana looked away, physically sick.

"Aren't the UN troops going to do anything to stop the killers?" one of the other passengers asked.

The driver shook his head. "This is their country, and we've been ordered not to intervene. Besides, we're outnumbered. A few days ago, the ten Belgian peacekeepers who were guarding the prime minister were tortured and killed."

"But why don't our governments send more troops? If ever there was an international crisis, this is one."

"I don't know. You'll have to ask someone in a higher pay grade," the driver said, bringing the discussion to an end. Rosalind buried her face in her hands.

Finally they crossed the blockade into Goma. They were in the Congo now, though it called itself Zaire, a country as politically explosive as Rwanda, only just not at that moment. The passengers all fell silent.

❖

The convoy wound through streets that seemed shabbier than those in Gisenyi and drew onto a wide square. One or two individual cars turned off and left the cortege, presumably people who had contacts or friends in the Congo. The bus with teachers from the missionary college also separated and drove off. Toward the airport, Dana guessed.

The others, including Rosalind's van, stayed with the convoy until it pulled onto an open field, where they climbed out.

It was not a welcoming sight. On a grassless expanse the size of a soccer field, some hundred white, half-cylinder tents stood in rows, like so many oil drums half buried in dirt. The letters UNHCR were stamped in blue on each one. Two larger square tents some distance away carried signs: LATRINE. Spotlights on poles at the four corners illuminated the entire field. It looked like a concentration camp.

"What does UNHCR stand for?" she asked their driver. "Uh..." He had to think for a moment. "United Nations High Commissioner for Refugees, I think. Yeah, that sounds right. They've just set the units up, so your group will be the first." He slid out of the driver's seat and began unloading whatever luggage still remained on the roof of the van. "Four to a tent," he announced, "and you can pick whichever one you like."

"I'll take the one farthest from the latrine," Rosalind said and began dragging her own suitcases toward one of the half cylinders. Passengers in the several other vans chose tents in a cluster close by.

"Are they going to distribute any food or blankets?" Dana called after the soldier as he climbed back into his van.

"The camp's just opened and none of that has arrived yet. In a couple of days, probably. But water's over there." He nodded toward a green tank truck at the periphery of the camp, then drove away.

Rosalind seemed to collapse into herself, like a puppet whose strings had gone slack, and Dana recalled her age. "Give me that," she said, picking up one of the suitcases and marching toward the designated tent. Kristen took the other one and linked her arm into Rosalind's. "Well, we have each other. And tomorrow, we'll be out of here."

"Yes, you're right, my dear. I was just struck with a bit of self-pity. And it's true. This is a refugee camp, but we aren't refugees the way the people are who'll be coming here. Even if we've lost everything, we have resources, money, influential friends. We mustn't feel sorry for ourselves."

At the tent they dropped onto the ground with their baggage, and Rosalind managed a weak smile. "And what's more, I have food for us." She opened one of the suitcases. Throwing back a protective layer of blanket, she revealed paper packages of flatbread, salami, and hard cheese, and a bag of small tomatoes.

"How wonderfully generous of you," Kristen said. "For our part, we'll provide the entertainment." She held up her transistor radio. "As long as the batteries hold out."

Ravenous from the two-day hike fueled only by wild-celery pith and melons, Dana ate gratefully while Kristen tuned the radio to the local station. The reports were even worse than they'd anticipated. A massacre at the Nyarubuye Catholic Church, where a thousand Tutsi had taken refuge. That they followed the same religion had not stopped the attackers from first tossing grenades into the building, then entering to finish off the victims with guns and machetes.

"It still seems so unreal," Dana said. "Even though we were almost killed, it doesn't help me grasp the larger scale of things." She finished off the last of her crackers and washed them down with some of Rosalind's bottled water.

"Almost killed? Oh, my goodness, dare I ask what happened to you?"

"It's too long a story, really," Kristen answered. "Essentially an attempt by a man who'd already killed some gorillas. Funny how easy it is to take the next step and kill people as well. Anyhow, we…uh… dissuaded him."

"Well, you were very lucky," Rosalind concluded as she tucked away the uneaten cheese and bread, and shook out the blanket. "In any case, we're safe here for the night. I packed only one blanket, but since the ground is so dusty, I think we should sleep on it rather than under it. We can try to stay warm with each other."

"I think we can manage that for one night," Kristen said.

"What are your plans for tomorrow?" Rosalind looked back and forth at them.

Kristen glanced toward Dana. "We haven't had time to make any plans, other than getting out of danger. We're at the mercy of the UN right now, but I suppose we'll try to get back to the States. What about you?"

"Oh, I have friends in Burundi who'll put me up for a while. From there I'll contact people back in the US. In fact, I don't *want* to leave Rwanda. It's been my home for so many years. I had to leave my dogs and my cat and my parrots."

Kristen nodded wistfully. "We were looking after a few dozen gorillas. I can't bear to think what will happen to them now."

"The same thing that happened to them before Karisoke existed," Rosalind observed mournfully.

Dana shook her head. "I keep struggling to make sense of the whole thing. I mean, what caused this sudden savagery. It's almost as if something cracked the veneer of civilization and the evil bubbled up from below like lava." She stared into the middle distance, then added, "And I can't help but wonder if Dian's murder wasn't a miniature version of that."

Kristen looked puzzled. "I don't really see a connection. Dian was almost certainly killed by a corrupt politician."

Rosalind tilted her head. "I think Dana's right."

"How so?" Kristen's puzzlement took on a frown.

"My dear, when you've been here as long as I have, you appreciate the historical context. Which is to say, that for all her good intentions, Dian upset the balance of power in Rwandan politics, and it exploded in her face. Moreover, you can't simply assert that Dian was good and righteous because she favored the animals, and her murderers were evil because they didn't and got her out of the way."

"Excuse me," Kristen said, the half-frown becoming a scowl. "But that's exactly what I assert. Dian was right to save the gorillas, and her murderers were vicious bastards."

Rosalind slid onto her side and rested her weight on her elbow. "It's not a question of who's right or wrong. For centuries, the Rwandans hunted their wildlife, for meat or for profit. Then this white woman arrived with the notions of sustainability and animal rights— concepts completely foreign to them. And when she tried to force those ideas, with her masks and her pistol, they killed her."

Now Dana scowled as well. "So what has that got to do with the massacres going on right now? You can't blame those on white interference."

"Not directly, no. But the *umuzungu* exploited Africa in general for a century and in Rwanda upset the balance among the three tribes by depriving the Batwa of hunting grounds and by making the Tutsi their agents."

Kristen wasn't convinced. "Perhaps so, but the hard, unsentimental reality is that the Rwandans are subject to the same pressure as the rest of the world—overpopulation and destruction of native species. If white people like us must convince them of it, then so be it."

"Isn't that a little racist? The white man knows better?"

"I don't know the answer to that. But if I have to choose between a sort of Darwinian survival of the fittest species or Dian's program of sustainability and animal rights, I stand with Dian."

Rosalind sighed and got to her feet. "I think we'll have to settle for amicable disagreement. And if you'll excuse me, this romantic, sentimental old traditionalist has to use the facilities. I shudder at the thought, but I guess we're lucky to be the first, eh?" She struggled to get to her feet and plodded from the tent toward the camp latrines.

Kristen stretched out on the blanket and Dana curled up next to her, drawing in her warmth. "I like her," Dana said. "She obviously loves Rwanda, warts and all, and you have to admire that. She's also the toughest little old lady I've ever met."

"That she is, and she's right about being a traditionalist. She wants Rwanda to be what it was when she arrived thirty years ago. No matter, she's a survivor and will do well wherever she goes after this."

"I wonder if *we* will. I mean, we have to go back too, don't we?"

"Yes, we do. At least until this is over. But we can stay together. I know people in New York, at the Bronx Zoo. With a recommendation from the Leaky Foundation, I'm sure I can get some kind of part-time work there."

Dana winced. "That's not what I meant. You've forgotten that I'm a fugitive."

"Oh, God. I'm sorry. I know you're afraid, but listen. The police can't still be looking for you. Why would they even suspect you? And even if they do, they've no way to trace you to Africa and back. They're not as brilliant as they're portrayed on television, you know. We'll get a place in the Bronx, near the zoo, and you won't even come up on their radar."

Dana scratched her scalp, feeling the grit of too many unwashed days in hiding and on the run. Maybe Kristen was right, and the sense of being unwashed simply added to her hopelessness. "You're pretty sure about this zoo thing."

"Yes, I am. The curator of gorillas in the Bronx Zoo is a friend. I helped him get a grant from the Leaky Foundation, so he sort of owes me. I know he'll find something for me to do, especially if I don't ask for a lot of money. And for your part, you just have to lie low until things cool down in Rwanda."

"So it wouldn't be permanent, would it? Just until we can go back." Dana clutched at the straw. "Yeah, I can see doing that."

"It'll all work out. I promise. Let's just get some sleep and figure out how to get out of this camp tomorrow."

Dana lay down and, with her face resting again on Kristen's shoulder, she mumbled agreement. At that moment, Rosalind returned.

"All right, break it up, you two. I see you've warmed a spot for me that will do nicely for an old lady," she said as she wiggled between them.

❖

Dana awoke when she felt Rosalind slide away from her side, and she stared up at the white tent roof, reconstructing reality: the camp, the convoy, and the massacres happening behind them in Rwanda. She also remembered the trap she'd sensed closing around her the night before.

But something had happened while she slept, as if her subconscious had continued weighing duty and responsibility against hope and happiness, and had reached a conclusion. For the first time since the beginning of all the slaughters, she felt nearly at peace.

Kristen began to stir, and Dana rose on one elbow to watch her. "Good morning, darling," she whispered.

"Ummm. Kristen rubbed her face. "Good morning yourself. Where's Rosalind?"

"Latrine, I suppose. You know how it is for old folks."

Kristen turned on her side and reached for Dana's hand. "You seem in a better mood than last night."

"I am. I've made a decision."

Kristen sat up. "That sounds…um…decisive. To do what?"

"Hey, you two." Rosalind's head peeked through the entrance. "Ready for breakfast?"

"After we make a quick trip to where you've just been, definitely," Dana said. "Why don't you start the bacon and eggs while you're waiting for us?"

Rosalind snorted. "Sure thing. But hurry up. I've got news."

Outside the tent and with boots laced up, Dana took a deep breath. Even in the grim setting of a bare refugee camp, the symbol of the desperation of an entire people, the fresh morning air gave her a sense of hope.

Kristen took her arm. "Tell me your decision."

"I'm going back to New York with you, of course, but I'm going to stop running away."

Kristen halted. "You mean you're going to turn yourself in? To the police?"

Dana pulled her forward again. "Yes. I have to. I told you I don't regret doing it, only that I have to hide. Being with you and taking care of the gorillas, that's given me something to live for, something to be honest and open and clean for. After all the bloodshed I've seen, I don't want to be counted among the revenge murderers. If I go to the police and explain, they'll still arrest me, but then it becomes something…well…honorable, not something to run away from. And I can stop being a fugitive."

Kristen slid her arm around Dana's back. "I understand. Besides, you said those men were carrying guns. I'm sure you can argue it was self-defense."

"They may not see it that way. But whatever happens, I'm going through with it."

Kristen stroked Dana's cheek. I know you're frightened, and I am too, but I'll be there with you the whole time, whatever the outcome. Never forget that." She gazed at Dana for a long moment, then kissed her on the cheek. "But first, I have to pee."

After seeing to that basic need, they marched over to the tanker where UN Relief operators had set up a long trough for washing. The water was ice cold, but at least they could do a cursory scrub of face and neck.

Returning to the tent, they found Rosalind had packed the blanket, and on top of the suitcase she had set out a breakfast of the last crackers and cheese.

"Eat up, my dears. While I was out, I talked to one of the UN people. They expect masses of refugees in the next days, so they want us to move along. The American Embassy has arranged a chartered flight to take US citizens to New York and Washington, and they have a van waiting to give us a ride to the airport. I'm going to Burundi myself, but you'll be able to get out on the charter."

Kristen nodded quietly. "So, there it is. We're saved. At the cost of...everything we've worked for."

Rosalind chewed her portion of the cheese, obviously more hopeful than she'd been the night before. "In a way, yes. But Rwanda won't disappear from the face of the earth. The war will be over one day, and you can come back to it. I'm sure I will."

"Oh, I'm certain we will too, for the gorillas," Kristen said. "I hate to abandon them this way."

Rosalind nodded. "You're a lot like Dian, you know? Strong-willed and intelligent. I suppose that's why she hired you. But you have something in your character she didn't have. Flexibility, the sense of when to bend and when to stand up."

She crumpled the paper that had held the cheese. "And now it's time to stand up."

Kristen also got to her feet and patted her side pocket. "We don't have any luggage, just the clothes on our back and this." She drew out the revolver. "It belonged to Dian, but I'm not so 'strong-willed' that I want to keep carrying it. It did save our lives, but I'm sure they won't let us on the flight with it. Would you put it in your suitcase and keep it as a remembrance of her?"

"Yes, of course. Though I can't promise where it'll end up. I'm homeless myself at the moment." She slid the gun into the suitcase amid the folds of clothing and clicked it shut again. "All right then, let's take advantage of our white privilege and get on that van. We have miles to go before we sleep again."

Their white privilege, in fact, became blatant as they reached the entrance of the camp. Busses and trucks were pulling in with African refugees, and behind them others were streaming in by foot from all directions, men with wheelbarrows or carts piled with belongings, women with babies on their backs or staggering next to them. Tutsis, probably, Dana thought, though by now surely the RPF had sent some Hutus fleeing as well. Their land was on fire, and hundreds of thousands were fleeing somewhere…anywhere.

Two UN trailer trucks pulled up and began unloading more tents and equipment, and behind them a small white van waited. The van of the privileged. It already held four passengers.

Rosalind handed over her two suitcases to be loaded on the luggage rack, and the three of them boarded. One of the passengers, an elderly gentleman who still wore a clean white shirt, greeted her by name as she sat down, and they began to talk. The conversation indicated he was connected with the missionary school. They too had come with good intentions, to save souls, not gorillas, but they too had been rendered irrelevant.

Her hand brushing against Kristen's, Dana stared out the window with a mix of emotions: relief that they were escaping the carnage, anxiety at what awaited her in New York, and a profound sorrow at leaving Mwelu and all the dead at Karisoke.

"I don't understand this," the white-shirt man said, interrupting her reverie. "This paroxysm of vengeance."

Paroxysm of vengeance, Dana thought. Wasn't that what had gotten her into trouble in the first place?

CHAPTER TWENTY-THREE

New York
April 20, 1994

Dana watched as Kristen tugged her shirt straight before the mirror at the front door. "You look great. Besides, you've lectured dozens of times, and you're already a star, no matter how you're dressed."

"I can't help being nervous. It's my first day on the job, and I have to prove that I can charm kids. Completely new skill for me."

"But they know who you are. All those years running Karisoke have given you stellar credentials as a primatologist, not to mention a certain Indiana Jones glamor. You'll dazzle them. The men will swoon and the kids will adore you."

"Sweet of you to say, but I'm still grateful that David was able to invent this part-time position for me. Lecturer in the education department of a zoo is not quite the same as heading a major research facility or fund-raising. And it's important I get this right. The income pays the rent on this apartment, and I'd like him to consider me for a full-time position. Assuming we stay in New York." Her voice trailed off and she turned toward the door.

Dana let the silence linger. She knew Kristen's sojourn in New York depended completely on her own trial and sentence for murder. But for that she had to surrender, and she hadn't had the courage to do that. Not yet.

She leaned past Kristen and opened the door for her. "You look smashing. Now go and let the public see how wonderful you are." She kissed Kristen in passing and closed the door softly behind her. Then she took a long breath. Today was The Day for her, also.

She had delayed surrender because getting their feet on the ground in New York seemed paramount. The job, the apartment, the reporting and coordination with the Leaky Foundation and other sponsors of Karisoke—all took priority, and even then their struggles had seemed trivial compared to the ongoing catastrophe they had left behind them.

Every day they had monitored the events in Rwanda, had followed the accelerating genocide. The Interahamwe was no longer killing by the score, or even by the hundreds. In mid-April they had lured over 12,000 Tutsi into a soccer stadium in Kibuye, then blocked their escape and slaughtered them with hand grenades, rifle shot, and machetes. The next day the report came of an even worse massacre in the mountainous region of Bisesero, where the Republican Guard had aided the local Interahamwe in eradiating the resistors, estimated to be some 50,000.

Paroxysm of vengeance. The nameless missionary had been right. As in her hideous dream, all of Rwanda had become a vast cellar of blood, and for her it had changed the meaning of murder.

In the midst of their repatriation, Kristen hadn't reminded her of the promised surrender, and Dana was grateful for her sensitivity. But now that Kristen had a source of income—and thus a means to stay in New York—it was time for Dana to live up to her part of the plan.

She took the Number 2 subway line to 125th and Lenox Avenue and began the walk. The late-April day was warm and the trip along Harlem's commercial street pleasant, or could have been. She tried to window-shop at the endless discount shops along the way, but her increasing dread kept her from concentrating. On what would likely be her last day "outside," she was suddenly filled with nostalgia for the freedom to shop.

Too soon, she reached Frederick Douglass Boulevard and had to turn left. In a few blocks, the dull-brown building of the 28th precinct became visible, and her stomach began to hurt. Perhaps she should have waited a day and asked Kristen to accompany her.

Breathing through a dry mouth and with her heart pounding, she tugged open the heavy door to the reception area, half expecting armed officers to surround her the way the Rwandan soldiers had done. But the place looked rather like the Department of Motor Vehicles, with clerks behind various counters and half a dozen people waiting in an alcove on spindly chairs. The air smelled faintly of disinfectant and old clothes.

The sergeant at the reception desk was a black woman in uniform. She was reading something in her ledger and didn't look up. "Good morning." Dana began in an unpleasantly high voice. Still no reaction from the woman. "I...uh...I'd like to talk to a detective, please." Finally the sergeant raised her head.

"And what would this be in regard to?" she asked with a mixture of boredom and condescension. "Would you like to report a crime?" She reached for a clipboard and a ballpoint pen.

"Uh, no." Damn, she'd rehearsed her speech in her mind a dozen times. Why was it all falling apart now? "I...uh...have information regarding a homicide committed last...uh...December. Can I talk to the detective who worked on that?"

With lowered head, the desk sergeant glared upward at her, as if over the rim of invisible glasses. The expression was of controlled exasperation from having to deal with an imbecile. "A homicide. In December."

"Yes, I think the date was December 15. About then."

"In Harlem?"

"Yes, ma'am." She declined to give the street name, not sure why. Perhaps because she already disliked this woman.

"And what is your connection to this crime? How is it that you want information about it?"

"You misunderstood. I don't *want* information. I *have* information and would like to talk to the detective in charge."

"Take a seat. I'll try to get someone for you," the desk sergeant said in a monotone.

Dana obeyed, her heart pounding somewhat less than it had when she arrived. She hadn't reckoned with such resistance. She took a seat on one of the plastic chairs and waited, glancing around at the shabby interior of the station. Police precincts on television seemed filled with colorful and courageous people energetically bent on solving complicated and horrible crimes. But if any such individuals were present, they escaped detection. All around her were depressed-looking people, obese women, elderly, disheveled, and unshaven men. Occasionally a uniformed officer came in or left, always unhurried. Others sat behind the counter typing into computers. Perhaps it was just a quiet day in the precinct.

Some fifteen minutes later a uniformed officer approached and stood over her. "Can I help you?"

Dana repeated her announcement, this time without the pauses, only to listen to the exact same questions. As if in a comedy routine, he even repeated the order. "Wait here. I'll try to get someone for you."

Now she was getting annoyed. She was about to confess to a double homicide, and she couldn't get anyone's attention. What the hell good were the New York City Police? She considered leaving. Obviously no one would pursue her. No one cared about her or, apparently, about the crime. She drummed her fingers on her knees. *I'll count to a hundred, and if no one shows any interest in what I have to say by then, I'm out of here.*

She'd reached forty-seven when a second black man stood over her, this one about forty-five and in civilian clothes. He held out his hand. "I'm Detective McIntyre. How can I help you?"

Dana stood up and, for the third time, recited, "I have information regarding a homicide in December of last year. Can we talk some place quieter than here?"

"If you wish." He led her through the noisy open space in front of the reception counter along a corridor to an office. She was relieved to see that it was an office and not an interrogation room. The ones she'd seen on television were rather frightening. She didn't even see any interior windows that could have held one-way glass.

But as they stepped in, she noticed a small television on a shelf overhead with the CBS news report running. She halted just inside the doorway as video footage showed dead bodies lying alongside a road, then jumped to endless rows of white UNHCR tents. Even with the sound off, she recognized the refugee camp at Goma.

"Please sit down," he said, but she remained standing, staring at the screen. It was what she'd been watching for all week, though the US news service was very slow at revealing video coverage of the killing.

"I was just there," she said spontaneously. "In that camp, but we got out after one day. The people who came in after us were Tutsi. The dead bodies on the road, too. There must be hundreds of thousands by now." Finally she obeyed and sat down on a chair in front of his desk.

"I don't understand. You're saying you were just in Rwanda?"

No doubt it was the fear wound up so tightly inside of her. Suddenly the Rwandan tragedy seemed vastly more important than her confession, and now, with someone to hear them, her words poured out in a stream. "Yes. I was studying gorillas in the mountains when the president's plane crashed and the slaughter started. We had no idea they'd actually come up into the Virungas, but they did. They butchered all of our staff, and my friend and I survived only because we hid in the forest for a couple of days. Finally we escaped through Gisenyi, and a UN convoy took us to Goma in Zaire. To the refugee camp they're showing on the news. Except it was empty then. Now it's full. Of Tutsis, I suppose, and maybe a few Hutus who wouldn't cooperate with the Interahamwe."

The detective stared at her in obvious disbelief, but she had merely paused for breath. "And nobody tried to stop them. The UN forces were recalled. And when President Clinton and the Europeans finally sent in a few troops, it was just to evacuate white people. And on and on it went. We saw Hutus stop people at roadblocks, and anyone with Tutsi on their ID cards—women, children—they hacked to pieces."

"And you were just there? How did you manage to get out?" he asked, sounding incredulous.

"I told you. I was in the Virungas. At Karisoke, a gorilla-research center. And when some of them came up to kill us, we hid until we could hike over to Gisenyi, where the Americans evacuated us along with some missionaries."

"Virungas. Interahamwe. Roadblocks. You've given me more information in one minute than they've broadcast all week on television. And I can't believe you were at Karisoke."

"How do you know about Karisoke?" she asked, the surprise now on her side.

"My daughter just did a report for her tenth-grade science class on Dian Fossey. Did you know Fossey?"

"No, she was before my time. But my friend, the one I escaped with, was her assistant. I never thought I'd meet a policeman who knew about Dian Fossey."

"Well, I *had* never heard of her. But when you live with a chatty fifteen-year-old, you go with the flow. All she talked about for the last week was Karisoke." He frowned slightly. "But this can't be the information you came here to give me, Miss..uh…you never told me your name."

"Uh, no. Sorry. My name is Dana Norland. So you're the detective in charge of the homicide last December 15th?"

"One of them. How do you know about this case?"

"Well, I was, uh…there when it happened."

He looked puzzled for a moment, then said, "Just a second. Let's make sure we're talking about the same case." He typed for a few minutes on his keyboard, peering at the monitor, mumbling to himself. "Let's see." He ran down the dates "December 2, burglary, assault; December 3, burglary, indecent exposure, armed robbery, breaking and entering; December 4, assault, rape. Then he fell silent as he worked his way through the days leading up to December 15th.

"Here we are. Double homicide. On 118th Street. What can you tell me that we don't already know?"

"Um…well, I can tell you the dead men were pornographers, really vicious ones, and they made videos of killing animals."

"Yes, we know that. How is it that *you* know it?"

"Well, one of the animals they killed was mine."

"I'm sorry to hear it. Then you probably aren't mourning the death of his killers."

"No, I'm not. But I know who killed them."

"We do, too. We caught him, convicted him, and closed the case."

"You do? You did?" She heard how high her voice was again and tried to keep from appearing astonished.

"Yes, though it was a strange case. In fact it was the coroner's assistant, or, more precisely, the coroner's assistant's assistant, who helped us out on this one. I was working on three cases, so she did a lot of the legwork. Just a moment. I think she's in the precinct right now. Let me call her and she can tell you how it went."

He picked up the phone and punched a few buttons. "Reilly, could you come into my office?"

He hung up, and taking his pen between his first and second fingers, he tapped it on his desktop while they waited. "We don't usually share this kind of information with the public. It just confuses things. But for a friend of Dian Fossey, I can make an exception."

A few minutes later the door opened and a young woman entered. "This is Megan Reilly, our coroner's assistant's assistant."

Dana blinked in confusion. The person who stood before her looked vaguely familiar, but it was hardly possible that they'd met. She had no friends in New York, and the twenty-something woman looked more like a college student than a coroner's assistant.

College student. A light went on. It was Blond Ponytail...without the ponytail. Her hair was cut short and combed stylishly, and she stared back in equal puzzlement.

"I know you," Dana said. "You were at Kristen Wolfe's presentation at Columbia last winter. I thought you were a student about to graduate."

"I was, but a couple of days later, I was hired here."

"Miss Reilly was made liaison with the Medical Examiner's office and got involved in the case because, well, we were short-handed. It was the Christmas holidays and half the staff was on vacation. In the end, she was indispensible in tracking down the felon."

Deeply confused, Dana forced neutrality on her face and nodded faintly. "So you caught the murderer."

Megan took a seat and crossed one leg over the other, a posture of relaxed confidence. "Yep. Guy named Chongo who resented them doing business in his hood. A commercial rival, so to speak."

"We know of several snuff pornographers currently in a turf war in Harlem and the Bronx," McIntyre interjected. "It's a lucrative business, and sometimes one takes out the other for cutting into his profits."

"You mean lots of people make videos like that? There's a market?" Dana was suddenly sick.

"Well, three less, now." Megan snorted.

Detective McIntyre added, "We think maybe this guy had a partner who led the patrol officers on a wild-goose chase while

Chongo finished the victims off. We never tracked down the other one, but forensics proved the fatal shots were from Chongo's gun, so a conviction was straightforward."

"Well, you're the forensics specialist, so you have the last word," she said amiably to Megan. "And you're not interested in the fourth guy?"

Megan shrugged. "Not really. If he's in the business, he'll probably show up eventually. If not, we don't much care. The investigation ended with a good conviction, and we saw no reason to go any further. Two slimy bastards were taken out by a third slimy bastard, who did us all a favor. And he's doing thirty to life."

Dana studied the young assistant's assistant as long as she dared. She remembered her remark to Kristen at the Columbia lecture. *I keep finding conflicts between legal justice and moral justice.* Did she recall how breathless Dana had been, and that she'd arrived only at the very end of the presentation? And still made no connection with a crime committed a few blocks away on the same afternoon? But then, her field was forensics, not investigation, a lab geek doing the legwork for detectives on vacation. And then fate had interposed another slimy bastard to finish off the first two. Her mind reeled.

And then she remembered another remark Blond Ponytail had made.

"Hey, how's your old dog?"

Megan all but twinkled. "How nice you remembered. She's doing well and shows no sign of imminent departure. So I guess it'll be awhile before I take off for Africa. You know how it is when you love an animal."

"Yes, I do," Dana said solemnly. "And that reminds me." She looked toward McIntyre. "Um…could you tell me what was done with the remains? Of the animals, I mean."

He frowned slightly. "That's not really my department. But I'm pretty sure city ordinances would require them to be incinerated. Cremated, if you wish."

"I see," she repeated, running out of steam. "Well, then, I guess I've taken up enough of your time, Detective McIntyre, Ms. Reilly. Thank you for indulging me, and I wish you a pleasant day." She stood up smiling and turned toward the door.

"Just a moment, Miss Norland."

She froze, cringing. Stupid to think she would get off so easily.

"You say you worked at Karisoke?" McIntyre asked.

Dana rebuilt her polite smile and turned to face him again. "Yes, but only for a few months, before the genocide began. My friend has worked there since Dian Fossey's time."

"Your friend, is she here in New York, too?"

Where was this going? The last thing she wanted was to bring Kristen into the case. But it was too late to lie.

"Um…yes. She works part-time at the Bronx Zoo, in connection with the gorillas, of course."

"Could I…would it be imposing or out of line if I asked to meet her? Not me, actually, but my daughter. She's really crazy for gorillas right now, and to meet someone who worked with Dian Fossey would be fantastic for her. But only if your friend wouldn't mind."

The release of tension made her slightly giddy, but it wouldn't do to laugh. "I'm sure she'd be delighted. Her name is Kristen Wolfe, and she'll be giving her next gorilla talk on Saturday. Why don't you bring your daughter to the zoo then?"

He squinted at his desk calendar. "That's the 23rd, isn't it? Should work out fine. We'll be there. Please tell Miss Wolfe she'll have a young admirer in the audience."

After warm handshakes with McIntyre and his mysterious assistant's assistant, Dana strode through the dreary reception area and out the door onto Frederick Douglass Boulevard. She stood for a moment on the sidewalk in front of the station, slightly stunned. So much anxiety, and now, with a simple declaration of "the case is closed," she was exonerated.

Was she still a murderer? In her heart, yes, but a righteous one, though in the eyes of the law, she wasn't. How very strange. She wondered what Plato would think.

She stared up at the blue April sky and took a deep breath of free air. As she began to walk her eyes filled with tears.

CHAPTER TWENTY-FOUR

Saturday, April 23

Kristen waved her employee's pass at the guard and, linking arms with Dana, passed through the Asia Gate of the Bronx Zoo. They strolled along the border of the newly created African Plains field, and she bumped Dana's shoulder. "Happy?"

"God, yes. It feels so good to be free, really free. Every day since we came back to New York I had a heart attack at every patrol car, every cop on the street. But now I can breathe again." She gazed at the "plain" where various predator and prey species roamed giving the appearance of freedom, though, to the frustration of the predators and the relief of the herbivores, they were invisibly separated.

"I'm happy, too. I can't tell you how terrified I was that I'd lose you. How could we make a life together if you were in a maximum-security prison for the next twenty years?" She shook her head, as if to dispel the terrible thought. "We both anguished so much for nothing. Thank God for the incompetence of the NYPD, which was so happy to have a perp-in-the-hand, they ignored the one in the bush."

"I've been thinking about that, and I'm not so sure it was incompetence. Of course the detective just seemed happy to close the case, but the medical assistant—Megan was her name—I think she figured out what happened. Fate added this Chongo guy, who should have been irrelevant, but she presented the case to the detectives in a way that would focus on him and not on me."

"But why would she want to protect you?"

"Do you remember her from the Columbia lecture? She was the blond woman you gave your address to."

"Yes, I remember vaguely. A student in forensics, wasn't she?"

She was, and she had a dog. That's why I blurted out that I'd lost one, and even mentioned his breed and color. She was the medical assistant's assistant—yeah, that was her title, and she helped investigate the case. Megan, to use her name, knew what monsters the dead men were, and she knew I'd just lost a dog. It wouldn't have taken much to put it all together and realize that I did it, and that the dog was the reason."

"Especially not if she saw Nikki and figured he was yours."

"Exactly. I think she was not only *not* incompetent but was *so* good at her job, she was able to control the direction of the case."

"A victory of justice over law. If only the same thing would happen in Rwanda."

"What do you mean?"

"Our government knows what's happening in Rwanda—it's all over the news—but they refuse to call it genocide because then international law would require them to intervene. They call it intertribal violence and close their eyes. From what I've been reading, it was President Clinton himself who washed his hands of the UN mission and urged its withdrawal. That's legal, of course, but despicable."

They arrived at the giraffe building, where the animals, two adults and an adolescent, had just come swaying out into the sun. The doe-eyed creatures gazed down at them with giraffe condescension, then turned their attention to their fodder. Dana found the discussion of genocide in the midst of such serenity hard on the brain and could add nothing.

She smiled up at them, then grew serious again. "Dian would be horrified. Do you plan to talk about her in the presentation? She's rather important to the plot."

"Yes, of course. She's where the plot began. Unfortunately, I had to leave all my slides of her behind when we fled Rwanda. I've contacted National Geographic for photos of Dian and Digit, but for now, stock gorilla images will have to do."

"Do you think we can ever go back to them, our gorillas?"

"God, I hope so. I can't imagine abandoning them. I also owe it to Senweke to find out if any of his family are left and, if so, to help them in some way."

"Yes, and speaking of owing, I want to contact Emily and Tony Bailey, the people I was staying with last December. Unfortunately, I lied and said I was going to England, but they're kind, forgiving people, and if they take a shine to you, maybe we'll both get invited back to St. John's for the Blessing of the Animals."

Kristen glanced dreamily at her. How lovely she was when she looked that way, with half-closed eyes. "Animals in church. Charming. Do they have gorillas?"

Dana snickered. "Can you imagine a silverback lumbering down toward the altar? But you'd like it. The sermon was good, about responsibility toward animals, and the concert mass was about nature. New Agey stuff. Nice, though. Nature needs all the friends it can get."

She leaned against Kristen, sliding an arm around her back. "Strange, to be back in New York with you again. I'm even carrying your slide carousel, just like before."

They arrived at the gorilla exhibit and the court where benches had been laid out in a semicircle. Some two-dozen people had already gathered, and others were meandering in leading children by the hand. One of the visitors looked familiar.

Detective McIntyre spotted them at the same moment and came forward offering his hand. "Pleased to see you again, Ms. Norland, and to meet you too, Ms. Wolfe. This is my daughter Angela."

A girl who Dana knew was fifteen, but looked more like eighteen, stepped forward. Tall and angular, she bore a strong resemblance to her father, with a narrow face and long jaw. She immediately thought Tutsi, then felt ashamed at falling into the racist trap. The girl was dressed in cargo pants and a sort of jungle shirt, with epaulets, but what struck Dana most was her hair, which she wore in a single long braid over her shoulder. The last time she'd seen hair like that was in a photograph of Dian Fossey.

"Nice to meet you," Angela said, beaming. "I'm really looking forward to your talk. We've been studying mountain gorillas, and I want to learn more about them."

Kristen smiled back. "Unfortunately, the gorillas here at the zoo aren't mountain gorillas."

"I know. These are *Gorilla gorilla gorilla*, rather than *Gorilla beringei beringei*, which are critically endangered, and very few zoos have them. And these lowland-gorilla populations are spread over five or six countries while *Gorilla beringei beringei* live only in the Virunga mountain range."

Kristen chuckled. "Well, you've really done your homework. Good for you." She glanced at her watch and moved toward the stage.

"Oh, it's not my homework. I love gorillas." Angela's speech seemed to speed up as she kept pace with her. "Scientists say that the chimpanzee is closer related to us than the gorilla, but I don't believe it. All you have to do is look in their eyes, and you know they have feelings just like us. Some day the scientists will do genetic studies and they'll prove it. So when do you think you'll go back to Karisoke? I mean, I know there's a civil war going on now, but the gorillas are still there and—"

"I'm so sorry, Angela." Kristen laid a hand lightly on the girl's shoulder. I'd love to talk with you about all those things, but I have to set up for my talk now. I'll be happy to chat with you afterward about gorillas, or anything else you'd like."

"That'd be super," Angela said, nodding energetically. "So I guess we better go and get the good seats. Okay, see you later." She turned away and led her father toward the rows of benches. Her father glanced back with an expression that said, "Yeah, I know. She's a handful," and followed her.

Kristen set down her notes on the lectern, then measured out the optimum distance for the slide projector, while Dana attached the cable and the electric extension cord to the carousel.

"Nice kid. Very bright." Kristen gathered up her notes and tapped them square. "Why don't you go sit with them and then take them to my office after I'm done."

"Good idea. Have a good lecture." Dana gave her a quick, publicly acceptable kiss on the cheek and hurried out to the audience. She squeezed into the last sixteen inches of space on the bench next to Angela and turned her attention to the stage.

Kristen began with the familiar material, presumably the same she'd presented at Columbia, though the fugitive Dana had never heard it. It was a rundown of gorilla facts, their habits and habitats, and their critically endangered status. The slides showed an appealing assortment of chest-pounding silverbacks, bamboo-munching females, and adorable gorilla babies. The sort of lecture, Dana was convinced, any good primatologist could have given in her sleep.

But then Kristen turned off the slide projector and stepped to the front of the stage. The talk became personal and deeply earnest. She talked about Ndengera and Amahoro, her voice tightening, compared their slaughter with that of Dian's beloved Digit. She described the tenderness of the parents, the self-sacrificing bravery of the silverbacks who tried to protect their families, the horrors of poaching that regularly mutilated them or killed them outright for their infants and for their heads. She described the storage room of the trafficker Bizimana and the complicity of some of Rwanda's own politicians. She was relentless.

Dana glanced to the side at Angela, who was watching the stage, hypnotized and nodding in sympathy.

Kristen moved on to the loss of Karisoke, the possibility that it would never open again due to Rwandan politics and the genocide. The audience fell silent as she described the slaughter of the Karisoke team, of its veterinarian, and of hundreds of thousands of Tutsis.

That was a tragedy of another sort, which urgently had to be addressed. But it was a tragedy of now. The gorillas, on the other hand, had been in Central Africa for thousands of years, long before the Batwa, Tutsi, and Hutu migrations, and in the midst of the human depredations, they were desperately hanging on in the Virunga mountains.

"Please remember them," she concluded. "And when the human depravity is over, support their preservation. *They* are innocent."

During the warm applause, she packed up her notes and slides and waved to Dana to bring the guests around to her office.

Kristin's office was part of a complex of inconspicuous wooden buildings at the edge of the Congo Gorilla Forest. Adjacent to her office was a food-storage shed and, more importantly, a space for the confinement of sick or injured gorillas or their neglected infants.

As Dana and the McIntyres entered, Kristen handed out surgical masks.

"What's this for?" the father asked.

"It's so we don't infect the gorillas with our germs, Daddy." Angela turned to Kristen, clearly excited. "Does this mean we're going to see a gorilla up close?"

"Better than that. I'm going to let you hold a baby gorilla, and that's why I want you to be careful."

"Oh, gosh. Of course." Angela slipped the elastic strap of the mask over her head.

Kristen disappeared into the next room and returned with a surgical mask over her own face and holding an infant gorilla. The lowland gorilla reminded Dana of Mwelu, though her fur was shorter and dark brown rather than pitch black. Angela's reaction was predictable. "Oooooh, how adorable. Is she sick? Why is she here?"

"She's in our infirmary just for a couple of days. One of the adolescent gorillas bit her, and we want to keep an eye on the wound. She's a healthy girl, but the bite was quite nasty. Here, you can hold her. Her name is Tuti and she's fifteen months."

Angela's face was radiant with love as she took the young gorilla into her arms and scratched gently behind its ear. The animal stared up at her with the same infant curiosity that Mwelu had shown, and from across the room, Dana felt a pang of envy.

"Oh, she's so precious. And her hands are just like ours, with long fingers." Angela made a series of kitchykoo-like sounds and tickled under the baby's chin and arms and across her belly. Tuti clawed the air and responded with little pants of apparent delight.

"She likes it, but of course she should be with her mother. They need to nurse until they're two or three, don't they?" Angela cooed as the little furry hand tugged at her braid.

"Yes, quite right, and she'll go back to Mama tomorrow. While she's with us, she gets a bottle twice a day. She's also eating soft fruit—bananas and mangoes—and likes to chew on celery. Speaking of which, it's time for her supper." Kristen held out her arms for the baby.

"Can we take a picture before I give her up?" Angela begged.

The instant Kristen nodded, Detective McIntyre snatched a camera seemingly out of nowhere, snapped two photos of his daughter and the infant, and dropped it into his pocket.

"Oh, I so much want to take care of her. Of all of them." Angela kissed the gorilla's head through the surgical mask and, with obvious reluctance, surrendered her to Kristen.

Stepping away from the baby, she removed her surgical mask and dropped it onto a table. "Thank you so much. I'll never forget this." After a few more greetings and salutations and head nodding, the two visitors left.

Dana claimed the discarded mask and slid the elastic over her ears. In two steps, she was by Kristen's side and embraced both her and the infant gorilla. A wave of optimism came over her, in spite of the horrors they'd left behind. "Did you see that girl's face?" she asked.

"I saw a very smart young woman with strong maternal instincts. A good scientist some day."

Dana tightened her hug and laughed. "Think about it, my darling. Apparently, you and I aren't the only ones haunted. We've just seen Dian's ghost in a fifteen-year-old."

POSTSCRIPT

Dian Fossey (January 16, 1932–December 26, 1985). Primatologist. Inspired by Louis Leaky and funded in part by his foundation, Fossey spent eighteen years in the Virunga mountains studying gorillas. She began in 1967 in the Congo (at that time Zaire) but was forced by Congolese unrest to relocate to the rainforest of Rwanda, setting up the base she named Karisoke. She made the first thorough record of gorilla sounds, behavior, and diet in the wild, identifying individual gorillas by "noseprints." The local people referred to her as Nyiramachabelli, roughly translated as "The woman who lives alone on the mountain." Primary research for this novel was from Farley Mowat's biography *Woman in the Mists* (1987) and Fossey's own book *Gorillas in the Mist* (1983). A film by the same name appeared in 1988, starring Sigourney Weaver.

Karisoke. Fossey founded the Karisoke Research Center in September 1967 in Ruhengeri province in the saddle between Mount Karisimbi and Mount Visoke, using syllables from both names to make up the word. Dian's cabin and the other structures were destroyed during the civil war of the 1990s, though the project was later greatly expanded and, under the name Dian Fossey Gorilla Fund, now has facilities in Ruhengeri (currently called Musanze) and elsewhere. Tourists can hike up the mountain to view the gorilla cemetery and the grave of Dian Fossey.

Mountain Gorillas. Not to be confused with lighter-brown lowland gorillas, mountain gorillas (*Gorilla beringei beringei*) are found in the Virunga volcanic range of Congo, Rwanda, and Uganda. As of November 2012, the estimated total number of the critically endangered species was around 620. Having been driven by habitat encroachment up into the fog-drenched mountains, the survivors have longer and thicker fur. Adult males develop silver fur on their backs and midriff. Standing upright, they are over six feet tall, have an arm span of more than eight feet, and weigh about 500 pounds. Gorillas live in stable social groups of five to thirty individuals guided and defended by a dominant silverback, though younger silverbacks and blackbacks are usually present as well. When the group is under attack by animals or humans, the silverback will protect it even at the cost of his own life. He is very protective of his own offspring, though he may kill an infant not his own (e.g. if taking over a group) in order to make its mother sexually available. Gorillas typically build night nests from local vegetation, which they share with infants, thus enabling researchers to make a rough population count. They are herbivores but will snack on insects and are generally non-aggressive, except for silverbacks from competing groups. The greatest threats to the species are agricultural expansion, which has reduced Rwanda's national park by more than half; fragmentation of habitat, which encourages inbreeding; respiratory disease from living at high altitudes in the rain; and infection from humans via gorilla tourism. Constant civil unrest, cutting of trees for firewood, and oil exploration are also a threat.

Murder of Dian Fossey. Fossey was killed by a machete blow in her own cabin on the night of December 26, 1985. First assumptions were that it was a poacher or disgruntled staff member, and with little evidence, authorities charged Emmanuel Rwelekana, a recently fired tracker, and Wayne McGuire, her American research assistant. McGuire was allowed to "flee" back to the United States, and Rwelekana died under suspicious circumstances in jail. Subsequent research suggests that both men were innocent and that the most likely instigator of the murder was Protais Zigiranyirazo (in the novel Zigirazo), brother-in-law to the president. It appears that Fossey was about to expose him and his circle as being behind poaching and smuggling operations of endangered species and gold. During the 1994 genocide, Zigiranyirazo was implicated as one of the creators of the Hutu death squads.

Plato. In his *Dialogues*, Plato explores the question of what constitutes moral (pious) behavior through conversations between Socrates and others. In the dialogue *Euthyphro*, a man is laying manslaughter charges against his father, who had allowed one of his workers to die, though the worker himself was a murderer. Socrates, who is in prison charged with immorality (impiety), attempts to find a definition that will apply to his own case. Euthyphro uses a religious definition: that any action contrary to the will of the gods is immoral (impious). Socrates demolishes this argument by pointing out that if morality is defined as the will of a deity, moral behavior is merely blind obedience. If, on the other hand, morality is absolute and the deity commands it because of its *innate* goodness, then the deity is unnecessary to goodness. Dana is familiar with this puzzle and, applying it to her own situation, is unable to decide whether her killing of the two men is moral or immoral.

Poaching. With young gorillas worth from $1000 to $5000 in the world pet trade, animal trafficking is a persistent problem in the Virungas. In seizing the infant, poachers inevitably kill the silverback and other members of the group protecting it. The surviving family usually disbands. Fossey's study groups had not been direct victims of poaching until 1978, when Fossey's favorite gorilla Digit was speared, decapitated, and his hands cut off to be sold to souvenir hunters. A year later, another silverback was killed protecting a mate and her infant by poachers cooperating with the Rwandan park conservator (sic!). The young gorilla was not captured but died slowly and painfully of gangrene from a poacher's bullet. Fossey subsequently created the Digit Fund to finance anti-poaching patrols. During four months in 1979, the four-man Fossey patrol destroyed 987 poachers' traps in the research area, while the twenty-four official Rwandan national park guards destroyed none. In park areas not patrolled by Fossey, poachers killed a dozen gorillas and wiped out the entire elephant population. Other international gorilla funds arose to accept donations in light of Digit's death, but this infuriated Fossey since some of these were used fraudulently for unrestrained gorilla tourism, fake conservation, and to pay Rwandan park officials who had ordered the gorilla poachings in the first place. In 1978, the Rwandan park conservator (sic!) killed twenty adult gorillas in order to capture two young gorillas for sale to the Cologne zoo. These episodes caused Fossey to turn her primary attention away from research to poaching prevention. Her methods, by her own admission, were extreme and alienated many Rwandan officials and some of her own staff.

Rosamond Carr (Rosalind Carver). American socialite who arrived in Rwanda with British explorer/game hunter Kenneth Carr in 1949. After divorce in 1955, she bought and maintained a flower plantation called Mugongo. She met Dian Fossey in 1967 and, though she disapproved of Fossey's policies, remained a friend until the latter's death in 1985. Forced to flee during the 1994 genocide, she returned later the same year to set up the Imbabazi Orphanage in Gisenyi and later on her own land at Mugongo.

Rwandan Politics and Genocide. It is beyond the scope of these notes to lay out the complex Rwandan history, except to summarize that historical tensions between Tutsis and Hutus were exacerbated during colonialism when the German (up to 1919) and Belgian (1922–1962) rulers favored Tutsis as more European and included them in their administrations. Hutus thus associated Tutsis with the colonial regimes, and in the wave of independence movements (1960s) Hutus gained dominance. Repressed Tutsis (some 150,000) fled to neighboring countries, from which they staged frequent attacks on Rwandan Hutu forces throughout the 1960s. By means of a military takeover, General, then President, Habyarimana formed a one-party Hutu state through the 1970s and 80s. At the same time, many Tutsis massed around Paul Kagame in Uganda, to form the Rwandan Patriotic Front, and they invaded Rwanda in 1990, sparking three years of civil war. The parties maintained a cease-fire in 1993, but on April 6, 1994, the presidential plane was shot down upon arrival in Kigali. In the next days the Rwandan army, the National Police, and militias calling themselves *Interahamwe* joined forces to gather and kill all known Tutsis. The UN peacekeeping forces withdrew after some of their men were tortured and killed. Refusing to acknowledge the mass murders as genocide, the United States, Britain, and Belgium also declined military intervention, allowing the massacres to continue unhindered. Hutu forces killed between 500,000 to 1,000,000 Tutsis, moderate Hutus, and a scattering of Europeans, mostly with machetes, until the Rwandan Patriotic Front seized control of the country in mid-July. President Clinton later apologized for US inactivity. The immediate end to the fighting did not end hostilities, for while Tutsi refugees streamed back into Rwanda, Hutus fled, fearing prosecution/retribution, and the refugee camps (particularly in the Congo) became breeding grounds for Hutu militias. Consequently, the Tutsi government led attacks into the Congo in two subsequent wars. Though Rwanda is currently calm, refugee camps throughout the region still hold large populations of both Hutus and Tutsis.

About the Author

After years of academic writing and literary critique, Justine Saracen saw the light and began writing fiction. With nine historical thrillers now under her literary belt, she has moved from Ancient Egyptian mysteries (*The 100th Generation*) to the Crusades (2007's *Vulture's Kiss*) to the Italian Renaissance. *Sistine Heresy*, which conjures up a thoroughly blasphemic backstory to Michelangelo's Sistine Chapel frescoes, won a 2009 Independent Publisher's Award (IPPY) and was a finalist in the ForeWord Book of the Year Award. The transgendered novel, *Sarah, Son of God,* followed, taking us through Stonewall-rioting New York, Venice under the Inquisition, and Nero's Rome. The novel won the Rainbow First Prize for Best Transgendered Novel. *Beloved Gomorrah* marked a return to her critique of Bible myths—in this case an LGBT version of Sodom and Gomorrah—though it also involved Red Sea diving and the hazards of falling for a Hollywood actress. Having lived in Germany, Justine was well placed to write her three previous World War II novels: *Mephisto Aria*, (EPIC Awards finalist, Two Rainbow awards, 2011 Golden Crown award) *Tyger, Tyger, Burning Bright*, which follows the lives of four homosexuals during the Third Reich (2012 Rainbow First Prize), and *Waiting for the Violins*, a tale of the French and Belgian Resistance, which just won a Golden Crown award. Her most recent work, *The Witch of Stalingrad*, won the 2015 (first) Sandra Moran prize.

An adopted European, Saracen lives on a charming little winding street in Brussels, venturing out only to bookfests in the US and UK, and to scuba adventures in Egypt. When she's home and dry, she listens to opera.

Books Available from Bold Strokes Books

24/7 by Yolanda Wallace. When the trip of a lifetime becomes a pitched battle between life and death, will anyone survive? (978-1-62639-6-197)

A Return to Arms by Sheree Greer. When a police shooting makes national headlines, activists Folami and Toya struggle to balance their relationship and political allegiances, a struggle intensified after a fiery young artist enters their lives. (978-1-62639-6-814)

After the Fire by Emily Smith. Paramedic Connor Haus is convinced her time for love has come and gone, but when firefighter Logan Curtis comes into town, she learns it may not be too late after all. (978-1-62639-6-524)

Dian's Ghost by Justine Saracen. The road to genocide is paved with good intentions. (978-1-62639-5-947)

Fortunate Sum by M. Ullrich. Financial advisor Catherine Carter lives a calculated life, but after a collision with spunky Imogene Harris (her latest client) and unsolicited predictions, Catherine finds herself facing an unexpected variable: Love. (978-1-62639-5-305)

Soul to Keep by Rebekah Weatherspoon. What *won't* a vampire do for love... (978-1-62639-6-166)

When I Knew You by KE Payne. Eight letters, three friends, two lovers, one secret. Can the past ever be forgiven? (978-1-62639-5-626)

Wild Shores by Radclyffe. Can two women on opposite sides of an oil spill find a way to save both a wildlife sanctuary and their hearts? (978-1-62639-6-456)

Love on Tap by Karis Walsh. Beer and romance are brewing for Tace Lomond when archaeologist Berit Katsaros comes into her life. (987-1-162639-564-0)

Love on the Red Rocks by Lisa Moreau. An unexpected romance at a lesbian resort forces Malley to face her greatest fears where she must choose between playing it safe or taking a chance at true happiness. (987-1-162639-660-9)

Tracker and the Spy by D. Jackson Leigh. There are lessons for all when Captain Tanisha is assigned untried pyro Kyle and a lovesick dragon horse for a mission to track the leader of a dangerous cult. (987-1-162639-448-3)

Whirlwind Romance by Kris Bryant. Will chasing the girl break Tristan's heart or give her something she's never had before? (987-1-162639-581-7)

Whiskey Sunrise by Missouri Vaun. Culture and religion collide when Lovey Porter, daughter of a local Baptist minister, falls for the handsome thrill-seeking moonshine runner, Royal Duval. (987-1-162639-519-0)

Dyre: By Moon's Light by Rachel E. Bailey. A young werewolf, Des, guards the aging leader of all the Packs: the Dyre. Stable employment—nice work, if you can get it…at least until silver bullets start to fly. (978-1-62639-6-623)

Fragile Wings by Rebecca S. Buck. In Roaring Twenties London, can Evelyn Hopkins find love with Jos Singleton or will the scars of the Great War crush her dreams? (978-1-62639-5-466)

Live and Love Again by Jan Gayle. Jessica Whitney could be Sarah Jarret's second chance at love, but their differences and Sarah's grief continue to come between their budding relationship. (978-1-62639-5-176)

Starstruck by Lesley Davis. Actress Cassidy Hayes and writer Aiden Darrow find out the hard way not all life-threatening drama is confined to the TV screen or the pages of a manuscript. (978-1-62639-5-237)

Stealing Sunshine by Tina Michele. Under the Central Florida sun, two women struggle between fear and love as a dangerous plot of deception and revenge threatens to steal priceless art and lives. (978-1-62639-4-452)

The Fifth Gospel by Michelle Grubb. Hiding a Vatican secret is dangerous—sharing the secret suicidal—can Felicity survive a perilous book tour, and will her PR specialist, Anna, be there when it's all over? (978-1-62639-4-476)

Cold to the Touch by Cari Hunter. A drug addict's murder is the start of a dangerous investigation for Detective Sanne Jensen and Dr. Meg Fielding, as they try to stop a killer with no conscience. (978-1-62639-526-8)

Forsaken by Laydin Michaels. The hunt for a killer teaches one woman that she must overcome her fear in order to love, and another that success is meaningless without happiness. (978-1-62639-481-0)

Infiltration by Jackie D. When a CIA breach is imminent, a Marine instructor must stop the attack while protecting her heart from being disarmed by a recruit. (978-1-62639-521-3)

Midnight at the Orpheus by Alyssa Linn Palmer. Two women desperate to make their way in the world, a man hell-bent on revenge, and a cop risking his career: all in a day's work in Capone's Chicago. (978-1-62639-607-4)

Spirit of the Dance by Mardi Alexander. Major Sorla Reardon's return to her family farm to heal threatens Riley Johnson's safe life when small-town secrets are revealed, and love may not conquer all. (978-1-62639-583-1)

Sweet Hearts by Melissa Brayden, Rachel Spangler, and Karis Walsh. Do you ever wonder *Whatever happened to...*? Find out when you reconnect with your favorite characters from Melissa Brayden's *Heart Block*, Rachel Spangler's *LoveLife*, and Karis Walsh's *Worth the Risk*. (978-1-62639-475-9)

Totally Worth It by Maggie Cummings. Who knew there's an all-lesbian condo community in the NYC suburbs? Join twentysomething BFFs Meg and Lexi at Bay West as they navigate friendships, love, and everything in between. (978-1-62639-512-1)

Illicit Artifacts by Stevie Mikayne. Her foster mother's death cracked open a secret world Jil never wanted to see...and now she has to pick up the stolen pieces. (978-1-62639-472-8)

Pathfinder by Gun Brooke. Heading for their new homeworld, Exodus's chief engineer Adina Vantressa and nurse Briar Lindemay carry game-changing secrets that may well cause them to lose everything when disaster strikes. (978-1-62639-444-5)

Prescription for Love by Radclyffe. Dr. Flannery Rivers finds herself attracted to the new ER chief, city girl Abigail Remy, and the incendiary mix of city and country, fire and ice, tradition and change is combustible. (978-1-62639-570-1)

Ready or Not by Melissa Brayden. Uptight Mallory Spencer finds relinquishing control to bartender Hope Sanders too tall an order in fast-paced New York City. (978-1-62639-443-8)

Summer Passion by MJ Williamz. Women loving women is forbidden in 1946 Hollywood, yet Jean and Maggie strive to keep their love alive and away from prying eyes. (978-1-62639-540-4)

The Princess and the Prix by Nell Stark. "Ugly duckling" Princess Alix of Monaco was resigned to loneliness until she met racecar driver Thalia d'Angelis. (978-1-62639-474-2)

Winter's Harbor by Aurora Rey. Lia Brooks isn't looking for love in Provincetown, but when she discovers chocolate croissants and pastry chef Alex McKinnon, her winter retreat quickly starts heating up. (978-1-62639-498-8)

The Time Before Now by Missouri Vaun. Vivian flees a disastrous affair, embarking on an epic, transformative journey to escape her past, until destiny introduces her to Ida, who helps her rediscover trust, love, and hope. (978-1-62639-446-9)

Twisted Whispers by Sheri Lewis Wohl. Betrayal, lies, and secrets— whispers of a friend lost to darkness. Can a reluctant psychic set things right or will an evil soul destroy those she loves? (978-1-62639-439-1)

The Courage to Try by C.A. Popovich. Finding love is worth getting past the fear of trying. (978-1-62639-528-2)

Break Point by Yolanda Wallace. In a world readying for war, can love find a way? (978-1-62639-568-8)

Countdown by Julie Cannon. Can two strong-willed, powerful women overcome their differences to save the lives of seven others and begin a life they never imagined together? (978-1-62639-471-1)

Keep Hold by Michelle Grubb. Claire knew some things should be left alone and some rules should never be broken, but the most forbidden, well, they are the most tempting. (978-1-62639-502-2)

Deadly Medicine by Jaime Maddox. Dr. Ward Thrasher's life is in turmoil. Her partner Jess left her, and her job puts her in the path of a murderous physician who has Jess in his sights. (978-1-62639-424-7)

New Beginnings by KC Richardson. Can the connection and attraction between Jordan Roberts and Kirsten Murphy be enough for Jordan to trust Kirsten with her heart? (978-1-62639-450-6)